CALI

FINN

CALL ME
FINN

PETE LAIRD

Call me Finn
First Print Edition

Copyright © Pete Laird, 2022
All rights reserved.

This book is dedicated to all lost souls

'Be kind, for everyone you meet is fighting a hard battle.'

Ian Maclaren

Contents

Author's note

Working-class Glasgow in the 1950s could be rough and violent, and yet it was a happy place with a strong and proud community spirit. People's memories were still vivid of the unity they'd felt during the Luftwaffe bombings of Clydeside in the Second World War, and people worked together and helped to look after one another. Together they formed impregnable, tight societies.

Lay-offs, unemployment and poverty contributed to the city's slums, though, and the condemnation of such inadequate housing and the creation of new council estates started to break this community bond. Life became about the survival of the fittest. This in turn contributed to an increase in juvenile delinquency, with new gangs forming all over the city.

An old expression was often cited in Glasgow at the time: 'If you fly with the crows, then you get shot with the crows'. You either sided with the gang and risked getting into trouble with them, or you were on your own. Most people chose the safety of the gang.

I, myself, chose the safety of the gang as a teenager in the late 1960s, following a troubled childhood. This book is a fictional expression of my own real experiences.

x

Wee Rosie

Ina McGill heard the wail and cry of her youngest boy Finlay through the window.

'Mammy! Mammy!'

Ina rushed to the door to see what was wrong. She caught Finlay's eye. 'What the fuck?' she said.

Finlay struggled to get the words out. 'Tam Fleming punched me and now my nose is bleeding,' he sobbed.

'What!' exclaimed Ina, and she gave Finlay a hefty slap around the ear that sent him flying across the back green. 'Did he hit you as hard as that then?' she blared, standing with her arms folded. 'And stop that fucking greeting!'

Snivelling through his tears, Finlay tried to catch his breath. 'No, Mammy.'

'I've fucking told you to fight your own battles. Go and hit him back or you'll get another slap from me.'

'Aye, I will, Mammy,' said Finlay. He was barely six years old.

In the tight space of the tenement, the McGills managed to jam their eight children into a second-floor single-end flat. Every inch of living space in their single room was occupied. It was as if Wullie had taken a mell and hammered them all in like human wedges. He was indeed very handy with wood and he'd constructed army-type drop-down triple bunks for the children who were comfortable sleeping head to toe. Their abode was in the centre of Southall, just five minutes' walk from the Clyde shipyard where most of the men in the area worked, including Wullie.

Wullie was a tall, thin man who believed that no matter how little money you had, you should always look your best. At the shipyard he would present himself in a fresh pair of overalls each week, and he always wore a flat cap and highly polished hobnail boots. His motto was: 'Cleanliness is next to godliness'. He instilled this ideology into his boys. 'If it's torn mend it! If it's dirty wash it!' he would tell them. 'Soap and water cost nothing. Better a clean patch than a mucky tear!'

Wullie was a man's man, but he loved and adored Ina so much he would do anything for her. He did his utmost to provide for his family, and was a constant and diligent hard worker, often doing double shifts in his job as an oxyacetylene burner. Every Friday payday, without fail, he would hand Ina his unopened wage packet. He was a soft-spoken man who avoided confrontation; he would rather agree with his aggressor than argue.

Ina though was tough. Born on the morning of King Edward VII's death in May 1910, the youngest of six and the only girl, she was brought up in a hovel in the Gorbals area of the city. She'd learned the hard way to be as tough as her older brothers and could give as good as she got. But people liked her straight-talking. With Ina you got what you saw; there were no airs or graces. She was blunt and straight to the point.

Small in height, eight births had taken their toll on her body. She was so overweight she was almost round, and her oval face and heavy chin hid her true beauty, but she was proud of the jet-black hair that flowed down her back.

Ina was, however, her youngest son's nemesis. She was a hard woman with Victorian values, and she loathed six-year-old Finlay. He had been her last hope for a girl and was consequently the biggest disappointment of her life. Her bitterness ran deep. She often thought back to the excitement that had been in her heart before his birth, if only to stoke her resentment.

She would remember the cold crisp morning in November when her waters broke, and the ambulance was called. Though Ina had delivered her seven other babies at home with no complications, she wasn't taking any chances with this one. She

3

was determined to get the best care for her precious wee girl whom she'd already named Rosie. The hospital had been built less than four years before and was fully equipped for all emergencies and complications, so she felt confident that nothing could go wrong.

It was to be a long, drawn-out affair though. Ina assumed her eighth birth would be a doddle, especially as her last four babies had each popped out like a jack in the box. But this was the worst labour of them all. In the fathers' waiting room adjacent to the labour room, Wullie sat with his head in both hands and his fingers in his ears to deaden the sound of Ina's cries. Eventually, after she had endured six long hours of fruitless pushing, the doctor gave into his pleas to let him be with his exhausted wife.

By then, Ina had reached her lowest point. Anxiety crept over Wullie like a cold mist at the sight of her, and it chilled him to the bone. She looked crushed. Beaten. Her eyes were dying candle flames sunk deep into darkly ringed sockets. Her gaze was blank. Wullie knew she needed him. Though Ina was a force to be reckoned with, Wullie was her rock. He stroked her face lovingly and took her hand.

'You all right, hen?' he said softly.

Ina's eyes burst wide open at his voice, and a deep gulp of air slammed into her lungs. His presence was what she needed. With Wullie beside her, she felt an invigorating surge of energy. Gripping his hand, her head rocked from side to side and her face contorted as she endured another wave of agonising, all-consuming pain. She screamed as though the Grim Reaper himself was about to collect her soul.

'Push Ina,' urged Wullie. She roared with the effort. 'I think she's coming!' she cried.

Gripping her hand tighter, Wullie worried Ina could not take much more of this labour. 'That's my lassie. Go on, hen. Wee Rosie will soon be here,' he murmured encouragingly.

As the pain began to recede again, Ina prayed. *Lord Jesus, this is pure torture. Please let it be over soon.* It would all be worth it in the end, she told herself. The thought of holding her wee girl in her arms gave her the strength to carry on.

Ina had the name Rosie picked out the day the doctor confirmed she was pregnant. So convinced was she that she was finally having the little girl she'd always yearned for that, over the months before the birth, she'd regularly taken herself down to the local department stores, happily looking at all the baby girl clothing and making many a purchase. Ina would take the pretty little dresses, lace slips and tiny hats home, lock the bedroom door and secretly place them at the back of her Victorian mirrored wardrobe.

In the run-up to her labour when the house was empty, Ina would lay the clothes all out on the bed and individually hold every one of the garments up to the light at the bedroom window. She would chuckle and smile to herself at the size and beauty of each one. Her favourite was a little pink cardigan that she would hold and caress before examining the rest. With eyes closed, she would gently stroke the clothes over her face, imagining the happy days that lay ahead for her and little Rosie.

Ina saw herself pushing the pram in the park, feeding the ducks and going to the fair. At times she would even act out her imaginings, talking gently to the clothes as though the baby were in them, and singing joyous nursery rhymes as she cradled them in her arms.

She had no misgivings whatsoever: it must be a girl. This pregnancy felt different from all the others. Besides, who had ever heard of anyone having eight boys! Having convinced herself, she had then succeeded in persuading Wullie and most of her friends and neighbours in the tenement close. And all their seven boys believed their mother would be bringing them home a little sister.

Her daydreaming done, she would take her time folding the clothing again neatly before replacing them in the wardrobe.

From her heavy breathing and grunts that had been getting systematically louder, Wullie knew the end must be in sight. Trying to keep her mind off the pain, he said, 'She's a wee bugger! She's hanging on in there but our wee Rosie's definitely on her way.'

'Oh! I can see the top of her head,' said the midwife. Ina let out a massive yelp as the midwife inserted forceps and began to assist in delivering the baby. With one last almighty push, the baby slid into the midwife's hands, and she quickly cleaned the baby and wrapped it in the pink shawl that had been warming over the radiator.

'Congratulations! It's a wee healthy boy!' the midwife cried.

Wullie heard Ina's gasp and his heart sank in despair. He knew how much having a little girl meant to her. Looking down, he saw her mouth wide open and her eyes like dinner plates, her face frozen in shock. He composed himself but before he could say anything he heard Ina's trembling voice.

'No! It cannae be! It cannae be! You're mistaken!' she cried, shaking her head from side to side and clutching her hands to her chest. Her heart was pounding at its epicentre. Every beat sent rippling shock waves through her body. This was not something Ina had ever contemplated could happen. She was unable to think straight.

'God, Wullie, please say it's not true! I've given birth to seven laddies, nurse. You must be mistaken with this one!' She held up her outstretched arms towards the midwife holding the baby, flapping her fingers frantically towards herself. 'Give it to me!' she demanded.

Shocked at the change of atmosphere, the midwife was unsure what to do. She looked over at Wullie uncertainly, but he nodded towards Ina and gestured that she should hand the baby down to her.

'Mrs McGill, it is a wee boy,' confirmed the midwife.

Snatching the bundle from her arms, Ina clutched it tightly to her chest, shaking with fear at what she might find. There was no way this was going to be a wee boy! Her mind was a whirlpool of twisting thoughts. Nothing seemed real. This just wasn't happening; she needed to wake from this nightmare! Then her face erupted into a smile and she laughed out loud.

'I see now, Wullie! You're playing a joke on me!'

Wullie stood up in readiness, watching Ina's shaking hand as she pushed the corner of the shawl aside.

'No! No!' she screamed.

That moment the plug was pulled: every drop of hope drained away. Every dream she'd had for her wee Rosie died. She scowled at the little boy in Rosie's place, her empty heart filling with contempt. *Oh my God, another boy! What am I going to do? I have seven boys already at home. I can't do this again!*

Ina thrust the baby back towards the midwife's arms. 'Take this fucking thing away! Get it out of my sight! There's no way that wee bastard's coming home with me.'

The midwife gathered up the loose shawl and wrapped the baby tight. 'I'll away with the baby to weigh him and check him out.'

Ina's loud crying could be heard echoing along the corridor of the hospital as the midwife left with the baby. She hurled her face into the pillow, wrapping it around her head, and curled herself into the foetal position as she wept.

Wullie attempted to console her, lovingly rubbing her back. 'I know how much you longed for a wee lassie, but it's not to be. The wee boy is healthy, so we must thank God for that at least.'

Through her crying Ina listened to Wullie's muffled words. Anger flared inside her and, removing the tear-soaked pillow, she stared scornfully at him, her eyes bulging as if about to burst out of their sockets. Thrusting her head forward to an inch away from his, she flung her arm towards the door and snarled, 'Get out, Wullie!' The fury on her face was to be imprinted into Wullie's mind forever. He would never forget it.

Noticing his despair, the midwife gently touched the back of his hand. 'Leave her with me, Mr McGill,' she said quietly. 'Don't worry. She'll come round, I'm sure. I can assure you it's not the first time I've heard this, and it sounds as though she has a wee touch of the baby blues.'

Looking down, he sighed at the sight of Ina curled up and crying. He felt helpless but was reluctant to leave her side.

'Look, she's only tired,' said the midwife. 'It was a hard birth. Come back tomorrow – she'll have perked up by then.'

'You think so?' he replied. 'I'm not so sure.'

He bent down to kiss Ina on the back of her head, but she flinched away from him. Looking at him through her tears, she said in a calm, cold voice, 'Go away, Wullie. Just leave me.'

The midwife put one arm around Wullie's waist and another on his shoulder and tried to manoeuvre him away. He turned to look at Ina again and made to return to her bedside, but the midwife gripped him tighter. 'Come on now, Mr McGill. You'll see her tomorrow. I'll get the doctor to give her something to settle her down and help her sleep.'

Once outside the hospital, Wullie stopped and lifted his flat cap off his head. His comb-over blew and curled around his face, and his thin hands shook as he ran his fingers through his fine, greying hair. Lighting a cigarette, he stood contemplating what to do with the rest of the night. He was proud that he'd fathered eight healthy boys and he didn't want to go home. He wanted to celebrate.

A shudder ran down his back. Like a startled cat, his eyes widened and his hair stood as proud as porcupine quills as a sudden thought struck him. What would happen when Ina awoke in the morning and realised she'd not been dreaming?

His thoughts were interrupted, however, by the sight of Irish Paddy a neighbour who lived on the next landing of the same tenement as Wullie. 'Paddy! What are you doing at the maternity?'

'Bejesus, it's yourself. I've just been up to see my cousin Mabel – she's just had twin girls and I brought her a wee bit of fruit and some flowers.'

Wullie spluttered mid-drag of his cigarette. 'Jesus Christ! Twin girls!' he barked. His heart missed a beat at the thought of the consequences should Ina hear the news. 'For Christ's sake, Paddy, please don't let on to Ina about Mabel having the girls.'

'Oh? Begorrah, I don't understand.'

'Ina has just given birth to our eighth son. As you and everyone else knows, she desperately wanted a lassie, so if she gets wind of this news, well, who knows what she'll do. One thing I do know, it would certainly break the poor woman's heart.'

'Now then, my good friend, don't you be going worrying yourself now. Not a word will pass my lips,' assured Paddy. 'I will tell the family to keep away from Ina for a week or two.'

'Thanks, Paddy, you're a good friend. I owe you a pint.'

'Come on now – eight boys! Boy o' boy. I'm buying you a pint of the black stuff because that is something to celebrate!'

Pride rose inside Wullie and flooded his heart when he heard those words. He puffed out his chest and for that split second he forgot about Ina. A pint in the local pub would be most welcome.

'Aye, you're right, Paddy. It is something to be proud of.' Paddy shook Wullie's hand and they headed straight for the pub.

The homecoming

When Wullie stepped out into the street a week later, the morning air was slight and chilled, and the cloudless sky a beautiful shade of eggshell blue. The low autumn sun cast long shadows which draped over the town as if a curtain had been drawn across the open sky.

What a beautiful morning to pick up the wean, thought Wullie as he headed into the maternity ward and looked over towards Ina's bed. It was empty. An uneasiness fell over him as he glanced around the ward. She had been upset all week, he knew, and wasn't at all herself. His heart began to pound.

'Excuse me, where's Ina McGill?' he asked a passing nurse.

'She's in isolation room number two, over in the corner.'

Looking through a gap in the curtained window, Wullie saw the room was dimmed to almost total darkness. Ina's bulbous body lay motionless on top of the bed, her back to the window. Unopened congratulations cards lay in a pile on the table and still-wrapped flowers sat inside a waterless vase. Ina's long black hair hung down like burnt straw. That was when Wullie knew she really was not herself. Ina was proud of her thick hair and took great care of it, combing it regularly.

Pulling up a chair, he sat beside her but before he could say anything, he heard Ina's cantankerous voice. 'I'm not sleeping if that's what you are thinking.'

Kissing the top of her head, Wullie said, 'It's nice to see you looking so relaxed'.

Ina's body jolted at this. Relaxed she was not! She was too busy worrying about what the future had in store for her and the unwelcome pile that lay in the little cot close by. She tightened her lips, determined not to reply, but couldn't let it go.

'What do you mean by that?' she snapped. 'Relaxed! Do I look fucking relaxed? Well, do I?'

Knowing Ina was wound up like a clock spring at breaking point, Wullie had to try and calm her down. Speaking softly he said, 'I have been worried about you, hen. Did you sleep okay?'

Anger flared in Ina's eyes. She could not comprehend why he would even think she was able to sleep when she had all the worry of looking after yet another boy. *Oh, it's all right for him out working and in and out the pub, while I run after another one of his weans! Well, I'm not doing it!*

13

'Did I sleep okay?' she repeated incredulously, glaring at Wullie. 'No, I did not!' Her blood had boiled straight from a simmer. 'Why?' she demanded. 'Did *you* sleep okay? I bet you fucking did!' Tears filled her eyes and began to fall.

Wullie wrapped his arms around her and held her close. 'How am I going to cope, Wullie? I cannae cope at the best of times. I so wanted a wee lassie!' she wailed.

Wullie held her tight, his forehead creased, as she rocked her head and sobbed. He too was worried about Ina's future. He gazed into space, thinking hard, when an idea jolted him.

'Ann!' he blurted. 'Your pal Ann – she will help! She always has. And no doubt she'll be at the house this afternoon to see you and the wean – although we cannae keep calling him the wean. I was thinking we could call him Finlay after your brother. I've always liked that name.'

Turning her head and casting her eyes away, Ina muttered, 'You can call that thing whatever you want because I couldnae give a fuck.'

He had been with her since their teens and Wullie thought he knew Ina. She had always been a loving and caring person; her rejection of this child was out of character. He couldn't deal with it. 'Okay, Ina. Finlay it is.'

At 10.25 am, Ina was awakened by the sound of her baby crying. Half asleep, she nudged the bed covers with her elbow to rouse Wullie. Feeling no resistance, she snapped her head to the side and saw that he was gone. He'd left for work hours ago. Her heart sank and her stomach churned. She just hated the sight of Finlay, and the less time she spent with him the better. Knowing she had to do something but unable to cope, she shouted, 'James! James, are you there? James!'

No one answered. James was her eldest son whom she depended on to ensure the younger children got some tea and toast before they set off for school. Scowling, Ina dragged herself out of bed, but as she reached down towards the baby she was struck by the sudden and unbearable thought of all the years ahead she would be stuck looking after him. She snatched her arms way as though red hot metal were about to burn her. Ignoring the baby's cries, she opened the door of the bedroom and made her way out. Glancing back at him, she saw his nappy was full, and his little arms and legs flapping about in the air. 'Wee bastard. Fucking greet all you want,' she muttered, closing the door behind her.

Ina made her way to the kitchen and put the kettle on. Cupping her hand round her warm teacup, she had just sat down on the sofa when the living room door swung open. She looked up to see her good friend Ann.

'Hello Ina. How are you feeling today?'

'Aye, not too bad. Just fed up is all.'

Ina was relieved that Ann had called in, knowing she would sort out little Finlay. Cocking her ear up toward the ceiling, she said, 'Ann, can you hear the

15

wean crying? Och, aye, it is. Will you do me a wee favour, because my head's bursting? Would you bring the wee one down?'

'Aye, nae bother. I'm dying to see the wee boy anyway!'

Entering the bedroom, Ann reeled back in horror when she saw what the baby was lying in. His nappy had leaked, badly soiling the mattress and bedding. The congealed mess lay dry and sticking to the baby's skin; it was obvious he'd lain in that state all night. What on earth was wrong with Ina? Ann wondered if she had just been too worn out to notice. She slid open the cot gate and, noticing some fresh nappies lying on the drawers nearby, proceeded to undo Finlay's dirty one.

She jerked her head back and contorted her face in disgust at the smell of ammonia and excrement. *Poor wee thing, he's dehydrated*, she thought. She cleaned him up, murmuring softly to him. 'Hush, my wee laddie, your aunty Ann is here now.' Then she laid him in the middle of the bed, opened the sash window and leaned the stained cot mattress near to air.

Ann brought the baby downstairs, patting him on the back. 'Ina, I think he might be hungry. Has he been fed?'

'Aye, Wullie fed him this morning.'

'What time was that then?' asked Ann.

Ina fidgeted in guilty agitation at Ann's question. 'I don't know!' she snapped. 'Five o'clock or somewhere around that time.'

'Ina, no wonder he's hungry, poor soul. It's twenty past ten – five hours since his last feed! Where do you keep his milk?'

'I have some in the coal bunker. Top shelf. Wullie made it up this morning.'

Ann worried for her friend. Ina was staring at the wall, oblivious to what Ann was doing. *I need to get Ina motivated*, she thought to herself.

'Right, I will see to him. Put the kettle back on. I know it's early but I brought us a wee Paris bun to share.'

'Thanks, Ann. You're a godsend.'

Ann Goldie was a lifelong friend of Ina's. They'd grown up together and had always been very close. Ann had no children of her own, but had supported Ina with all of hers. Despite never having given birth herself, she was of a similar stature to Ina – small and rounded. Eating was a comfort to her during her own problems, and boiled sweets, chocolate and biscuits were always on hand in her home. Working in the local baker shop, and well off by the day's standards, she hoarded large stashes of treats around the house which she'd eat to her heart's content while her husband Gus was out drinking.

Gus was a happy-go-lucky man who, when sober, was a good man and a gentleman. But he liked a pint or two of the demonic liquid gold, and too much of that could make him cantankerous. Ann put up with him giving her a hefty slap now and again because she loved him. Besides, what would the neighbours say if she left him? No one knew he hit her; they kept

17

it to themselves. So it helped Ann to help Ina and get out of the house.

Still holding the baby, Ann sat down. 'Look, Ina, we'll have a wee gab and a cuppa and a Paris bun. Then, you get in the bath for a good soak. I'll look after the wean for a wee while.' She leaned forward and slipped a ten-shilling note into Ina's palm, and patted her leg. 'He's so beautiful. Aw, look at his wee feet and toes! Bless his little cotton socks.'

Ina looked away and rolled her eyes into the back of their sockets. 'Thanks Ann, I don't know what I'd do without you. You're my best pal and I do appreciate you.'

Smiling at her friend and patting her shoulder, Ann said, 'Aye, I know, hen! That's what friends are for.'

'What's the ten bob for?'

'I want you to get yourself off to the bingo for a wee break. I will keep an eye on the wean. But you better be back before your Wullie gets home from his dayshift – the less he knows the better.'

Smiling at Ann, Ina jumped up off the chair excitedly. 'Thanks, Ann! I'll put the kettle on.'

The baby was barely a week old, but Ina was glad to rid herself of him for half a day.

Arriving home after her session at the bingo, Ina walked into the living room and saw the baby fast asleep in the padded middle drawer of their pine chest. Her fourteen-year-old boy Sam sat on the chair next to him.

'Where've you been, Mammy?' he asked.

'I've been to see the doctor,' she answered. 'Where's Ann?'

'She had to go,' he said.

'Did she leave the wean with you?'

'No, she left him with my daddy.'

'What about your daddy? Where's he now?'

'He went out.'

'Do me a wee favour, Sam, because my head is thumping and I need to lie down. If the wean wakes up, give him a bottle. They're keeping cool in that large Quality Street tin that's in the coal bunker near the back door. You better put the kettle on ready for warming the bottle. I'll be upstairs in bed.'

This trend of palming Finlay off to anyone who would have him was to continue for the whole of the boy's childhood, with Ann and Ina's two eldest sons, James and Sam, bearing the brunt. When Ina had an audience, she would play the part of loving mother, but on her own with Finlay it was a different matter.

From the age of two, Finlay was frequently and for the slightest reason locked in the dark cupboard under the stairs. Threatening him if he so much as whimpered, he quickly learned to suppress any form of emotion. As he grew older, the time he spent in the cupboard grew and at times he was in there for over an hour. It was an easy out for Ina: she didn't need to look at him, hear him or even admit to herself that he was there.

Not long before his fifth birthday, Finlay was locked in the cupboard and badly needed a pee but was too frightened to ask to go to the toilet. He held it in for as long as he could but eventually the inevitable happened and he wet himself. He was terrified. He knew if his mother opened the door and saw what he had done, he'd be chastised or, worse, beaten. Even at this tender age he could take the beating, but it was the cruel way she treated him mentally that he feared most. One minute she was sweet to him, but the next she would scold and strike him.

'Finlay, you're an idiot and a useless, stupid, daft laddie!' was her usual put-down. Ina never stopped telling him how stupid he was, and he believed her.

She was always careful to only ever hit him on his buttocks and shoulders in an effort to hide any bruising from Wullie and the others. She loved all her other boys and regularly gave them hugs and kisses – particularly when Finlay was around to see it. She would be loving to them and then say hurtful things to Finlay. 'Look at Hugh's teeth and how nice and straight they are. You have ugly buck teeth, Finlay. Why aren't yours like his?'

Her damming words repeatedly crushed his confidence, as well as his trust in his mother, and his ability to learn consequently declined. His little head had so much burden to carry. As Finlay grew and the abuse from his mother continued, unhappiness festered in his soul. He was so afraid of her, he couldn't have mustered a smile even if he'd wanted to.

Growing pains

In 1955, Finlay turned five and was to start school after Christmas. Ina was over the moon. She would be rid of her burden for a few hours each day at least. *It will do me good to have him out of my sight*, she thought. With a few extra shillings from Wullie's sideline as a bookie's runner, she kitted Finlay out in old school clothes from Paddy's second-hand marketplace, and the money she saved there went with her to the bingo hall.

The morning of his first day at school arrived and Ann turned up to see him. Finlay was excited, drumming his feet as she gave him a penny for the tuck shop. She told him he looked a 'wee smasher' and then she left for work. Prince, the family border collie, was wagging his tail and smothering Finlay in tongue licks and saliva. Prince never left Finlay's side; he was the little boy's only friend so far in his short life and a great comfort. They often fell asleep snuggled up together.

Ina told Finlay she would show him the way to school today but after that he'd have to make his own way. Grabbing him by the wrist, she started to lead him down the road.

'Remember the church! Pass the church and up the road to the top,' she told him.

'Mammy, my legs are sore,' said Finlay.

'Never mind your legs,' she snapped. 'I'm telling you, don't forget your way or you'll get this!' and she showed him the back of her hand, bringing it to within an inch of his face.

Finlay flinched. Even at the tender age of five, he believed her and knew he had to get it right or she would hit him. 'I won't forget.' Ina led him up towards the school, and again he said, 'Mammy, my legs are sore.'

'Fuck!' she shouted. 'I told you, it's growing pains!'

Nearing the school, he began to walk slower, hobbling towards the classroom door where the teacher was waiting. His legs felt like they were set in cement.

'This is Finlay McGill,' said Ina. 'Is it all right if I leave him with you as I have something urgent I need to attend to this morning?' In fact, she was desperate to attend the matinee session at the bingo hall, funded by the money saved skimping on his uniform.

'Yes, that's fine. Leave him with me. By the way, I'm Miss Clyde – same spelling as the river. I'm going to be teaching Finlay for the coming year.'

'Thanks very much,' said Ina. Putting on an act for Miss Clyde, she got down on one knee and affectionately rubbed her hand over Finlay's head, running her fingers through his hair and neatening his parting. 'Now, you'll be a good boy for Miss Clyde, won't you, son?' she said.

'Aye, Mammy, I will,' he replied.

'Do you remember the way home?' He nodded his head up and down several times. 'Good boy,' said Ina, and she walked away leaving little Finlay with Miss Clyde.

Finlay's first day went well, and before he knew it, the bell rang to mark its end. Numerous parents were waiting to pick their children up, and he scanned the crowd for his mother but soon realised she wasn't there.

He walked out through the hall and into the corridor and, looking up, saw row upon row of windows that let the afternoon sunshine through, illuminating the corridor and the adjacent glazed classrooms. Each window appeared to project great sunbeams into the long narrow aisle, and for wee Finlay this was overwhelming. Frightened and confused by the vastness of it all, he took to his heels and ran to the door at the end of the corridor. He stepped out on to the asphalt path, panting and wheezing. The idea of returning the next day scared him. Even though his mother was cruel to him at home, he could deal with it: it was all he knew.

He managed to make his way home on his own, but when he tried to open the front door, it was locked.

He ran round to the back door but found that locked too. He banged on it, but no one answered. No one was there. Feeling very alone, he sat down on the doorstep with his elbows on his knees, and patiently waited for someone to come home.

'Wullie, I need to have a word with you,' said Ina. 'This place is doing my head in, with all eight boys and only the one room. We've put up with this for years now!'

'You'll just have to hang on for a wee while more,' Wullie answered. 'You know we have our name down for rehousing on the new housing scheme they're building up in Gallows Hill.'

'Aye, I know we do, but that's years away. And, besides, Finlay's getting a bit too big now to be sleeping in our bed.'

'You're right,' agreed Wullie. 'We'll move him out tonight and into one of the bunks with the other wee ones.'

'Thank God!' Ina was delighted and, wanting to reward her man, asked, 'What are you wanting for your dinner? You fancy liver and onions?'

Wullie smiled. 'You know I always like liver and onions any time you make it.' Kissing Ina, he added, 'I am away to my bed for a couple of hours or so – I'm on night shift tonight. Give me a shout around four.'

Ina got herself and young Finlay ready to take the short walk to the butcher's shop for Wullie's tea.

They hadn't gone far before Ina realised Finlay was a long way behind her and limping.

'Finlay! Hurry up!' she barked.

'Mammy, my legs are sore.'

'Fuck! It's growing pains!'

Grabbing at his earlobe, she twisted it and dragged him along the pavement. Finlay dared not protest or whimper about the pain she was inflicting on him, though he did complain constantly about his legs.

'My legs are sore, Mammy!' he cried, trying to run to keep up with her and alleviate the pain on his twisted ear.

Ina stopped walking. 'If you mention sore legs again, I will give you sore legs with the back of my hand. I have told you, it's growing pains! Now shift your arse.'

Finlay's legs were aching badly. He tried to walk faster but couldn't.

'For Christ's sake, laddie,' said Ina, slapping Finlay hard across the face. 'Move it!'

He could walk no further, though he tried hard so as not to upset his mother any more than she was already. His legs gave way and he crumpled to the ground, much to Ina's angry frustration. She had to get Wullie's tea.

'Christ's sake, what's up with you now? Get on your feet.' Finlay attempted to stand, but couldn't.

A passing man stopped. 'Are you okay, missus?' he asked.

Having finally grasped that there was indeed something wrong with Finlay's legs, Ina realised she had no alternative but to address the situation.

'Aye, but could you help me get him to the taxi rank? I need to get him to the doctor.'

The doctor examined Finlay and said, 'I'm going to refer Finlay to the orthopaedics specialist at the hospital. You should get a letter soon. In the meantime, keep him off school and limit his movement until we find out what's going on.'

Ina's face fell. The thought of being stuck in the house with Finlay for God only knew how long filled her with dread.

After various tests, it was found that Finlay had pockets of fluid on his spine, and he was admitted to the hospital to be operated on.

The hospital

Walking into the living room of his home, Wullie found Ina sitting by the window smoking a cigarette. 'Have you had a good day? And did you manage to get to the hospital and visit the wee boy?' he asked.

'Well, no, I've not had a wonderful day as when I tried to get over to the hospital, the first bus never turned up, and then the next one broke down,' Ina replied.

'But did you manage to see Finlay?' he asked.

'I got to see him, though I was a wee bit late.'

'Ah that's good,' said Wullie. 'How was he?'

'Aye, he was the same as yesterday. Just his normal self,' she said.

At no time had Ina been to see Finlay that day, or the day before. Nor the day before that. All in all, in the two weeks he had been in hospital, she had only visited him twice: once when she had to come in to sign some papers, and then five days later when she went only to show her face. Even then, she made excuses to the matron about having to go to the doctor's and rushed away.

Lying in his hospital bed with his legs in traction, Finlay was unable to move for weeks. He couldn't interact with the other children on the ward and just lay watching them play, pushing little cars along the floor and running around. He wanted to play with them.

One day, he pulled himself up with the bed handles and sat bolt upright, his face red and twisted. He punched the mattress in sheer frustration. Then he slowly shuffled down the bed, unhooked his legs, slid over the bedside and crawled over to the other children. He felt so happy as he pushed the cars and played. But less than five minutes later, it was noticed that he was missing from his bed.

'Finlay! What are you doing out of bed?' yelled the matron. Finlay jerked with fright at her voice. He disliked her. She was a bit of a harridan, small in height and with a face that often wore an unattractive and grumpy look.

She ordered that he be placed in a cot bed and tied to its sides with bandages. The nurses looked at each in disbelief but hurriedly prepared a cot bed, fitting the pullies above it and putting his legs back in traction. They then bound Finlay's waist, legs and hands to the sides of the bed as ordered.

'It's for his own good,' pronounced the matron. 'It's no wonder he keeps getting infections if he's crawling around the floor like a cockroach. Nurse Jones, I would like you to keep an eye on Finlay and keep me informed of his progress. Now, run along. I'm busy.'

Finlay's lonely little heart sank. He wondered why this was happening to him. But tired after his crawl across the floor and the ensuing turmoil, he soon fell fast asleep.

Wullie had walked out of work at two fifteen and, spotting the number 27 bus which passed the hospital, he'd decided to jump on and go and see Finlay.

Sitting on the bus, Wullie lit a cigarette and blew out blue smoke as he thought about his wee boy. He looked forward to seeing him. Although he had seven other boys, he has a soft spot for Finlay. Deep down in his heart, he suspected – although he didn't want to admit it to himself – that Ina struggled with Finlay's presence and did not give the boy her best. However, he couldn't bring himself to believe that Ina was anything other than a decent God-loving person. Little did he know what his wife regularly put wee Finlay through.

Grabbing a bag of sweets from the shop, Wullie made his way to the children's ward. Finlay's eyes lit up so brightly with excitement when he saw him, it was as though Wullie had thrown the switch to a happiness bulb. His father was the last person he'd expected. He had not seen anyone for more than a week.

'Oh Daddy, Daddy, it's you!' he cried.

Bending over the cot, Wullie gave Finlay a kiss and immediately noticed that his son's arms and legs were bound with bandages to the cot side. Outraged, he began to untie the bandages.

'We'll see about this!' he said. 'I can't believe this has been going on. Nurse! Nurse!' he called out.

'Yes, Mr McGill, how can I help you?' she asked.

He pointed towards young Finlay. 'How can you help me!' Wullie repeated incredulously. 'Come on now. Why is this wean tied up in this cot like a Christmas turkey? Could you please tell me what the hell is going on?'

The nurse's face flushed. 'If you have anything to say, you will have to speak to Matron,' she stuttered.

'Well, get her now. I have plenty to say.' Wullie shook his head as he continued untying Finlay.

When Matron approached and saw what Wullie was doing, she marched across the ward crossing her arms. 'What, may I ask, are you doing?' she demanded.

The normally placid Wullie turned his head and said in anger, 'What does it look like? I am untying my son. Who gave you the right to restrain him in this manner? The Japanese during the war wouldn't even do that to a child. What sort of person are you anyway?'

'I am the person who has your son's wellbeing at heart. How dare you question my nursing ability!' the matron retorted scornfully.

'Well, if I see this happening again, there will be trouble and you will be reported. No question about it. Now go!' Wullie would always fight for what he believed was right, and today he knew he was right. 'Go!'

Her face flushed a bright crimson; no one dared speak to Matron as Wullie had. He had embarrassed her in front of her staff. She snorted, throwing her head back, swung on her heels and marched military style from the ward.

For nearly eighteen months, Finlay was bed-bound with his legs in long-term traction. He'd suffered bone inflammation and several severe infections. But now, as he neared nine years of age, he was to finally leave the hospital.

He would also be leaving his favourite person, Nurse Davis. The morning he was to go home, she looked over at Finlay, knowing she was going to miss him. She felt sorry that he'd never really got much interaction with the other children except maybe for the last three or four weeks of his stay and, even then, she'd noticed him shy away from them. She strongly suspected there was a lacking in his social skills and wondered just how he would cope back at school. Nurse Davis stroked Finlay's hand. As he began to come round from his slumber, she said softly, 'You're going home today'.

'Will I see my daddy and Prince?' he asked.

'Yes, of course, and your mammy too.'

Finlay pushed his head back under the sheet and shivered. He'd felt safe in the hospital away from his mother, and was used to the daily routine of the hospital ward. Though he felt excited about seeing his father and his faithful dog, his body chilled with fear at the thought of going back home. The thought of seeing his mother again churned his stomach.

For some time, Finlay's glazed eyes stared out of the hospital window. He thought about running away through the open fields in the distance. He allowed himself a slight inward smile as he imagined running away from everything with his faithful dog Prince, just running and running. In his mind's eye, he saw Prince bounding over the grass and he saw himself tumble and fall over, laughing when Prince ran up to him, wagging his tail and licking his face.

His thoughts were soon interrupted. 'Come on, Finlay, you will have to get ready to go home.'

'Is my daddy coming for me?' he asked.

'No, you'll be going home in the ambulance by yourself, but someone will meet you when you get home.'

The nurses stood at the door of the ward and waved to little Finlay walking away slowly all by himself, aided by his sticks and supportive leg callipers. Reaching the waiting ambulance, he sat by the window and enjoyed looking out at the sights he passed on the way home. When the ambulance passed his road and turned up the hill towards the Gallows Hill housing scheme, Finlay looked back at his tenement building and wondered if they were picking someone else up. But the ambulance stopped outside 118 Riverside Road, Gallows Hill, and to Finlay's delight and surprise, his father emerged from the front door. Unknown to him, it was the family's new corporation house.

The second homecoming

Wullie scooped young Finlay into his arms and hugged him tight. Finlay pressed his face into his father's chest. He could smell the shipyard on Wullie's work clothes; for Finlay, it was a smell of contentment and safety. He felt more relaxed in his father's arms than he had done in over a year and he didn't want his father to put him down.

Wullie carried him into the hallway of the family's newly built three-bedroomed house. It all felt very new and strange, but Finlay was pleased to find there was an inside toilet and bathroom. And he did still recognise most of the living room furniture, although a new three-piece suite sat pride of place in the middle of the room and a new grey floral hearth rug lay in front of the fireplace. All this was due to Ina winning the £100 snowball jackpot at the bingo.

Bingo was also the reason Ina was not there to greet Finlay today.

'Are you okay, son?'

'Aye, Daddy, I am. Where's Sam and James and everybody?'

'James and Sam have moved out and got a flat down the road. And the rest of the boys are at school or work,' Wullie explained. 'But we do have a surprise for you, so close your eyes.'

Drumming his feet in excitement Finlay covered his eyes, but he stole a look through the crack between his fingers and saw his uncle Finlay enter the room.

'Look to the door, Finlay,' said his father. Uncle Finlay walked across the living room towards him, smiling. He rubbed young Finlay on the head, splaying his hair. 'Well, Finlay, my wee namesake, here you go. Here's a thruppence bit for you to get yourself a bag of caramels.'

A smile lit up Finlay's face as he took the money. 'Thank you, Uncle Finlay! Can I spend it today on an ice cream when Johnny comes?' His father and uncle both laughed.

Young Finlay hadn't seen much of his uncle in the last few years, but he was one of the very few people who had treated him kindly as a youngster and he liked him. He'd never noticed anything odd about the man's appearance before, but now, after being stuck in a hospital bed for such a long period of time, he had developed a habit of looking closely at people, sussing them out. He saw his uncle had become tubby and had actually quite an unpleasant face. His head was flat on the sides as though it had been squashed in a vice, and his over-large ears seemed pinned flat to those sides. He had a very big nose with extremely large nostrils that reminded him of a farmer's bull, and his eyes bulged slightly from their sockets. He looked rather like Quasimodo as played by Charles Laughton in *The Hunchback of Notre Dame* film, Finlay thought. He guessed that there was something not quite right with his uncle, but it was all hush-hush and he never found out what it might be.

He might like his uncle but he didn't trust him. Young Finlay had learned to trust no one in his short life, not even his beloved father. After all, if his father loved him, how could he let his mother treat him the way she did? It broke his already aching heart. He was too young to comprehend just how devious his mother was in fooling Wullie and everyone around her.

Meeting his uncle again and being home but in this new house all felt quite strange. Everything except his father was different and it was unnerving. Finlay asked if he could go to his new room.

'Of course you can. Your uncle Finlay will be staying with us for a wee while, so he'll be sleeping in your room, too.' Finlay nodded.

It took a good month or two for Finlay to settle back at home and for the doctors and all concerned to be sure he was fit enough to attend school. But the day finally came. He had looked forward to this for months and yearned to see his old classmates again.

His mother though had told him to make her breakfast in bed before he left for school. 'Tea and toast now!' she had hollered down the stairs. There was no one else at home to do it.

Already trembling, Finlay put the kettle on the hob and turned on the gas in the grill. He was frightened he'd burn the toast and anxiously watched it brown. 'Thank goodness,' he murmured to himself as he took it out from the grill. 'Perfect.' He covered it lightly in margarine, placed it on the tray with his mother's tea and made his way upstairs.

'Here you are, Mammy.' Ina was sitting upright in bed and he carefully placed the tray on her lap. He looked at her with trepidation as she took a sip of the tea and jerked with fright when she immediately screamed at him.

'For fuck's sake, that tea is peely-wally and tastes like dishwater!' She bit into the toast and shouted even louder. 'So is this fucking toast! It's fucking peely-wally, too!'

A tremor travelled down Finlay's spine.

'You daft bastard! You can't even get a cup of tea and slice of toast right, can you? A fucking monkey could do it better!' Ina threw the tray off her lap and on to the floor. Tea splashed up the walls and little brown rivers ran back down again, racing each other to the bottom.

'For fuck's sake. Go and make me a stronger cup of tea and get me toast that is light brown.' She pointed at the soaked wall. 'And you better clear up that mess that you've made, too!'

Overwhelmed with anxiety, Finlay bounced about robotically trying to clear up. He felt his hands shake. It was as though they were connected to puppet strings: they wouldn't move where he wanted them to go. As soon as he was done clearing the spillage, he ran downstairs out of his mother's sight.

Down in the kitchen, he still felt as though his body were underwater. A drowning sensation descended over him. His chest heaved as he fought for a mouthful of air – a mouthful that gave him momentary relief before the sensation of sinking returned. He gasped and gulped and sank again. He shuddered at the thought of burning this next slice of toast. She would kill him. He kept his eyes on the grill to make sure he got it right, but the kettle's whistle startled him and he ran over, grabbed a tea towel and took it off the hob. As he poured the boiling water into the pot, he realised with horror that the toast was smoking. In panic, he tried to quickly replace the kettle on the stove but dropped it, splashing boiling water over his right hand. Pain bit into his palm and thumb and Finlay screeched.

As he held his hand under cold water, Ina yelled, 'Where's my tea and toast? You better hurry up or you are going to be late for school!'

Finlay wanted to try again with the toast but knew he didn't have time, so he scraped the burnt bits off as best as he could and tried to hide its blackness in a thick layer of margarine. He climbed the stairs to her bedroom. 'Here, Mammy, I made this fresh,' he said, and he laid the tray upon her lap again.

'That looks much better,' she said. It was as though his mother had opened a relief valve in Finlay's head with these words, and all the pressure began to slowly deflate. He allowed himself a smile and began to relax. But then Ina tasted the tea.

'This is like fucking tar!' she bellowed. 'And your other cup was like fucking dishwater! Do you want me to drink dishwater?'

Lips trembling, he squirmed and his eyes appeared unpleasantly bright. 'No Mammy, no Mammy, I don't want you to drink dishwater,' he stammered.

'Well then, do you want me to drink tar?'

'No, Ma-m-mmy,' he stuttered again.

Finlay fought hard to stifle a sob but couldn't manage it. A tear ran down his face. Ina was quick to pounce on it. 'What the fuck are you greeting for now?'

'I'm not greeting, Mammy, I'm not. Please, Mammy!' he begged.

She snapped her fingers at him and he flinched. 'Come here. Come here now,' she commanded.

Holding back his tears, Finlay stood shaking. 'Oh Mammy, don't!'

'Don't what? Come here!' Ina screamed, pointing to the floorboard in front of the bed. 'Stand there, and I will give you something to greet for.'

Sweat poured from Finlay's brow, his mind flashing back to the bad days before he was in hospital.

'Fucking stand there!' she ordered again. He took a hesitant step forward.

'What the fuck have I told you about greeting? I told you that I would give you something to greet for. Lean over!' she said.

'No, Mammy, please don't!'

Reluctantly, Finlay leaned towards his mother, but he was still too far away for her to reach him. She jabbed her finger repeatedly at the floor in front of her. 'Fuck me! Nearer!' she yelled.

Moving closer, he got within striking distance and without hesitation she slapped Finlay square on the face with such force that it almost toppled him over. 'You're a fucking waste of time. Now, get yourself ready and washed for school and make sure you wash your neck.'

Finlay felt a scream fill his mouth but he dared not let it out. He gulped it down his throat and swallowed it. He could not show any emotion. The throbbing in his head and in his burned hand intensified, but he knew he dare not let out so much as a murmur. Finlay held his hands to his ears as a heavy cloud of helplessness engulfed him. It was like a freezing mist rolling in from the sea, icing everything to the spot. He stood by the side of the bed motionless, his mind numbing with every heartbeat. Like stinking slurry slipping down a drain, his emotions ran down into his gut and simmered.

'What are you doing standing there like a big daft laddie for? Get to school now.'

Making his way out of the bedroom, Finlay turned to close the door. Looking back, he saw his mother opening her women's magazine and biting into the toast. It looked very much as though she were enjoying it. It was as though nothing had just happened at all.

'Come up and let me see you before you leave for school,' said Ina, 'and hurry up. You're going to be late!'

'Right, Mammy, I will.' Finlay held his burned hand under his armpit and rubbed his red swollen cheek with the other. He grabbed his school bag and left.

Finlay was relieved to be out of the house and looking forward to his first day back, but when he walked into his old classroom he was immediately dismayed. He could only see the unfamiliar faces of children smaller and younger than himself. He ran out of the classroom in confusion and bumped straight into his old teacher Miss Clyde. Bouncing off her, he fell face first to the floor and bumped his head.

'What have you all been told about running in the school!' shouted Miss Clyde. Not realising it was Finlay, she proceeded to take her three-tonged belt out from her waistband. 'Stand up and hold your hand out,' she demanded.

Finlay got to his feet and instinctively offered her his right palm. Miss Clyde lifted the belt in readiness for the punishing swoop and drew it down firmly across his hand. The crack could be heard resonating along the hallway's stone floor. Finlay recoiled and flicked his hand to cool it. He had mistakenly offered his scalded hand and the pain was excruciating.

When Miss Clyde looked at him properly and saw it was Finlay, her heart sank. 'Oh, it's you,' she said. 'How are you, Finlay?'

He was still waving his hand around in agony but dared not show any emotion. He had learned that much. 'I'm okay, Miss Clyde. Where is everybody?'

Miss Clyde's eyebrows knitted together. 'What do you mean by everybody?'

'Where's everybody that was in my class before?'

'Oh, Finlay, I'm sorry to tell you this but they have moved up to a different class,' she explained. 'You will now be in Miss Brown's class two doors up. You had better go there now. Good luck in your new class.'

Finlay got to the door of his new classroom but it was closed. Peering through the glass, he could see everyone already sitting with their books on their desks. His hand shook as he knocked on the door.

'Come in!' was the cry.

'Hello, miss. My name is Finlay McGill.'

'Where have you been? Your first day back and you are late!' said Miss Brown. Opening the drawer of her desk, she pulled out a well-used five-fingered tawse and slammed it hard on her desk. The noise made the class all jump. 'Now, young man, if you are late again you will get this! Go on and sit down.'

***

When the bell rang for morning break, Finlay made the long walk out into the schoolyard. He felt alone and frightened. The yard was surrounded by a large sandstone wall, with wrought iron double gates that opened on to the playing field. Finlay walked slowly to the far corner and stood with arms and eyes lowered, trying to blend in against the wall. He no longer knew how to interact with other children: his time in hospital had seen to that.

Only a minute or two before the bell rang again to signal the end of break, two boys from the class below approached him.

'What's your name?' they asked.

'My name's Finlay McGill.'

'Where d'you live? And what class are you in? Do you have any sweeties? Do you have any money?' they pestered.

When they saw Finlay tremble, they knew they had an easy target. They attempted to ransack his pockets even though he was a good few inches taller and more well-built than them. Finlay turned to face the corner of the wall. 'Leave me alone! Just leave me!' he cried helplessly. They both started punching his back, only running off when they heard the voice of Mr Burns, the teacher who taught the oldest children.

'Hoy, you two! Stop that!' The bell to return to class was ringing in the distance. He turned to Finlay. 'What happened, boy?'

'Nothing, sir.'

43

'Well, we'll have no more fighting in the playground. Got it?' Finlay stood silent. 'I will not ask you again,' Mr Burns growled. 'Have you got it?'

He knew that tone of voice and immediately responded. 'Yes, sir, I've got it!'

'Got what?' he barked.

This is so unfair, thought Finlay. I've done nothing! Why is it always me people pick on? What is it about me that makes everyone hate me? 'No fighting in the playground, sir.'

'Well, there had better not be, or you will have me to deal with. Now, get to your class before you're late!'

Finlay hurried back to class only to discover that, yet again, the door was closed. He was late again. His stomach sank to its deepest depths and a cold sweat waxed across his brow. He steadied himself before knocking on the door, knowing he was visible to the class through the large windows.

'Do enter!' called Miss Brown sarcastically.

The other pupils didn't lift their heads from their desks but all eyes were on him. Finlay hesitantly turned the handle, crept into the classroom and closed the door as softly as possible behind him. His stomach churned and he felt unsteady on his feet as he headed straight for his desk.

'This is beginning to be a bit of habit. Your first day back and late twice in a row,' said Miss Brown.

'B-b-but, miss! I was talking to—'

Miss Clyde stopped him before he could explain. 'Shut up, McGill!' she bellowed. 'Did I ask you to speak?'

Dragging her desk drawer out, she extracted her tawse and stood by her desk. Finlay looked up nervously at her. She was very tall, dressed all in black and rather frightening-looking. Her narrow face seemed to elongate her high forehead, and her short, greying hair looked rather like a grey squirrel sitting on her head, Finlay thought.

Miss Brown seemed to take pleasure in swishing the tawse back and forth through the air to frighten Finlay. 'Don't you "but" me! You are late again – and that is twice today. Twice on your first day, might I add.'

'Yes, miss. Sorry, miss.'

'Now, hold out your hand.'

Finlay did not want to be belted on his right hand again. The scalded skin stood proud and had blistered after Miss Clyde hit him. He offered Miss Brown his left hand instead.

'Right hand, McGill, right hand,' she instructed.

'But, miss, please, I—' he pleaded.

Miss Brown wasn't interested. 'If you say "but miss" one more time, you will be strapped on both hands. Now hold out your right hand.'

Her two feet lifted clean off the ground in a little jump when she brought the tawse down on Finlay's hand. It cracked like a whip. Finlay's face screwed up as stinging pain ran up his arm. Now he knew why the older pupils nicknamed her Miss Whippy.

'Now sit down open and your book at page forty-three.'

Throbbing and aching, Finlay sat at his desk feeling wronged. *Why does no one like me?* In despair, he covered his face with his fingers, unable to cry even if he'd wanted to.

When Finlay arrived home later and walked into the living room, he was met by his uncle Finlay.

'Hiya, wee Finlay. Have you had a good day at school?'

'No, Uncle Finlay,' he replied. 'I have not had a good day at school. I hate school!'

'You hate school? Why do you hate it?' his uncle asked.

'I just do.'

Uncle Finlay

One Friday evening in the summer of 1959, when Finlay was nine and a half years old, he tried to stop his father leaving for his night shift at the shipyard. 'Please, Daddy, don't go to work. Stay here with me,' he pleaded, pulling on Wullie's arm.

'I can't, son. I need to go to work. That's what daddies do. I'll bring you back one of my corned beef pieces and you can toast it in the morning for a wee treat.' Wullie kissed Finlay goodnight and rode off to work on his pushbike.

Finlay took himself up to bed, but found his bedroom overly warm and stuffy. The double doors to the hot-water tank had been left half open. He went over to close them and spotted a large glass jar of petroleum jelly sitting on top of the tank. Curious, he lifted it down, feeling its warmth in his hand, and unscrewed the top. He dipped a finger in: the jelly was warm, too, and soft. He wondered why it was there. Maybe it was for Uncle Finlay's hair, he thought. He put it back carefully and went to open the window.

Later that night, he was awakened by his drunken uncle flinging the bedroom door open – a regular occurrence on Friday nights. Turning over in his bed, he tried to ignore the sounds of his uncle wrestling with his trousers, staggering and falling to the floor.

'For God's sake, please go to your bed, Uncle Finlay,' he said under this breath in tired irritation.

His uncle was now on the floor on his hands and knees and he crawled over to Finlay's bedside. He slipped a hand under the bed covers. Young Finlay froze. The hand moved over his leg. Finlay's heart raced. He was too frightened to even breathe. The hairs on the nape of his neck jutted from their roots. Goosebumps erupted all over his body.

He pretended to be asleep, but the stinking reek of cigarette smoke and alcohol was getting stronger as his uncle slavered over him. A whisper came in his ear. 'You're my wee namesake and my wee best pal, aren't you, son?'

Young Finlay sweated and shivered as the hand moved ever nearer his genitals. His uncle made sickening grunts and groans as he fondled both the boy and himself. Through his fear, Finlay felt horror and shame as his penis responded to the first caress. Then he heard the sound of a jar being twisted open. The petroleum jelly jar, Finlay realised with a jolt. He lay rooted to the spot in terror and confusion.

'Please don't, Uncle Finlay!' he begged.

'You are my wee namesake and I love you,' his uncle answered softly as he smeared the petroleum jelly on Finlay's bottom.

His uncle turned him over and lay heavily on top of him. Unable to breathe under the weight, and with stale liquor-soaked saliva still dripping over him, Finlay pleaded again more loudly. 'Please don't do that, Uncle Finlay! Please don't!'

Hundreds of butterflies fluttered frantically in his stomach, bashing against each other as if they wanted to escape too. They were ripping his throat and insides away. In another desperate attempt to stop his uncle in his tracks, he cried out, 'Uncle Finlay, I don't feel well!'

'Shut the fuck up!' his uncle hissed. 'Your mother is in the other room. Keep your mouth shut or you will get a fucking slap! You hear me?'

Feeling dead inside with the weight of his uncle still upon him, a tear dripped from Finlay's eye, and then another and another until there was a river of tears. He emitted no sound. His mother had seen to that. But a quiet scream swirled and pounded inside his head. He lay motionless until he could bear no more, and then slowly wrapped his body within his arms. He hoped it would all end soon.

Uncle Finlay dismounted and rubbed young Finlay's head. 'I am your uncle and I love you. It's okay. Don't worry,' he said. And then he went to his own bed, leaving his young prey to his own thoughts.

Finlay felt a wet substance running from his bottom. He crept downstairs to the bathroom and sat on the toilet until it had all run out of him, and then ran himself a bath. His whole body was numb with pain. His head was numb. Everything was numb. Nothing seemed real. All he wanted was for it all to have been a bad dream. *I've just had a nightmare*, he told himself. *That did not happen.* And he sat in the bath until the water was cold.

Finlay lay in bed until dawn unable to sleep, furious that he had let this horrible thing happen. He was so ashamed and confused about the way his body had responded. It would haunt him for many years to come. In desperation, he grabbed a knife from the kitchen and pulled his penis out, wanting to cut it off. He slid the blade lightly across his skin and watched it bleed. But he couldn't go through with it and threw the knife in the sink.

Morning broke and, with mind and body numbed, Finlay found himself downstairs with his mother. She was angry with him as usual. 'Get ready to run to the shop and get me my fags!' she shouted at him just as his Uncle Finlay walked in.

His uncle did his usual rubbing of young Finlay's head.

'My wee namesake,' he said. 'Here you are, son.' He slipped his hand into his pocket and pulled out a florin. Finlay's eyes shone like torch lights. It was a lot of money for a child. 'That's for my wee namesake Finlay. But don't dare tell your mammy I gave you that or she will take it off you. It's a secret between you and me!'

The abuse continued almost every drunken Friday or Saturday night. Being young and smart, Finlay soon realised he could limit the damage: by doing certain things his uncle enjoyed, he could get it all over with sooner and without the trauma of penetration and rape. But he couldn't make it stop.

He had nowhere to turn and nowhere to run and no one to talk to. If he told his father, his uncle Finlay would no doubt beat him. And he had gladly accepted the two shillings his uncle had given him to keep quiet. Telling his mother would only get him a slap for telling lies. Who would believe a nine-year-old? And even if his family did believe him, wouldn't they hate him for what he'd done? Deep-seated guilt hovered over all his thoughts – his penance for having allowed this awful thing to happen. He sank into depression and anxiety.

The janitor

Life didn't change for Finlay. The bullying, abuse and mistreatment occurred so often that he simply accepted it. Everywhere he turned cruelty stood in his path. He thought it was just how life was; he'd never experienced anything else.

He was, as he neared the age of eleven and a half, a tall and well-built youth and he was desperate to play in the school football team before he moved up to secondary school the following year. But Joe Durkin, the school janitor, ran and picked the football team, and Finlay was never picked. Durkin told him he couldn't kick his way out of a wet paper bag – but Finlay never gave up asking to try out.

On one such attempt, Finlay made his way to the janitor's room during his dinner break, peering in through the door window. The room was poorly lit and dingy. School supplies, buckets, brushes, paper reams and an assortment of other school-related items were dumped in the corner. Durkin was sitting on a wooden stool with his back to an old, rickety teacher's desk that was strewn with odd pieces of children's clothing and lost property. A pack of cigarettes peeped out of the top pocket of his blue boiler suit.

Durkin sat there smoking a cigarette. As he dragged the smoke into his lungs, he threw his head back to within a short distance of a grey metal lamp, the dusty light bulb hanging just inches above his face. Rounding his lips, he blew the smoke into rings. The lamp light that managed to escape cut through the haze of smoke and, flickering like will-o'-the-wisp, lit up the top of his head while eerie shadows hid his sunken eyes.

Durkin's other, cigarette-free arm was firmly placed around a young girl's waist. He was bouncing her up and down on his lap and she seemed oblivious to where his hand was wandering. She laughed as she poked her finger through the smoke rings, dispersing them with a swirling movement. Finlay recognised her as Fiona Yule, one of his classmates. She was quite well into puberty and one of the few eleven-year-olds to wear a bra. He also recognised the two other girls standing either side of Durkin. They, too, were popping the smoke rings. Finlay didn't find it particularly odd at the time but, later in life, he'd understand just what sort of predator Durkin really was.

Durkin noticed Finlay lurking outside the room. 'What the hell do you want, McGill?' he grumbled.

Nerves made Finlay stutter. 'C-c-c-can I get a trial for the football please, Mr Durkin?'

Durkin looked Finlay straight in the eye and, with cigarette in hand, he swung his arm out as if to sweep the desktop and beckoned Finlay into the room. In a deep ominous voice he said, 'You're a daft laddie, are you not? You ask me every week for a trial.'

'I've never had one,' said Finlay.

'Aye, and you will never get a trial from me either.'

'Why?' asked Finlay. 'I'm good enough to be in the team.'

'You! Good enough for the team! Never!' snapped Durkin. 'Who told you that?'

'My pals. And you won't even let me train with them. Why not?' he asked again.

'You haven't any pals. You're a loner. Naebody even likes you. Now go away and don't ask me again!'

Durkin couldn't stand Finlay. He'd harboured a festering resentment of the McGill family ever since Ina had given him a dressing down eight years before for ridiculing her son Sam in front of the other boys. Durkin had made fun of Sam for having holes in his socks and for not wearing underpants, so Ina had waited outside the changing room after a football match and chastised Durkin, embarrassing him in front of several other parents and teachers. He had never forgotten that day and took his resentment out on Finlay.

But staring at him now, Durkin realised Finlay had grown tall and was well-built for his age. He changed tack. 'OK, you might get a trial, McGill, but only if you do me a big favour.'

'What is it that you want me to do?' asked Finlay.

'Go outside,' Durkin pointed to the back of the room, 'and go through that brown door, and you will see all the coke for the water boiler and school heating at the rear of the building. It's backed up against the wall. Beside it is a small metal door that drops straight down into the basement. I want you to open the door and shovel all the coke into that hole. If you can finish that in three weeks, if you shovel all the coke into the cellar, then I will consider giving you a trial. Now, go on and get the shovel – it's leaning against the wall.'

Twenty tonnes of coke had been delivered to the school the day before, and Durkin knew it would take Finlay weeks to do it. *Let the daft bastard do my dirty work*, he thought to himself, enjoying the idea of it somehow getting Ina back.

'Thank you, Mr Dukin! I will do now.' Finlay's body fizzed inside with excitement. At last he had the chance of a trial. He rushed outside, eager to shovel the coke.

Durkin grinned to himself. *What a fucking stupid laddie.*

Every day without fail, in break times, and again before he left for home, Finlay would diligently shovel the coke through the little door into the cellar below.

He'd even go back after his evening tea for an hour or two and shovel. It was hard work for an eleven-year-old but Finlay was determined to get his trial. He would only stop long enough to stuff jam sandwiches into his mouth or to have a quick drink. Even in the rain he shovelled the coke, desperate to get the job done.

After two solid weeks of shovelling, a smile lit up Finlay's young face. He felt more than pleased with himself: he had managed to shift more than three-quarters of the pile. *Mr Durkin will be pleased with me*, he thought. *I've nearly earned my football trial. I will get it all shovelled before the three weeks are over.*

Finlay picked up a piece of coke and, closing one eye, aimed it at the small metal door that he'd spent so many hours shovelling coke through. He flung the coke with all his strength and smashed it dead centre with such force that the door rang like the first strike of a church bell. Finlay's face broke out into a massive grin.

'Yesss!' he shouted. The door was still ringing like a tuning fork as he turned to make his way home.

When his mother, standing at the window, turned and looked him, she saw that his face and clothes were black. 'Look at the fucking state of you!' she cried. 'Playing on the coke heap again?'

Rage ran through Ina's body. If it had been any of her other sons, it would have been all 'boys will be boys'. But Finlay was different. She seemed to relish any excuse to make his life a misery.

'Come here!' she ordered.

Finlay knew if he went anywhere near her, he was in for a slap. 'No, Mammy. I'll wash it all off and I'll wash my clothes now,' he said.

Her face contorted with anger. 'I said come over here!' she bellowed, a fine mist of saliva shooting from her mouth. 'And I won't tell you again!'

Finlay shuffled nearer to his mother, his stomach churning so much he felt sick.

'Stand there!' Ina pointed to a knot on the bare floorboard. 'What have I told you about looking after your clothes? They do not grow on trees! Lean forward!'

This, Finlay remembered, was what she'd said when he'd brought her the tea and toast in bed. He knew what was coming. He leaned forward but was at the ready to pull his head away. Ina swung her arm up, her palm facing forward as if she were about to salute Hitler. With a swift hard swing, she brought the flat of her hand down on Finlay's ear. A loud crack rang out as his eardrum burst. The force threw him backwards halfway across the room. As he hit the floor he rolled out like a flicked carpet, and lay dazed and still.

'Get up!' Ina shouted, an edge of panic in her voice. 'Get up or I'll slap you harder!'

Finlay clasped his bloodied ear in his hand and screamed. The pain was like nothing he had ever felt before. It was a red-hot knitting needle thrust deep in

57

his ear canal. It throbbed in a rhythmic pulse, worsening with every beat. He threw himself to the floor, repeatedly head-butting the ground in a frantic attempt to dull the pain.

Ina stood screaming profanities at him and ordering him to get up on his feet. Finlay was past caring. There was no pain she could inflict that could surpass what he was already going through, and at that moment he felt he was going to die. She desperately tried to lift his dead weight but he was too heavy. 'Get up!' she screamed. 'Get fucking up! Stop being a cunt!'

There was no response from Finlay. Ina's panic turned to fear. Wullie would kill her for this, she knew. Grabbing the boy under his armpits, she managed to haul him on to his feet. He stood disorientated and unsteady, bawling and clutching his ear. She steered him to his bed and gave him two aspirin and a cup of water.

Finlay turned away and moved himself into the foetal position for comfort. His ear thumped and pounded as if someone was inside with a battering ram, trying to break out. Every beat of his heart sent a sharp dagger-like pain into his ear canal.

Ina knew she had gone too far. Prodding her finger in his face, she hissed, 'If you so much as tell your father about today, I will make sure your life is a misery!' Her face was stern and twisted. 'Not one fucking word to anyone, do you hear me? Not one word.' And she left the room.

It was Friday night and Finlay was lying in his bed, dreaming of playing in the school football team. His mind and body were exhausted and his ear was very sore, but he was still determined to finish the shovelling and earn his chance to try out for the school team. Interrupting his thoughts, the bedroom door swung open and the light switched on. Finlay pretended to be asleep.

'My wee namesake Finlay,' his uncle said softly. Finlay felt his hair being rubbed and the covers pulled back. He was wearing a sloppy joe to cover his modesty. He heard his uncle laugh as he tickled Finlay's abdomen, brushing his penis several times in doing so. Finlay lay rooted to the spot. Then his uncle switched off the light and left the room. It was a close call. Finlay was relieved that this unpleasant ordeal was over for tonight, but he knew another visit was likely on Saturday.

Saturday morning saw Finlay working hard again at shovelling the coke. He had carefully picked his clothing. Knowing no one would see him, he stood shivering on the coke pile naked except for the black wellingtons on his feet. A bucket of cold water he'd had the foresight to fill during his Friday dinner hour sat ready for his end-of-shift wash. He had a week to go and looked forward to getting his trial with Durkin and a chance of playing in the team. With that thought, he shovelled even harder.

Four hours went by and the coke was nearly all gone. After Sunday and Monday he should have no more shovelling to do. Exhausted, he threw the shovel down. Coke dust covered his sweating body and he looked like someone from a minstrel show. Finlay had brought a small slice of soap with him and he washed himself with the cold water from the bucket, meticulously scrubbing his face, neck, hands and legs. He would cover the rest of his body with clothes and sneak into the bathroom to finish his wash properly.

Sunday saw Finlay hard at it again, naked and shovelling. The pile was minuscule compared with two weeks ago and he knew he should have it finished by Monday teatime at the latest, and definitely within the three weeks Durkin had allocated to him. He would be glad when it was all over. His body ached and his back made a crunching sound when he bent down. He was worried he might end up in traction again. That night he was unable to move in bed without wincing. Every muscle in his back, legs and arms throbbed as though a mob had given him a good beating.

On Monday morning, Finlay rushed to school to get the last of the shovelling done. But when he made his way around the back towards the coke pile, he stopped in his tracks. The small pile had gone. The shovel was gone. And the yard had been swept. Finlay ran towards Durkin's office and met him at his door.

'Hi, Mr Durkin. All the coke has been shovelled and cleared up. When can I have my trial?'

'You never finished on time. I had to finish it,' said Durkin. 'You will be getting no trial.'

'But I would have finished if you'd left the last bit for me!'

Durkin had underestimated the young boy and had been shocked when he'd turned up at the school on Monday morning to find only a small pile of coke left. He had quickly cleared it up himself as he no intention of giving Finlay McGill the promised trial.

'I said two weeks to finish, so no trial.'

Finlay's stomach wrenched. 'No. You gave me three weeks to do it. I want my trial!'

Grabbing Finlay by the collar of his jacket, Durkin yanked him forward to within an inch of his face and spoke firmly. 'Listen, you're nothing but a daft wee cunt to do all that work. You're always asking for a trial and you've never got one. And you didn't finish shovelling the coke in time. So fuck off and don't come near this office again!' Durkin went inside and slammed the door.

Finlay was always submissive, but this was something he dreamed of and Durkin had promised. He would not let it go. He twisted the office door handle and went in.

'I want my trial,' he said again. 'You promised!'

Manhandling Finlay out of the office, Durkin tossed him on to the ground. 'I told you to fuck off. Now do it!' he spat.

Rage engulfed Finlay. He flung himself at Durkin and began thumping him with closed fists. Taken aback, Durkin gave Finlay a strong slap across the jaw and in one fell swoop lifted him off his feet and threw him on to the ground. Finlay lay crumpled up in a heap, shaking with anger.

'Just you wait until I grow up…' he raged. 'You'll be sorry!'

'Aye, I think we'll both need to wait a hell of a long time before I'm sorry. Now fuck off.'

Miss McGregor

Between the regular onslaught of the school bullies, the prejudiced teachers and the sadistic janitor, school was no relief for Finlay from his torments at home. No one seemed to take to this quiet, shy boy except for old Miss McGregor, a softly spoken music teacher who saw potential in all her pupils. Though she didn't teach Finlay, she felt sorry for him: a frown seemed almost permanently tattooed upon the boy's forehead as if there were a sadness he couldn't shift.

Whenever she saw him in the corridor, she would offer a kind word of encouragement, and sometimes she'd go out of her way to bump into him and have a chat. She knew instinctively that there was more to his demeanour than met the eye. In all the time she'd known him, he'd never seemed to find his smile.

Walking along the corridor one day, eyes bowed to the floor, Finlay felt her tap him on his shoulder. Miss McGregor was his favourite person at school and his eyes and mouth opened slightly in a faint attempt at a smile.

'How are you, Finlay?' she asked, concerned.

Finlay stood in front of her, gazing down at his feet. He pulled at his oversized grey school jumper before sniffing his dribbling nose. He caught a whiff of Miss McGregor's perfume, a fresh and clean smell that he liked, and wondered if the other kids would like him more if he smelt nice like that.

'I'm okay, miss,' he said slowly into the air as if sedated, not meeting Miss McGregor's eyes.

'That's good, son. Would you like a wee bit of apple pie? I made it this morning.'

When making the pie, Miss McGregor had Finlay and one or two of the other kids who were going hungry in mind. She had an apple tree in her garden and had made good use of a recent windfall.

'Oh, Miss McGregor, that would be smashing,' he answered quickly.

Miss McGregor showed a stern face. 'But hear you me, Finlay! Don't you dare tell anyone I gave you the pie,' she said.

'No, I willnae, Miss McGregor!' he promised, excitedly snatching the slice of pie from her hands and stuffing it up his jumper. He gave a little skip as he started to walk away, and then turned back to face Miss McGregor, winking and mouthing thanks. A slight smile had cracked across his face at the thought of his special treat. Miss McGregor felt pleased with herself. It was so rare to see him look happy. She skipped the last two steps into her office herself.

Born in 1888 and now in her seventies, Isobel McGregor was a spinster well past retirement age, but making a difference to children's lives was her great purpose in life. She loved her job. Caring and compassion ran through her family: her father had been the local doctor while her mother had served in the Church of Scotland Women's Guild. Marriage had never really been on the cards. It was the will of God. Though she had courted a few men in her younger days, she'd always managed to find fault with them. She preferred her own company, and nothing was better than a good book.

Known as Bel to her friends, she had lived the same handsome four-bedroom detached house all her life. It was, as people often said to her, far too big for one person, but she loved it and was not prepared to live anywhere else. She'd been born in it and she was determined that she would die in it. It held so many happy memories for her. Her mother and father's influence could still be seen in the furniture and décor, but she would not change it. She liked it just the way it was.

She was a slight woman, and age had given her a distinctive forward stoop, but her warm blue eyes sparkled somewhat like a young teenage girl's. She had a silken white face, tight lips and her thin grey shoulder-length hair, set with kirby grips, lay flat and tight against her head. She carried a book under her arm everywhere she went, and her long black skirt covered her shoes, making her appear to glide across the floor.

Finlay always looked forward to seeing Miss McGregor. He felt safe in her company and she lifted his spirits. She never shouted at him and was always softly spoken and kind. He would have done anything in his power for her, she had only to ask. It was Miss McGregor that kept him from dodging school altogether.

One summer's day, Finlay decided to go to Miss McGregor's office and pay her a visit. He had not seen her all morning. Her door was less than an inch ajar and he peeped through the crack and scanned the room. There was no sign of her, so he nudged the door open a little more and craned his neck to look for her reflection in the large mirror above the fireplace. His heart sank.

Then a glimmer of hope flashed through him like lightening, breaking a smile across his face. She might just be having a cup of tea with the other teachers. He began running at full pelt towards the staff room, only to be met by bully boy Drew Cowan. Drew tried to grab hold of Finlay running past at a thundering pace but the weight of Finlay was too much and they both ended up falling to the floor.

'Where are you going, you daftie? You got any money?' badgered Drew as they dragged themselves back to their feet.

'No. Leave me alone.' Finlay shrugged him off and ran on towards the staff room.

Approaching the tall opaque-glazed door, he wiped away the dribble on his nose with his sleeve, wet his fingers and ran them across his wellington boots to clean them up a bit, pulled at his jumper and straightened his hair. Miss McGregor was always nice to him and he wanted to make her proud of him and present himself as best he could. Standing with one foot turned on edge, his ankle just about off the ground, he clasped his hands in front of his grey school shorts and knocked.

'Yes, McGill? What can I do for you, my boy?' said Mr Ritchie, the headteacher.

'Please, sir, is Miss McGregor there?'

'No, I'm afraid she's not in today.'

Finlay's heart sank to a new low at the news. 'When will she be back?' he asked.

'She'll be back next Monday. Can I help you?'

'No, sir, it's okay. I just wanted to see if she was okay,' Finlay answered.

'Run along. I will inform her that you wanted to see her when she gets back.'

Finlay desperately hoped Miss McGregor was happy and well. He knew he would worry about her all over the weekend and would feel anxious until he saw her on the coming Monday.

Wee Wullie Wilson

One Friday morning at school, Finlay's teacher Miss Brown was discussing the African slave trade. She asked the class if they knew the name of the mark left on the slaves' skin after they'd been whipped. Lots of hands shot up eagerly, including Finlay's. He fidgeted frantically over his desk as he waved his arm and said, 'Me, miss! Me, miss!'

'Okay, Finlay, do you really think you know the answer?' she asked.

Confident that he did, he replied, 'Oh yes, miss.'

'Now, I will ask you again: are you sure you know the answer?'

'Yes, miss, I think so.'

'My goodness, wonders will never cease. I believe you do know. Go on then, surprise us all. Tell the class.'

Sure that he was indeed correct, he said, 'Please, miss, it's a scar.'

'Now see this, everyone. Here we have a stupid boy who thinks he knows it all, but in fact he knows sweet nothing! The answer is not a scar; the answer is a wheal.'

The classroom erupted with laughter. Her humiliation of Finlay was cruel. She knew every one of the pupils would have given the same answer, but she had deliberately chosen Finlay. In contrast, Miss Brown would boost the confidence of the more privileged children by picking them to answer easier questions that she knew they would get right.

Miss Brown had no time for children of a working-class background. In her mind, they were only fit to be labourers or servants, and therefore trying to teach them was a waste of her time. If they fell behind in their schoolwork, then she left them behind and they could never catch up. And she was not frightened to punish them harshly. Today was one of those days.

'You have made me look a fool! You made me believe you knew the answer,' she said. 'Come out here!'

She pointed to the middle of the floor, turned and opened her desk drawer and pulled out her tawse.

'Right, hold your hand out.'

Holding his hand out, Finlay screwed up his face in anticipation. Miss Brown grunted as she slammed the heavy-tailed piece of leather down on to his hand, and she intentionally went further up his hand to catch his wrist.

Finlay yelped as it hit him. The cruel blow bit into his wrist as if he'd been stung by a giant bee. He grasped his wrist and rubbed it. It was so much more painful than being struck on the palm, almost unbearable. His brow began to sweat and his wrist began to swell. Finlay whipped his hand back and forth in an effort to cool the sting.

Miss Brown could see the pain in Finlay's face. 'Stop that flapping, McGill,' she smirked, 'and show me your hand.'

Finlay reluctantly held out his throbbing hand, expecting another belting.

'Ah! Now, see, that's perfect! Simply perfect!' She grinned. 'Now, hold your hand up and show the class.'

Finlay wondered why she would ask him to do this but didn't hesitate to do as he was told. Miss Brown grabbed him by his wrist and twisted it towards the class. 'Now, class, see this bright red and blue mark that has sprung up on Finlay's wrist. Does that by any chance look like a scar?'

There was complete silence.

'Well, does it?' she barked.

Sensing annoyance in her voice, the class replied in a musical chorus. 'N…o, miss.'

'Correct! Well done, everyone. We know that is not a scar.' Miss Brown pulled his hand towards her and growled, 'Right, Mr McGill? This is not a scar! N.O.T. a scar. Do you hear me, you dunderhead?' She turned towards the class. 'Who can remember the name of the mark that's on Finlay's wrist?'

Several hands shot up, including that of the local accountant's daughter Morag.

'Go on then, Morag! Will you tell the class?'

'Please, miss, it's a weal,' she said triumphantly.

Miss Brown looked at Finlay and gave a slight snigger. 'Well done, Morag! You can have a gold smiling face to stick in your rewards book. You answered correctly with no hesitation whatsoever.' To add further insult to Finlay, she went on, 'That was exceptionally good, Morag. You answered correctly – unlike some know-it-alls we all know!'

Morag took the sticker from Miss Brown and thanked her. She made her way back to her desk, then stuck both her index fingers into her mouth to pull her lips apart, rolled her eyes and stuck out her tongue before she sat down and smirked at Finlay.

'Now sit down, McGill!'

Sitting at his desk, despondent, Finlay stared at a knot in his desk. His body shook inside as he wept inwardly. The belting he could bear. But the belief that everyone was against him, the humiliation of being a laughing stock, scarred him mentally. *I wish I were dead*, he thought. He knew he could do nothing right; Miss Brown was on top of him for any small mistake in his work. And for every mistake she gave out punishment. Even his spelling a word wrong meant corporal punishment.

Miss Brown addressed the class. 'Now, we have got everything cleared up, get out your jotters for a written exercise. I would like you to use your imagination to write a short story. It can be about anything – just let your creative juices flow and see what you can produce. You have forty-five minutes starting now!'

Everyone got their heads down to write. Finlay was still reeling from his ordeal, and sat with his head laid on his forearm over his desk. His body trembled and a tear leaked from his eye. He knew things were going to get even worse as his father would be out tonight working his night shift. It was Friday – pay day for his uncle Finlay – and a drunken visit was highly likely. The thought of the jar of petroleum jelly softening in the warm boiler cupboard turned his face white and made his skin crawl. He was filled with despair.

His thoughts were disrupted by Miss Brown's repeated banging on her desk with a blackboard duster. She hit the desk so hard a little white cloud of chalk dust rose up around her hand. The sound startled the whole class.

'McGill! Are you sleeping, boy?' she bellowed.

Before lifting his head, Finlay dug his eyes into his sleeve and rubbed away his tears. 'No, miss!'

'Get on with it then! Only thirty minutes left, class.'

Fifteen minutes had already gone, spent wallowing in self-pity. Finlay had no idea what was in store for him that night. He turned his thoughts to the one good thing: his father would be home for tea at least, and would, if only for a little while, protect him from his mother's wrath (though not from his uncle Finlay later). His lip curled to as near a smile as he could get.

If he didn't get this work done, Miss Brown would be on his back. Finlay thought for a minute or two before writing his heading: 'Prince McGill by Finlay McGill'. He loved his dog so much that he wanted to write about him, but he soon rubbed the heading out. He'd been asked to use his imagination and feared the belt if he wrote about his dog.

I know, he thought, I'll try and write a story using as many words as possible starting with W. Eagerly he wrote his heading and started scribbling words.

Wee Wullie Wilson by Finlay McGill

Wee Wullie Wilson, the Welsh welder, was walking with Walter Watson. Walter was wearing work wellingtons, while Wullie was wearing white walled wellingtons. Walter watched Wullie walk with a wilted wooden walking stick. He wondered what was wrong with Wullie, while they wandered. Walter watched a woman work with watercolours...

Miss Brown noticed Finlay was frantically sifting through his school dictionary. 'McGill!' she shouted. 'What are you up to now?'

'Please, miss, I am searching the dictionary for words beginning with W,' he explained.

Annoyed, she barked back, 'What do you mean words beginning with W? Bring that paper to me. Let me see what you've been doing all this time.'

Panic gripped Finlay at the angry tone of her voice. He gripped his exercise book with a trembling hand and slowly made his way to her desk. Miss Brown tutted impatiently. 'Hurry up, boy!' she urged, before snatching the book from his hand.

Most of the class lifted their heads to watch. They knew what was coming. It always did.

'I don't believe this! Everyone, put your pencils down and listen to this. We have the Robert Burns of Gallows Hill Primary here!' The children tittered nervously as she began to read out Finlay's story.

'What a load of rubbish!' Miss Brown shouted into Finlay's face, drawing a red line across the paper so hard it cut the paper in half. 'What are you trying to do? Make a fool out of me? And disrupt my class for the second time in less than an hour?'

Miss Brown opened her drawer and pulled out her tawse. 'Hand!' she demanded, before swiftly whacking Finlay again. 'Now get over there in the corner and put that dunce's hat on. Go on now.'

Finlay took the white makeshift coned hat that was marked with a large black D and placed it on his head.

'Stand there on that X that's drawn on the floor,' ordered Miss Brown.

Humiliation engulfed Finlay as the minutes ticked by. He could hear his fellow pupils sniggering behind his back. The hot radiator beside him was slowly baking his body, leaving him nauseated and sweating profusely. He felt his head lighten and for a moment it was as if the lights had gone out. He lost his balance and stumbled off the mark.

'Where do you think you are going?' Miss Brown barked, unable to pass up an opportunity to be cruel. She knew full well he'd simply stumbled.

'Please, miss, it was an accident. I didn't mean it,' Finlay pleaded.

'Oh, you didn't mean to move from the X? Well, you did move and I told you not to. Take that stupid hat off and go and stand outside the classroom door. I can't bear to look at you.'

The sash window

Finlay felt his body relax in relief: he would escape not only the heat of the radiator but the wrath of Miss Brown also. He gladly stood outside the classroom, still and quiet, the cold corridor cooling his sweltering body. But his thoughts soon returned to the evening that loomed before him.

Time and time again, his uncle Finlay rubbed young Finlay's head and continued to call him his 'wee namesake'. The more he did it, the more Finlay detested him. And the more he detested him, the more he hated the sound of his own name. Young Finlay had the weight of the world on his shoulders and he was desperate. With nowhere to turn, he felt he would be better off dead. With no real happiness in his life, he felt dead anyway.

Finlay looked up at the sash window in front of him. It was one of a series of six huge, tall windows that lit the main corridor. Sunlight streamed through each one like a giant spotlight. Each window had a long, looped cord running all the way up, enabling easy opening and closing. The nearest window ledge was four or five foot off the ground and Finlay was unable to see out of it except for some rooftops and sky. He noticed the chair outside Miss McGregor's office for pupils waiting to see her.

With sure deliberation, Finlay dragged the heavy chair towards the window. He stood on it and climbed up on to the window ledge. Finlay could hear the birds singing and, recognising the robin's song, he stopped and listened. The warm sun beamed through the window and caressed his young body as a musky smell of dampness filled the air around him. Gripping the cord, he carefully wrapped it around his neck twice.

He felt forsaken by everyone. I just want to die, he thought sorrowfully. I have no life. Who would even care if I weren't here? Well, I don't care either.

His last thought was of his beloved dog, his wee Prince. Finlay fretted about who would look after him if he weren't there, and was pleased when he realised his dad surely would. Tears dripped from his eyes. 'Goodbye, Prince. I love you, boy.'

With the cord firmly around his neck, Finlay did not hesitate. He took a leap off the ledge and launched himself up into the air, dropping down like a stone. The rope took hold, shuddering and tightening around his neck, and his young body lurched as it burned deep into his flesh. In reflex, his thin skeletal frame began thrashing at the end of the rope, his arms and legs spasmodically jerking – until it all stopped. Finlay's body swung, still and lifeless.

Sitting at her desk, Miss McGregor looked up and noticed the movement of the cord through her office window. Her immediate thought was that some of the children were up to mischief. She leaped out of her chair and scrambled to open the door and catch the culprit, only to be met by the horrific sight of young Finlay's limp body hanging motionless.

'Oh my God! Finlay!' she screamed in horror.

As she ran towards him, the cord around his neck began to unravel and his body jolted, dropping down on to the next loop. His pale figure swung and turned as the unravelling continued, dropping gradually until it reached the end of the rope. With the last jerk, his dead weight snapped the cord, setting him free. Finlay dropped to the floor with a thump. His head hit the stone floor and his body lay crumpled and still.

'Oh my God! Oh my God! Finlay! Call an ambulance!' Miss McGregor shouted out.

Miss Corbitt, the nit nurse, popped her head out of the medical room and threw her hands to her gaping mouth to quell a scream. Pale-faced, she ran to the telephone. Miss McGregor lifted Finlay's limp body and carried him to her office, pushing the paperwork off her desk with his dangling feet, and laying him down on the wooden surface. She felt for his pulse, muttering anxiously to herself. 'Please let him be okay, Lord, please!' When she found one, she let out a joyful cry. 'Thank you, Lord!'

By pure chance, part of the cord that Finlay had wrapped around his neck had been rotting away for some time in a little pool of rainwater that had penetrated a small crack in the windowpane and accumulated on the window ledge. If he had picked any other of the windows, he surely wouldn't have survived.

Finlay was still unconscious but Miss McGregor knew now there was hope. She loosened his shirt collar and put her ear to his chest to make sure he was breathing. Reassured, she carefully placed him in the recovery position and put her cloak over him. She clasped her hand over his and began to fan his face with a hanky, only stopping briefly to dab her own eyes. She glanced anxiously towards the door every few seconds, waiting for the ambulance to arrive.

Miss Brown walked into Miss McGregor's office and saw Finlay laid out on top of the desk. She tutted loudly. 'Typical! That boy will do anything for attention,' she said coldly. 'He'll be putting it all on, mark my words. That boy should get an Oscar for this performance!'

Miss McGregor's normally pale face reddened to a deep crimson. She was livid. It was not the first time she had noticed Miss Brown's unkind treatment of some of the children, and this time she could not stay quiet.

'My whole life I have tried to respect other people's beliefs and opinions, but what you have just said is totally unacceptable. This poor child could die!'

Miss Brown was taken aback. She had never heard Miss McGregor be so abrupt. 'Look Bel, you don't teach Finlay. You don't know the boy. You have no idea about his behaviour! He's always crying wolf, the little devil that he is, and I just can't have any sympathy for that wretch of a boy.'

Anger surged through Miss McGregor's body – an anger she'd not felt since the night she'd waved clenched fists at the sky after the Luftwaffe's devastation of her city. 'Miss Brown, I am not prepared to have this conversation right now while little Finlay is lying here,' she growled. 'But rest assured, we will have it later. Now please get out of this room while I deal with Finlay.'

'I say, you've got me all wrong, Bel—'

'Leave now!' Miss McGregor said, jabbing her finger towards the door and struggling to retain her composure. She looked Miss Brown in the eye, and with a low and deliberate voice, added, 'You, madam, are a vile and wicked woman who should never be allowed near another child!'

'But Bel!' protested Miss Brown.

'Go!'

The infirmary

With the ambulance bells ringing, Finlay and Miss McGregor soon arrived at the hospital. Miss McGregor was still holding Finlay's hand as he was wheeled inside to a ward, and the ambulanceman held an oxygen mask over the boy's mouth. Miss McGregor saw a slight flicker behind Finlay's eyelids and dabbed his brow with a cool flannel given to her by a nurse. When his eyes opened, his first sight was of Miss McGregor sobbing into her hanky.

'Hey, miss, don't cry,' he said in his soft-spoken voice.

'I'm okay, Finlay. I'm just happy,' she replied, smiling through her tears.

'Why?'

'Because I am. I just am. And I'm happy that I can sit with you for a wee while.'

Wearily, Finlay felt his eyes grow heavy and he closed them. 'Miss McGregor, don't leave me please…'

'Doctor!' she cried out in alarm. The doctor, who had been standing behind her, quickly felt Finlay's pulse and cast his eyes over his chart. 'Don't worry, he's just fallen asleep. Leave him with us,' and he prised Miss McGregor's caring grip from Finlay's hand.

Crying all the way home in the taxi, Miss McGregor wondered what anguish had made the boy do such a thing. It was certainly no accident: he'd dragged the chair over to the window in order to climb up on to the ledge. It had to have been a deliberate act. She clutched her chest as her heart raced. Finlay had truly wanted to kill himself. What could make an eleven-year-old child want to try and end his young life? Miss McGregor committed herself to finding out the answer. *My gosh, what a terrible mess*. She shuddered at the thought of how close he'd come. She had to find out why.

Ina was in the kitchen with Wullie, making sandwiches for his evening's work at the shipyard, when there was a heavy knock at the door. Ina pulled the curtain back just enough to see out.

'Fuck me, Wullie, it's the police!'

'The police! What are they wanting? I hope it's not for our Robert. He's been up to no good lately.'

'Christ, what's that laddie done now?' said Ina, worried. She made her way to the front door and opened it wide, folding her arms tight to her chest. 'What?' she demanded.

The police officer looked at her momentarily. Ina, now fearing the worst, repeated her question. 'What? What are you wanting with us?'

The police officer opened his book and asked, 'Are you Ina McGill?'

'Aye, what about it if I am?' she responded coldly.

'I'm afraid I have sad news about your son Finlay.'

'What's that laddie done now? When I see him I'll kill him!'

'Well, I'm sorry to say you might not need to,' the police officer said grimly. 'We have received a phone call from your son's school and it seems Finlay has tried to take his own life.'

'What do you mean take his own life! Kill himself, do you mean?'

'Aye. He's in the infirmary, and the last I heard he was still unconscious.'

'Wullie! Wullie!' Ina shouted. 'Our Finlay's in the hospital and unconscious.'

'My God, what's happened to him?' asked Wullie, coming quickly to the door.

'I can't believe this. The policeman says he tried to kill himself!'

'Nae way would Finlay kill himself! Why would he?' asked Wullie.

'I can run you to the hospital in the police van,' offered the officer.

Gazing into space, Wullie took a moment to reply. 'Aye, if you would, officer. I thank you kindly.'

In the van on their way to the hospital, Ina started to talk gibberish. 'That wee bastard has done nothing but bring bad vibes to this house since the day he was born,' she said with a growl. 'I have put up with him for the last eleven years.'

Placing his arms around Ina, Wullie said, 'Hush now, hen. Hush. He'll be all right, I'm sure.'

But when Wullie saw Finlay lying on the bed, the bright red weal on his neck illuminated by the soft nightlight, his heart sank in despair. Finlay lay staring at the ceiling, his eyes open wide.

'You okay, son?' Wullie asked him. Ina stood behind him.

Without breaking his stare, Finlay replied, 'Aye, Daddy, I'm okay.'

In a low and soft voice, Wullie asked, 'What made you do that, son? What were you thinking?'

Finlay hesitated, thinking hard. He sensed his mother was angry. She'd punish him for what he'd done. He rocked his body nervously and, feeling his throat tighten, he gulped and fought for air.

'I don't know, Daddy. I don't know,' he said once he'd caught his breath, his voice quivering. 'I'm sorry.'

Looking down, Wullie saw his son fidgeting anxiously. He was flustered. 'Don't worry, Finlay,' he said quietly. 'It's okay.'

'You have brought nothing but trouble to our door,' burst in Ina. 'Oh, how I wish that fucking rope had held!'

Wullie started. 'Don't you be saying that to the wean!'

At his mother's voice, Finlay slipped himself further under the bed covers.

Ina had always been careful never to show her cruelty to Finlay when anyone else was around. Now though, she was truly frightened she would be found out. She knew she had pushed Finlay too far too many times. And she had betrayed herself with those words in front of Wullie. She quickly changed tack.

'Oh no, Wullie! What have I done?' she wailed theatrically.

'It's all right, Ina, it's not your fault.'

'Aye, it is Wullie. It is!' She began to cuddle Finlay so tightly that he was crushed in her grip. She had never cuddled him before.

Finlay looked at his dad and Wullie winked at him. Finlay smiled back before closing his eyes to savour the moment. His little heart pounded. This was all he had ever wanted: to be loved. And he never thought he'd be loved by his mother.

'We'll get you home in a couple of days and things will be different, I promise,' she said.

At first light the next morning, Miss McGregor was sitting next to Finlay's bed, patiently waiting for him to wake up. Her pretty, long black dress and lace jacket contrasted well with her pale face, and a velvet-bowed straw hat sat on her lap. She held grapes wrapped in a brown paper cone in one hand and a small chocolate bar in the other. When Finlay opened his eyes and saw Miss McGregor, he was more than happy to see her.

'Hiya, miss. What's that in the brown poke?' he asked her excitedly.

'It's for you! Here, take a wee peek in and see.' Finlay took the small cone from her and like a cat clawing at a mouse he ripped it open.

'Grapes! I have never tasted grapes. Can I have one please, miss?'

'Of course, you can – after all, they are for you!' Thanking her, he eagerly plucked one from the bunch and popped it into his mouth. He bit into it and sucked slowly, savouring its sweetness.

'This is smashing, miss. Could I have another one, please?'

'Finlay, they're all for you!'

His face brightened with a beaming smile. 'All for me, miss, and nobody else?'

She smiled and nodded. 'Yes, and nobody else!'

'And what's that in your other hand, miss?' he quizzed.

'A Five Boys chocolate bar for you,' she told him.

'But, miss, you brought me the grapes.' Finlay was overwhelmed by Miss McGregor's unexpected kindness. No one apart from his father he had ever shown him such kindness. Even his adopted aunty Ann never came close to this.

Finlay wondered what would have happened if he had died. Would he have gone to heaven and not been able to see Miss McGregor? He would not have wanted that. He loved her for her kindness and caring attitude towards him. Guilt suddenly coursed through him and numbed his head.

'I don't deserve chocolate too…' Finlay's voice tailed away and he turned to the wall.

'Why don't you deserve chocolate, Finlay?' she asked him gently.

'I just don't!' He pushed the grapes away from his lap.

'Okay. I will put the grapes and chocolate in the bedside locker for you and you can get them when I am gone,' she said.

Uncle Finlay's departure

Before Wullie left to collect Finlay from the hospital, he gathered all the family in the living room.

'Look, everyone, the wee boy is coming home today,' he said. 'I'd like you all to be here to make a fuss of him. Unknown to any of us, he's been feeling incredibly low, and it's up to us to help build up his confidence.' The family all agreed. Wullie looked around the room and added, 'Hugh and Charles, he's closest to you two. Take him with you when you go out, please. It will only be for a wee while until he settles down, and that way you can keep an eye on him for me.'

When Finlay arrived home, the family were true to their word and made a fuss of him, giving him plenty of hugs and smiles, and Finlay felt their love. But his mother was nowhere to be seen and his heart flooded with disappointment. He had always yearned for his mother's love and had desperately wanted to believe her promises in the hospital. Her absence shattered those hopes of finally having a loving relationship with her. He sat on the sofa and cried inside. His brother Boyd saw the sadness in Finlay's face and began tickling him to make him smile. With that, Finlay let himself forget about his mother. The rest of the family really did care about him, and a tear dropped from his eye in happiness.

Miss McGregor made sure she kept in touch with the McGills, and when she heard that Finlay was home, she sent him an invitation.

Miss Isobel McGregor requests the honour of
Master Finlay McGill's company
for afternoon tea
at 1pm on Saturday 22nd July 1961
at Orchard House, 91 High Street,
Blackwood Gardens
RSVP

Finlay's heart missed a beat when Wullie asked him to sit on the sofa as he had something to show him. He sat sullen in anticipation of bad news. Wullie stood tall and read the invitation out loud to Finlay, watching his reaction closely. He laughed out loud as Finlay's gloomy expression transformed into a smile.

Finlay was overjoyed that Miss McGregor had actually invited him to her house. In his excitement, he grabbed the cushion off the sofa and began jumping all over the living room floor, banging the cushion on his head. No one had invited him anywhere before, except to maybe Tam or Davie's place for tea. But now his favourite teacher Miss McGregor had chosen him out of everyone at school. *Why me?* Finlay felt special at last. He alone and nobody else was going to Miss McGregor's house for afternoon tea.

When the day of the tea came around, Finlay ran around the house, dashing to and fro from bedroom to bathroom, excitedly getting ready. He was like an overactive caged budgerigar waiting for its food. Soaking in the bath, he wondered what food Miss McGregor would offer him and hoped it would be his favourite apple pie. He climbed out of the bath, dripping on to the towel, and reached into the bathroom cabinet for his mother's lavender bath cubes. He was pleased to see the box had already been opened, and then slowly and carefully so as not to leave so much as a crease on the foil wrapper, he took out one of the cubes.

He was careful not to overly dissolve the cube as he rubbed it on to his wet skin. Gently he brushed one side of the cube on to his chest, then used another side and then another, until the fragrant cube had scented most of his body. Finlay wanted to smell nice for Miss McGregor and he was sure his mother would never notice that the bath cube had been touched. He rewrapped it tight and slid it back into the box, returning it to the same position in the bathroom cabinet.

Finlay thought how Miss McGregor must like him to invite him into her home and he felt overjoyed. He had never heard of any other pupils visiting her house. His excitement lifted to a new high and he began to hum to himself as he pulled on his trousers and shirt. It was almost time to go.

Sighing to herself and rushing around, Miss McGregor opened the dining room window before setting the table for her young guest. She was determined to get to the bottom of Finlay's attempt to kill himself. She was perplexed. *I can't push him for answers*, she thought to herself. *I will just have to be delicate, take it slow and be understanding with Finlay, and maybe he might open up*.

Leaving his house, Finlay could smell the sweet perfume of lavender as it drifted from him in the gentle wind. The sun was bright and warm and made his body tingle as the lavender cube residue dried and tightened on his skin. He put his hand up his shirt and a small blue cloud blew from where he rubbed. He was careful not to rub too much off. He skipped along humming happily to himself and picking the odd wildflower as he made his way down to Miss McGregor's house in Blackwood Gardens.

He walked up the paved drive towards her huge red sandstone house and stood outside what seemed to him a giant door. He lifted the door knocker and banged it loudly. The house was so large it scared him. He was sure he would get lost in it.

The sound of the brass Kewpie-doll door knocker slamming resonated through the house. Miss McGregor swung the door open and saw Finlay standing in plastic sandals on the large front step, one foot on top of the other. A shy grin filled his face as he held out a bunch of flowering thistles, poppies and other wildflowers. 'Come away in now, Finlay,' she smiled at him. 'Are those beautiful flowers for me?'

Twisting his body timidly from side to side, he handed them to her. 'Yes, miss, I picked them for you on my way special.'

Walking into the house, Finlay gazed at the high ceiling. It felt like entering a church vestry. Through an open door into the dining room he glimpsed an enormous dining table and a massive sideboard with three silver salvers daintily set out with sandwiches and fancy cakes. In his excitement, he yelled and bobbed from one foot to the other. Putting her wrist over her mouth, Miss McGregor giggled to herself at Finlay's reaction to the spread.

'There you are, Finlay, take your pick. You can have anything you want – just tuck in,' she said. She had asked his father what he liked in a sandwich beforehand.

Eyes sparkling, Finlay pretended to faint as he looked at the dainty sandwiches. 'Yeeees! Corned beef, my favourite!' he hissed, punching the air.

After taking his pick, they both sat at the table and Finlay poured himself some tea.

'Please, miss, can I have a cake?'

'Why of course you can!' Miss McGregor could not stop smiling. It was so nice to see him happy and enjoying the food. She knew from his father that he'd choose either a fern cake or a pineapple tart.

'Why did you pick that one, Finlay, when you could have had any of the others?' she asked, surprised he'd chosen her homemade apple pie instead.

He grimaced slightly. He couldn't understand why she'd ask that when it was so obvious to him. Holding the pie high and over his plate, ready to take a bite, he said, 'Please, miss, I love your apple pie. It's the bestest pie in the world.'

Miss McGregor rocked on her chair and laughed out loud. She didn't know who was having a nicer time – her or Finlay. But she knew she had to find a way to approach the delicate subject.

'How are you feeling, Finlay, now that you're out of hospital? Are you feeling any better?'

He gave a quick shrug of his shoulders and chewed his lip, and then, clearing his throat, said, 'Aye, I'm all right, miss.'

'Are you sure, Finlay? I feel I know you … and this has not been you. I care about you and you can trust me. You know that.' She paused for a moment. 'What made you climb on the windowsill and do what you did?' she asked gently.

Enjoying his pie, Finlay looked away. 'Everyone hates me, miss, and I don't like what people do to me. That's why, miss.'

Leaning over, she gave him a reassuring rub on his back. 'What don't you like and who does it? You know you can tell me.'

Chewing his last mouthful of apple pie, Finlay said without hesitation, 'I know I can, miss. Well, he keeps touching me and I don't like it.'

Miss McGregor was stunned to silence for a moment. She lowered her voice. 'Who touches you, Finlay? Is it your dad?'

'No, miss, my uncle Finlay. He touches me, and he squashes me when he puts his thing inside me and it really hurts. I want him to stop it but he won't.'

Miss McGregor choked on her tea as a sickening wave washed over her and lay heavy in her stomach. She dared not show any emotion, though a teardrop ran down each cheek. She moved out of her chair for a moment, feeling the need to leave the room and compose herself, but quickly sat back down and wiped her eyes with her hanky. She leaned over and stroked his arm. 'Everything will be okay, don't worry.'

Fidgeting on his chair, Finlay looked Miss McGregor in the eye. 'You won't tell my mammy, will you? Or I will get into trouble.'

'Why would you get into trouble with your mammy?' she asked, holding his hand.

His eyes glazed as shame flushed his cheeks. He turned away and laid his trembling chin on his chest.

'I hate him! And I hate his smelly breath. He pays me two bob after he's done it. He says he loves me and that I shouldn't let my mammy see the money. It's our secret.'

Curling his arm over his head, Finlay pressed on his mouth with his other hand and held in a cry, his throat aching from doing so. 'I never wanted him to do it, miss, honest!'

Miss McGregor's face flushed with anger. She had seen the despair in his eyes. 'I know, Finlay, I know. Don't worry, everything will be all right, I promise.'

Changing the mood, she said, 'Well, now then, would you like a fancy cake now? Then you can take the rest of the cakes and sandwiches home – oh and the apple pie too – and eat that later?'

A smile broke across his face. 'Oh, thank you, miss!' Unsure what to take, his hand hovered over the salver before settling on a fern cake. 'This is my second favourite, miss.'

Miss McGregor knew she would need to take a slow approach. She knew she had made progress today, believing she had finally got to the root of the youngster's sadness. She could never have imagined what was truly going on in that house.

As she filled her shopping bag with the leftover sandwiches and cakes, Miss McGregor was preparing herself to report to Finlay's mother and father. 'I will help you carry these,' she said. 'The bag's too heavy for you.'

Arriving at Riverside Road, Miss McGregor told Finlay she was going to talk to his mam and dad about school things. 'Don't worry,' she said.

'Thank you, miss, for my tea. I'll give the sandwiches and cakes to my brothers,' he said, showing her a shiny smile. 'But they're not getting any apple pie!'

The next morning, Finlay looked over at his uncle's bed. His eyes squashed closed in a frown of puzzlement. His uncle Finlay wasn't there. He didn't work Sundays and normally loved a long lie-in.

Later that evening, his father was sitting reading his *Glasgow Evening Times*. Finlay tapped him on his shoulder and asked, 'Daddy, where is Uncle Finlay?'

Wullie had known this question would come and had feared it all day. With uneasiness, he looked over his paper at Finlay before folding it and patting his lap. Finlay grinned as he sat on his father's legs.

'Your uncle Finlay had to leave right away. He had another job to go to and he starts it tomorrow.'

Finlay gazed at the floor and blushed. He knew in his heart what had happened and felt guilty.

Call me Finn

1965 was a turning point in young Finlay's life. He was now fifteen years old, but the bullying and abuse at the hands of his mother and uncle had had such a devastating impact on his self-esteem that it continued to tear him apart.

Ina was sitting in the corner of the living room smoking a cigarette. When Finlay entered the room, she calmly blew out the smoke and turned to him. 'Right, you!' she spat. 'You will be leaving school next month, so you better get yourself a job quick. Me and your daddy have kept you for the last fifteen years and now it's time for you to pay us back.'

Finlay was taken aback. 'But, Mammy, I thought I'd be able to stay on at school and go to college.'

Ina's face turned red with anger. 'What! You want to stay on and go to college! Who is going to feed and clothe you, eh? Because it certainly won't be me! You seem to think money grows on trees! Well, you're not staying here with no money coming in. If you want to stay at school, you can move out and look after yourself, because I'm not going to be running after your arse. Either bring the money in or fuck off!' she said, and then she walked out of the room, slamming the door behind her.

'Aye, right, I will!' he shouted after her.

Finlay's dream of going to college and becoming an architect was crushed. He'd wanted to prove to himself that he was capable of a degree. His education had suffered but once his uncle Finlay left, he'd managed to make up some ground in his final three years at secondary school.

Now he had the bedroom to himself, Finlay had painted it psychedelically: the walls were orange and the ceiling purple. Though he'd never had much, he had at least the freedom and privacy of his wee bolt-hole, as he called it. But if he wanted to stay on in the house, he was going to have to find work.

Finlay called round to local architects, lawyers and other professionals and asked if they needed an office junior, but it was always the same reply: no vacancies. It was obvious they wanted a well-educated boy with academic qualifications. Despondent, he called in at the factory works to ask if they needed an apprentice – but again to no avail. He was determined to get himself a skilled job. He saw his father and all but one of his brothers labour in the shipyard and knew it was not for him. He wanted a better life than that and was adamant he would not follow suit. Day after day, he diligently plodded on, knocking on doors, but nothing was available and there were few places left to try.

Coming out of a factory one day, he noticed Irvine's Fuels, the local coal merchants and coal yard. Someone was walking towards him, his face covered in coal dust and his heavy black-rimmed spectacles magnifying his eyes. It took Finlay a moment to realise it was Charlie Berry who lived in Gallows Hill and drank in the Clachan.

'Oh, it's you, Charlie!' he said. 'I didn't know you worked here.'

'Aye, been here five years now. Ach, it's all right and they're good to me. It pays my bills.'

Finlay did not want to carry coal for a living but knew he was running out of options. 'Any jobs going, Charlie?'

'I'm not too sure … Away in and see Billy Irvine, the gaffer. He's sitting in the office now.'

Thanking Charlie, Finlay went in to try and his luck and came out very pleased and relieved: he had secured a job delivering coal to the locals. It wasn't the greatest of jobs or pay, but it would keep his ranting old mother off his back. And it would be a stepping stone to something bigger and better, he told himself.

He started work for the Irvines the day after the school term ended. It was hard work, but within a month or two he found the job much easier. In fact, he could carry two bags of coal – weighing a total of 224 pounds and equal to a one-hundredweight bag

– on each shoulder and walk all the way around the lorry, and was very proud of his bragging rights. It certainly was no mean feat for a teenager to be carrying hundredweight sacks of coal. To do the job you needed to be very strong, and strong he became.

With all the heavy lifting and shovelling, Finlay's six pack and arm and leg muscles developed rapidly and his broad shoulders became increasingly muscular. He was as solid as rock. And he had shot up in height and was now very nearly six foot. He had begun to feel good about himself. Flashbacks of his uncle's abuse still haunted him at times, sending him spiralling downwards into a depression he couldn't shift for weeks, but for much of the time it was all good.

With payday money coming in, Finlay was able to afford trendy clothing. Jeans and a black leather jacket were his choice – he thought they suited his rugged look – and he grew his black hair longer. And when he passed his motorcycle driving test, he celebrated by purchasing a black and chrome 1957 Triumph 500s Speed Twin with fitted extended apehanger handlebars. He always said he liked the sit-up-and-beg position.

One evening after work, Finlay stepped out the bath, wrapped a towel around himself and lay on top of his bed. A warm breeze fluttered through the open window and gently passed over his body, cooling his near-naked frame. He lay quiet and relaxed. One of his favourite songs by the Kinks, 'You Really Got Me', spun on his record player.

His ears pricked at the distinctive Greensleeves chime of Johnny's ice cream van outside his front door. *I could just murder a cone*, he thought. Jumping off his bed, he pulled on his jeans, grabbed a handful of pennies from his copper smash tin, as he called it, and made his way down to the van.

Eddie Cullen, who had constantly bullied Finlay at school, was headed for the ice cream van, too, and Finlay's stomach churned at the sight of him. Eddie was three years older than Finlay and had always exploited his age and heavy build to dominate him. A year or two previously, they'd both played football with the local boys of Gallows Hill and Eddie had taken a penalty kick. Finlay had lined up in front of the goal with some other players, all holding their hands over their privates and screwing up their faces in anticipation of the projectile that was about to head their way, and when Eddie had kicked the ball, it had curled and flown straight towards Finlay's face. Finlay had instinctively turned and the ball had bounced off his back and landed over the byline.

Eddie had been enraged. 'Away, you shit bag that you are!' he'd yelled. 'You are a fucking shit bag!'

'What do you mean?' Finlay had asked.

'I mean you are a shit bag. A scaredy cat. You're nothing but a wimp!'

'I am not!' Finlay said hotly.

'OK then, let's see you stand there when I kick the ball towards you. We will see if you flinch.'

Finlay stood bold, erect and defiant as Eddie placed the heavy water-soaked leather ball on to a spot marked with grit from the roadside path. He twisted the ball into the grit and made sure it was covered in the jagged material.

'Let's see how brave you are then.' Eddie walked ten paces backwards and lined up his shot. He ran towards the ball at full speed and kicked the ball towards Finlay. It was the perfect shot – though Eddie was hardly going to miss from just ten feet away. Like a missile, it flew straight and true towards Finlay. The ball ricocheted off the left side of his face and landed in the corner of the field. Instantly dazed, Finlay's body reeled the other way.

'You're a flincher,' said Eddie. 'A fucking flincher!' All the other boys stood by and said nothing. Frightened of Cullen themselves, they laughed as they walked away, leaving Finlay with his grazed and swollen face.

Ever since that day, Eddie had bullied Finlay whenever their paths crossed. Now, at the ice cream van, Finlay began to shake at the prospect of another confrontation. His mouth went dry as he breathed in the summer air. He knew Eddie would pick on him but continued to the van just the same. He got there just ahead of Eddie and ordered an ice cream cone.

'Will you put raspberry sauce on it please, Johnny?' asked Finlay.

Incensed that Finlay had got his order in before him, Eddie kicked him on the back of his leg. It was hard enough to numb it and make Finlay stumble. With no response, Eddie then punched him hard in the nape of his neck. 'Hey, you! I was before you, you fucking dick!' he goaded.

Johnny smiled at Finlay as he handed down the cone to him. Eddie's forehead and face screwed up and twisted with anger. He punched Finlay again. Finlay, still shaking, stiffened. Eddie assumed he was shaking with fear – but not this time. Finlay was shaking with anger. For the first time in his life, he felt a raging fire inside him that burned to his very soul, and a thick red mist descended, blurring his thinking. He rammed his ice cream cone into Eddie's face with left fist, punching him straight after with his right. The punch caught the dead centre of Eddie's eye socket. Finlay threw a further right and then a left to Eddie's nose, and it was enough to send the bully reeling backwards and collapsing on to the road.

Laughter filled the air and penetrated deep into Eddie's mind. It was obvious to the sniggering lads waiting by the van that Eddie was now tasting a mixture of his own blood and Finlay's ice-cream. Bleeding, bruised and visibly embarrassed, he wiped his reddening face with his sleeve and scrambled to his feet. That prick Finlay had finally fought back – and got the better of him.

Finlay's mist slowly evaporated. Still shaking with adrenalin, he jolted at the realisation of what he'd just done. Eddie would surely retaliate. He quickly moved into a boxing stance with his fists up, ready for Eddie's counterattack. But it never came.

Trembling himself now, Eddie covered his swollen and bleeding nose with a snotty hanky. His left eye was puffed up and red. 'I'm going to get my big brother Owen on to you,' he shouted at Finlay. 'He will kick your fucking head in!'

Finlay's jaw dropped in disbelief. He felt the tension in his body deflate. After all those years of being bullied, he realised his mother had been right all along. All he'd had to do was fight back. With new-found confidence, he marched off, his head held high. He felt as though a beam of pride and happiness shone from inside him, lighting up his whole self. Finally, he had got rid of the bully.

I will never let anyone take advantage of me again, Finlay vowed to himself, and I will always face confrontation head on.

A sudden shout broke his thoughts. 'Hoy Finlay, where do you think you are going?' It was Johnny, the ice cream man. 'That was so funny! You have given me a great laugh there. Here is another cone for you, on the house and with a double scoop. That bully boy was needing that!'

'Thanks, Johnny,' he said. 'But my name's not Finlay; from now on, it's Finn. Call me Finn.'

From now on, Finn would be fighting back. He would never back down from anyone again. In a fair fight, he realised, the worst outcome would be a sore face. He'd had worse knocks playing football than from some of his playground scraps.

He left his bullied past behind, and the transformation from immature boy was complete. He was now Finn the man.

The gang

Tam Fleming looked around and counted the guys that were standing around in the hangout near the shops in Gallows Hill. 'There is sixteen of us and we need to get organised and protect ourselves,' he said. 'We need to get a squad together. And someone to lead it.'

After some muttering amongst themselves, Tam spoke again. 'I personally think Finn should do it. He takes no shit from anybody, and I reckon he's the best fighter here. What do you say?'

The lads had begun to look at Finn differently. Since he'd beaten the Gallows Hill bully and so-called hard man Eddie Cullen, they'd noticed how Finn held himself in a different way. Privately, Finlay had vowed to himself that he would seek out and beat up all the people who had wronged him. He was prepared to wait for as long as it took. He was now a force to be reckoned with, and his friends knew it.

But Big Jed bristled at the idea of Finn being the best fighter. 'I don't think so! I mean, I could take him on a square go anytime.'

Giving Jed a side glance, Finn frowned. 'Behave yourself, Jed. You're a mate. It's not about the best fighter. It's about us all sticking together and working as a unit to look after ourselves. That way we can depend on each other and watch each other's backs.

'Don't get me wrong, Jed, you're a big guy,' Finn continued. 'But you're too much of a firebrand and we don't want to start trouble. My philosophy is if we don't start it, we can be the ones to finish it. We won't need to start trouble anyway; I am certain it will come to us. We just want to be like the Romans – organised and ready for any snash that comes our way.'

The gang held a vote on who would be the leader and Finn won fifteen to six. Jed was red-faced. 'I think the leader should be the best fighter!' he shouted, squaring up to Finn. 'Come on, you cunt. Try and take me, Finn "I'm not a daft wee lassie from the Gallowgate"!'

Finn knew that he could take on Jed and beat him but he chose to go down the diplomatic route. After all, he liked the big man – he made him laugh. But most of all, Finn craved popularity, and he knew Jed was popular too. Beating him would alienate some of the gang. So Finn played it cool.

'Fuck's sake, Jed, behave yourself!' he said, smiling. 'You are my mate and I want you to be my second in command. Together, we can challenge anybody who comes our way. But if we're to be at one another's throats, then we're just a couple of arseholes and not worthy of being leaders. Okay, we could fight it out and, aye, you might well beat me – but what would that prove? Let's work together for the sake of the team. What do you say, big man?'

The tension ran high as the gang waited for Jed's response. Jed was six foot two and well built, with square shoulders and a solid chin. His thin and frizzy blonde hair hung over his ears like golden candyfloss. He could be a bit slow on the uptake, though he was three years older than Finn, and he was unpredictable and well known for his troublemaking. In truth, he was a headbanger who was nearing the point of unhinged. Finn wanted him on side where he knew he could keep a tight rein on him.

'Aye, right, I'm in. But I'm my own man, gang or no gang. I'm my own man,' Jed replied fiercely.

The rest of the gang whistled and cheered as the two bumped shoulders and shook hands. 'Great stuff,' smiled Finn. 'What we need now is a good name. Have any of you lot got any suggestions?' After some discussion, the gang all settled on the Gallows Hill Executioners.

The main dominators in the gang after Finn were Jed and Tam, Peem O'Neil, Dal Daleny and Davie Fleming. Tam and Wee Davie were Finn's best friends and had really been his only friends growing up on the hill. They tended to do most things together. Though Davie was small, he was well built for his size, with heavy, square shoulders and long brown feathered hair. Davie mostly wore polo necks as he was embarrassed by the black mole that clung to his neck. Tam's long, thick brown hair framed his baby face, and he liked to dress in nice clothes for a night out.

Peem was a blue-eyed boy and rather debonair. He was good-looking and had his dark brown hair cut in the style of screen star Cary Grant. Dal, on the other hand, was a big guy whose near-charcoal hair was always scruffy, greasy and in need of a good wash. He was gaining a reputation for being a bit of an idiot on alcohol, and it was noted that he could start trouble in an empty house. As soon as he had a few pints of heavy in him, he'd become argumentative and a bit of a halfwit. Finn knew he had to keep Jed and Dal on friendly terms with each other – both of them at loggerheads would bring the others down.

The Gallows Hill Executioners gang was born. Finn felt overwhelmed with pride that they'd picked him to be their leader. This was what he'd always wanted: to be popular and liked. Things were heading in the right direction and Finn looked forward to what the future had in store.

Old Aggie

The dying sun laid its fading light peacefully in front of the houses of Gallows Hill, casting a dusky red glow along the rooftops and forming bizarre castle-like shadows. There was an eerie absence of bright light on the back green. Lingering rays weaved themselves through the closes and gable ends and sneaked up to the tenement doors like thieves trying to break in.

Davie and Tam were on the double-decker bus, returning from the city. As it slowed near their bus stop, they stood at the rear exit and waited to jump off. Tam couldn't help but notice the woman standing below the streetlamp across the street, loitering alone on the corner. Her bleached blonde hair and bright red lipstick had caught his eye. She was wearing a black pencil skirt, with a black Chanel coat draped over her shoulders. A half-smoked cigarette hung from her red lips as if about to fall. Tam looked straight at her. She caught his gaze and nodded.

In the dredges of light from the sinking sun and the weak glow emerging from the sodium streetlamp, Tam tried to guess her age. He thought she must be in her late forties. In truth, she was old enough to be his grandmother and was nearing sixty. She was Agnes Barnes, the local alcoholic and prostitute.

Agnes had once been secretary to the Lord Mayor, a pillar of society, well-liked and respected. She was a kind and gentle woman who had hit hard times after her daughter's tragic death. And while Agnes was in the house lying in a drunken stupor, her uncaring and philandering husband had taken another woman into their marital home and upstairs to their bedroom.

Looking her over now, Tam liked what he saw. She continued to watch the pair of them as the bus turned the corner into Clyde Street and drove them out of sight. They both swung on the steady pole and jumped off the bus before it came to a halt.

'Did you see that that woman, Davie?' asked Tam.

'Her! That's Old Aggie. She's a bit of a jakey, though a nice woman really. And she was good with us kids when we were weans.'

'My God, Aggie! I remember her. She had a daughter Bridie, about the same age as us. Didn't she, em…?' Tam tailed off.

'Aye. They say that the day her daughter died in that car accident, Aggie died too, poor woman.'

'Aye, a poor tormented soul, my mother said she is,' agreed Tam.

By this time, Aggie had moved a hundred yards up nearer to the bus stop and was now approaching the lads. 'Hiya, Davie. How do?'

Tam was staring at her open-mouthed and she gestured towards him with a swing of her handbag. 'I havenae seen him around here before. Who's your pal then, Davie?'

'My name's Tam. I'll have you know I have been looking after my mam for a year or two. She's not been too well.'

'Och aye, I recognise you now! Your mammy is Peggy Fleming from Park Close. You're Tam Fleming! Well, I never!' she exclaimed. 'Tam Fleming, look at you with your suit on, and all suave and sophisticated!'

Davie laughed and said 'You must be joking! What, him? Suave and sophisticated? Wait till I tell the gang!'

'Hey, wait a minute!' said Tam. 'Oh, I see now, Davie. You're just jealous, are you not?'

'Fuck off, Tam! There's no way I am jealous of you!'

Aggie interrupted their squabbling. She wanted her drink. 'Hey, wait a minute. Can one of yous lend us a couple of shillings? 'Cause I am gagging for a can of Tennent's lager.'

'Aye, maybe. What's in it for us?' replied Tam.

'I don't know…' she said. 'But have any yous two had your hole yet?'

112

Tam and Davie were both virgins. 'Aye!' they both lied.

'Och, aye, I believe you, but thousands wouldnae! So who took your cherries then?' asked Aggie.

They both struggled to think on their feet. 'It was a lassie from Fairglen. She was, eh, a bit of all right, you know...' Davie muttered.

'And I shagged a lassie from—'

'Never mind who you shagged,' interrupted Aggie. 'If you want your hole, it's a dollar each.'

'Fuck me! Five bob!' yelled Davie.

'No, Davie, its five bob to fuck me!' laughed Aggie.

'Hold on, Aggie,' said Tam, tugging at Davie's sleeve before whispering in his ear. 'Fuck's sake, let's just go for it, eh Davie? I want my hole; I'm fucking fed up pulling my boaby.'

'Aye, all right, let's negotiate. But you better not fucking tell anyone!'

'No, I won't, and you better not either.'

'That's great, lads! That's yous sorted.' Aggie held out her hand and swung it towards the pair. 'Money first.'

Tam thrust his hand straight into his suit pocket, excited that he was about to lose his virginity. He pulled out two half-crowns, nodded his head and pushed the coins towards Aggie. Aggie's painted lips smiled gleefully at Tam as she took the money and quickly stuffed it into her handbag.

Tam was over-keen to accomplish his goal and immediately unzipped his fly. Aggie cackled. 'Am I that attractive? Fuck's sake, Tam, there is no way are we doing it here! Come round the back of the bike shop. It's dry round there and it's pitch black – naeone will see us. It's where I always do my business.'

The bike shop's back door was in Clyde Street, at the rear of the tenement single-end housing and between the coffee shop, grocer, chemist and bookmaker.

Tam was by now over-excited and desperate. 'Right, Davie, I'm first,' he demanded.

'No, you're not! I'm first. There is no way I'm going in after you,' snapped back Davie.

Aggie broke in. 'Right, yous two, stop it now. I will toss a coin. That's fair, is it not?'

They both agreed. Aggie flipped her half dollar and shouted, 'Call!'

'Tails,' said Tam.

Tam and Davie's eyes locked on to the silver sputnik. Tam had his fingers crossed. Both their hearts missed a beat as the coin spun on its axis. Both gasped as it seemed to slow and pause briefly, almost floating, as it spun at its highest point. Following the coin keenly with their eyes, they both crouched down as it crashed to the ground and rolled on to its side, before disappearing into the darkness.

Aggie snapped the light on her cigarette lighter. It was just enough to see the glint of metal stop and fall over, but in the darkened corner, no one could make out whether it was heads or tails. Aggie bent down and picked up the coin. She brought the lighter and coin nearer to her eye and peered at its face. To Tam's delight he heard her say, 'Tails it is.'

'Fuck! I never win anything!' shouted Davie.

Tam did a little jig of delight. 'Ya dancer! I'm in there!'

Sitting on the window ledge, Aggie lifted her leg up on to a metal dustbin. 'There is no way am I taking my knickers off!' she told them both. 'It's too cold. You two will just have to get on with it the best you can.'

Tam approached her and fumbled at her underwear. Aggie whispered in his ear, 'I'm glad it's you first. Besides, it was heads all along!' Tam smiled, delighted. His act was over in seconds. Aggie chuckled to herself as she kissed Tam on his forehead, leaving a bright red lipstick mark. 'That was lovely, Tam,' she told him.

As he pulled his trousers back up and zipped up his fly, Tam was unaware of the heavy smell of pine. He walked away with a new swagger. 'Right, Davie, get in there,' he said.

Wee Davie approached Aggie like a praying mantis and grabbed her tight around the waist. His heart was pounding faster by the second. He desperately tried to enter Aggie but the window ledge was too high for him. Frustrated, he moved his hands down to Aggie's bottom and clenched her cheeks, accidentally pinching her. 'Shift down a bit, Aggie,' he demanded. 'I cannae get it in!'

'Oh, for Christ's sake, that hurt! Stand on your tiptoes and I'll move down a wee bit. But get on with it. The pub will be closing in an hour!'

Davie didn't notice Aggie placing both her hands on to his shoulders to steady herself, he was too busy fumbling around with her knickers. Though Davie did manage to start the act, he struggled to keep himself inside Aggie. Desperate to finish, he pulled her bottom towards him, yanking her off the windowsill. She squealed as her head banged off the sill and she slid down the wall. Davie stood with his trousers round his ankles and his eyes tightly closed. He was too far gone to be aware of what had just happened and he ejaculated on to Aggie's coat.

'Oh, for fuck's sake, man, that's my new coat! You better give me the money for it to be dry cleaned. Help me up!' she bellowed.

Regaining his senses, Davie yanked up his trousers and pulled Aggie to her feet. Davie got a whiff of a strong-smelling disinfectant lingering in the corner. 'Jesus Christ, Aggie, there's a hell of a reek of pine disinfectant in this corner!'

'Aye, I know. It's off me,' she said. 'I wash my knickers in it. I just love the smell.'

Davie's face dropped like a stone and his whole body shuddered. 'Fuck's sake Aggie, you wash your knickers in pine disinfectant!' He screwed up his face in disgust. 'You're a dirty fucking cow!' He scurried away from her.

'You werenae saying that a minute ago, were you, you fucking bastard! Calling me a cow!' Aggie took

116

off her shoe and launched it through the darkness in Davie's direction, missing him by quite a distance. It landed at Tam's feet. Tam grabbed the shoe and gently tossed it back into the abyss. They looked at each other, turned and ran off laughing.

'Fuck's sake! Tam, you realise it was at the back of the bike shop that we were both riding the local bike?' snorted Davie.

'Old cow!' said Tam, laughing even louder.

Aggie heard them both laughing in the distance. 'Fucking bastards! Calling me a cow!' she muttered to herself. She checked her money was in her pocket and headed off round the corner to the Clachan Bar for her wee drink.

Pail of Dettol

Nearly two weeks passed and a few of the gang met in the Clachan for a card school.

'Deal the cards, Jed,' said Finn. He looked over at Davie. 'Stop that clawing at your balls! What have you been doing? Fuck, I know what! Have you been humping Old Aggie?'

A tomato-soup colour stained Davie's neck and face. 'Stop taking the micky. I've got headlice on my balls!'

The gang all doubled up in hysterical laughter. 'Aye, I hit a sore point there! You fucking have! You humped Old Aggie! Headlice nothing…You've got fucking crabs!'

'Aye, all right, I did hump her. My balls are so fucking itchy and sore and I cannae stop clawing at them. What am I gonnae do?' whined Davie.

Winking over at the gang, Finn said, 'I see, Davie. That's nae problem. There's nae need to worry at all, wee man.' He patted Davie on the shoulder and looked him straight in the eye. 'You can sort this yourself. Just get yourself a bottle of Dettol. Dettol kills everything dead! It's so easy. Just get yourself a pail and make a strong solution of salt and the hottest water you can bear and fill the pail up to the top. Tip in some Dettol. Fire in about half a bottle – or more if there hundreds of the wee bastards – and sit your balls in that mixture for a good half hour. If you can stand it, that is. My cousin Stewart from Braesend done it. The water drowns them and the antiseptic kills the stragglers. They never came back.'

Downing the last dregs of his pint in one go, Davie slammed the empty glass on the table. 'Thanks, Finn. I have been worried all week about what to do, and I know now. My mam's got some Dettol in the house. I am away home to drown these wee fuckers.'

The gang waited patiently until Davie was out the door and well on his way home before erupting in laughter. Finn coughed his drink out and slapped his thigh. 'Poor Wee Davie!'

A couple of weeks later, most of the Executioners were enjoying playing cards in the Clachan again. 'Has anyone seen or heard from Wee Davie since his crab situation two Saturdays ago?' Finn asked.

Tam's body swayed from side to side and took on an obviously nervous shuffle. 'What do you mean, crab situation?'

'Fuck! You shagged her as well!' laughed Finn.

'No, I didnae!' Tam retorted. 'No way would I touch that cow Aggie. No way!'

'There you go, you *have* shagged her – because how did you know it was Aggie?'

'Come on, Tam, we know now!' said Peem. 'Did you get the seaside creatures too?'

Tam's face turned from peely-wally to a deep crimson. When he spoke, his voice quivered with shame and humiliation. 'Aye, all right, you might as well know. I did. So fucking what? I bet any one of you would have done her too, 'cause she's not bad looking.' The gang guffawed.

'Not bad looking! Way you go, Tam!' laughed Peem. 'She's an old cow. Though I don't see you scratching at your balls. How's that then?'

'Easy. I just paid the doctor a visit and he gave me some cream.'

'Ah, way you go. You pair of wankers that you are,' said Peem.

'Hey, Peem, have some respect. They are not wankers now, and because of that they are to be congratulated,' said Finn, and he lifted his glass and began patting Tam on the back. 'Here's to Tam and Davie, the kings of crabs!'

More hilarity followed as the lads joined in patting Tam on the back, adding to his humiliation. Finn put his hand on Tam's shoulder, and gesticulating in a sweeping motion towards the gang, said loudly, 'Don't feel bad, my man, because half these bastards here have been with Aggie long before you!' The Clachan boomed with laughter.

Davie crossed Finn's mind again. 'Fuck! I am a wee bit worried that we havenae seen head nor tail of Wee Davie. That's nearly two weeks now. Drink up, lads. We will take a donner down and see what's going on with him.'

The gang walked the short distance down the hill and arrived at Davie's door. Davie's mother was standing with her arms folded, chatting to her neighbour. 'Hi Finn. Thank God you have turned up! Are you looking for our Davie?'

'Aye, we came to see if he was all right. We haven't seen him for a week or two. Where is he?' asked Finn.

'He's upstairs in his bedroom. He's been not too well at all. Been there five days now! He just won't come down, and I'm awfully worried about him, Finn. It's just not like him to sit in his room. And the doctor won't tell me what's wrong. I need to know, Finn, I need to know. He's all I have got since his daddy died. Will you go up and speak to him?' she begged.

'Aye, of course I will, and don't you be getting yourself up to high doh now, Mrs Fleming. We will see what's going on with the wee man. Right, Tam, you come upstairs with me.'

Tam and Finn climbed the stairs and when they entered Davie's room, they saw him sitting on the edge of his bed in just his socks and underpants, looking pale and washed out. He was staring at a penknife in his hand.

Finn was appalled at Davie's appearance. 'Are you all right, Davie? Is everything okay or what?'

121

'No, I'm not all right! And it's nae thanks to you, Finn McGill,' Davie answered coldly. 'My balls and my boaby are red raw, the skin is flaking off my bell-end, and the doctor said if I had sat any longer on that pail, I would have needed a skin graft. Fuck me, that's not all. It could take up to another six weeks to fully heal. Six fucking weeks!' he screamed.

They both held back their mirth, feeling some empathy for their wee pal.

'Away you go, you daft cunt. I didnae think you would take me serious! Anyway, you're on the mend now,' said Finn. Holding in a snigger, he added, 'Did it do the job and drown the wee fuckers then?'

'No! It fucking didnae! And fine well you knew it would not drown them. You ripped the pish right out of me, Finn. I'm only glad the doctor gave me some cream that cools my fucking tackle.'

'You got it all wrong, Davie. My cousin Stewart from—'

'Fuck your cousin!'

'Never mind, Davie. Never mind, eh? Tam, give Davie that half bottle of Bell's we were about to open.'

Passing the bottle over, Tam said, 'Here, Davie,' and he mouthed, 'Sorry! Enjoy!' Davie took the bottle and slammed it down on to his bedside cabinet. 'Thanks, Tam, but it's not your fault.'

'Okay, wee man, we will see you in a week or two when everything has settled down in your nether regions,' said Finn.

'Aye, okay, will do. Fuck off then and give me peace.'

Finn and Tam both cackled as they made their way downstairs. 'He's in a wee bit of a huff, is he not?' said Finn.

'Nae wonder, poor wee guy. Six weeks of agony for him.' Tam let a grin slip from the side of his face.

At the bottom of the stairs, Davie's mother was pacing back and forth. She stopped in her tracks when she heard Finn and Tam and glanced up at them over the banister. 'Is he all right, Finn?'

'Aye, he's all right, Mrs Fleming. Don't worry, you can settle yourself down. He's going to be all right.'

'What's wrong with him?'

Looking over at Tam, Finn smirked. 'As I told you, Mrs Fleming, don't worry, he will be fine. It's all down to privates matters.' Both he and Tam turned and looked away, desperately trying to hold in their laughter.

'That's good, son. That's good news.'

Mrs Fleming watched the gang leave and when they were nearly out of earshot, she put her hands on either side of her mouth and cried, 'Thanks for coming, lads! I am so glad our Davie has great pals.'

'Thank God she doesn't know!' sniggered Finn.

Bernadette's trap

Baz Donaldson stood propped against the counter in the small dimly lit newsagent, talking to his sister Bernadette. One hand was stuck into the pocket of his ankle-length Gestapo-style black leather coat. His left cheek carried a razor scar that glinted in the sunlight seeping through the cracked-open door. An Elvis Presley pompadour hairstyle gave the impression of a small black chicken sitting on top of his head, while the pock marks on his face resembled the craters of a crumpet and gave him a hard edge.

Baz was the leader of the notorious BMB gang: the Bridgeburn Mad Bastards. He and his team ruled most of Bridgeburn with a heavy hand and were not a gang to mess with. They were one of the Executioners' many rivals that were dotted in and around Glasgow.

A well-known violent psychopath, Baz had no empathy and could be as dangerous as a rabid dog on the loose. His unpredictability frightened even the members of his own gang. He could change like the weather depending on the storm that blew inside his head. And he was a knife man who would not think twice about using it.

He was infamous for taking pleasure in frightening unsuspecting and vulnerable people. He would go into a public lavatory and waylay some gent whilst they were urinating, holding a knife to their throat. He'd watch them squirm and urinate over themselves as he forced them to hold their hands up, and would then swagger off laughing in a weird, lunatic way that verged on a death scream. And he'd say, 'Fuck's sake, that guy didnae find the funny side of that. He's not pishing himself laughing, but I am! No, he's just pished himself!' More of his frightening laughter would follow.

His sister Bernadette was blonde and blue-eyed with an hourglass figure. She was not especially pretty but she was stylish and presented herself well.

'Fuck me, Bernadette! See that guy who just walked in? Him with the Brando-style leather jacket. Well, that's Finn McGill from the Executioners. If he comes over to your counter, see if you can use your charm to get him to meet up with you at the Burns Hotel on Saturday night.'

'Baz! Who are you kidding! With him?' she asked.

'Not actually go with him; you just have to get him there. I have plans for that bastard.'

'No way, Baz. That's not gonnae happen.'

'How not? You are not exactly a fucking angel, Bernadette.'

'No, I don't mean that. It's just that I am not pretty enough for the likes of him.'

'Don't be daft, Bernadette. You're gorgeous and you just don't know it.'

Baz was frightened to take on Finn in a one-to-one fight. It would have to happen when he had back-up or when he was in one of his demonic frenzies. 'Right,' he said, 'he's coming this way!' Baz slipped out the back door of the shop and left Bernadette applying her red lipstick.

The game was on. Bernadette wanted to give it her best shot and hook this handsome man to please her brother. She covered her face with a false smile as she bunched her hair with both hands and watched Finn approach the counter. Smiling back at her, he laid a ten-shilling note on the counter.

'Hiya. Ten Woodbine and a box of matches, please.' Bernadette's slender fingers lifted the note from the counter and held it up to a beam of sunlight. She looked Finn in the eye as she deliberately and slowly began to lick her fingers on one hand and then the other before starting to wrinkle and snap the note several times in her two hands. Inspecting it closely, she flipped it over and slammed it down on the counter. 'A rich man, I see,' she said.

Through his laughter, he answered, 'No, not me. Besides, it's only a ten-bob note. It hardly makes me in the same league as Andrew Carnegie.'

Bernadette gave him a quick side glance. 'You are far travelled, are you not? Because I have never seen you around here before, and I know everyone and everything that goes on around here. So where you from then?'

'Oh, now that would be telling.'

Bernadette looked deep into his eyes and held his gaze, smiling, as she took his hand and slipped his change into his palm. Finn's smile widened, enjoying the sexual tension as she curled his fingers over the coins and squeezed. She winked at him. 'There's enough in your hand for a nice Bacardi and coke,' she whispered.

Finn frowned. 'I don't drink Bacardi.'

'No, but I do!' Bernadette giggled as she stuffed the cigarettes and matches into his jacket pocket. 'What you doing Saturday night then?'

Running his eyes over her, Finn liked what he saw. Her green tight-fitted chiffon blouse, high heels and matching green miniskirt all complemented her figure. 'Saturday night, you say? I'm usually out with the lads down at the Clachan. You fancy coming over?'

'I cannae. I'm going to a charity dance at the Burns Hotel.' Bernadette tucked the cigarettes deeper into his pocket. Turning away, she gave him a side-on puckered smile. 'You fancy meeting me there? It will be a good laugh.'

'I'm not sure about that. Bridgeburn might be beside the Clyde but come on! It's not exactly the Scottish riviera, is it? And definitely not the place for the likes of me to be seen in.'

Playing it cool, Bernadette stood squaring up the newspapers on the counter. She had not really expected him to bite anyway. 'Well, if you don't fancy it, that's all-right. Nae bother.'

'No, I'm not saying that! I want to think about it. What sort of dance is it anyway?'

'It's a charity dance run by the old folk of Bridgeburn. It's in aid of the local St Theresa's charity for the babbies in Africa. You will be safe there.'

'Somehow, I don't think so. But it's not only that – I just don't see me doing the Foxtrot or the Gay Gordons,' smiled Finn.

Bernadette laughed, throwing her head back. 'So are you going to the dance or not?'

'Aye, I might go if you have got any pals for my mate Tam.'

'Och, I have plenty pals for him, and good lookers too.'

Leaning over the counter, Finn stroked her pale cheek with his curled index finger and said, 'Well, one thing I know: none of them will be as good looking as you.'

Her heart thumped. No one ever spoke to her like that. Attracted to the warmth in his voice, she lost sight of her prime objective set by Baz. She looked forward to seeing this man at the dance. As Finn turned to go, she said, 'It starts at eight o'clock. Will I see you then?' And then in the same breath, 'My name is Bernadette, by the way. What's yours then?'

'They call me Finn.'

After a pause, she prompted him again. 'Will you be going Saturday then?'

'Aye, maybe I will, and maybe I willnae,' he said, and disappeared out the door.

Bernadette's heart sank for a second. Then Finn gave her a cheeky little wink as he popped his head round the door pillar before vanishing again. She covered her mouth with her hand and giggled to herself. She couldn't believe that he wanted to date her.

She stood looking at the reflection staring back at her in the shop window. An enormous smile cracked her face open. But seconds later a horrific shock ran through her body, a thunderbolt piercing her heart. She clutched at her chest and gasped at what she had done. She had just set him up for the kill. She ran out of the door and frantically scanned the area, wanting to warn him. But it was too late. He had gone, eaten up by the busyness of the street. Gazing widely into space, Bernadette muttered to herself, 'What have I done? Oh God, what have I done?'

The soup ladle

On Friday night, the lads were at their usual card game in the Clachan when Finn asked Tam, 'You fancy going to the Burns Hotel in Bridgeburn tomorrow night? There's jigging on.'

Tam stepped back, shocked. 'No way, Finn. The Burns Hotel? Fuck that! That's BMB territory – it will be rife with them nutters!'

'Aye, in a way it is jumping with the BMBs, but there will be no hassle because it's being run by the pensioners in aid of the babbies of Africa or something like that. It's a charity dance.'

'I don't know, Finn,' said Tam uneasily. 'It sounds dodgy to me.'

Finn flashed a smile at Tam and nodded his head. 'Yes, I know, but I have had reassurance from a certain young lady that the BMB won't be there. She's a smart, wee thing. Said she has a pal who will be there on her own … And there's bound to be a rockabilly band playing – it should be a good laugh if nothing else. Anyway, I am going with you or without you, so what do you say?'

'Ok, I will go if you can guarantee the BMB won't be there and that we'll be safe and if I'm definitely fixed up with a bird.'

'That's great, Tam. I will catch you in the Clachan tomorrow night, round about half seven.'

On Saturday night in the pub, Finn waited impatiently for Tam at the bar. As the clock struck seven thirty, the pub door swung open and Tam stood in the doorway with a self-satisfied grin. 'Right, Finn, mine's a heavy. Oh and by the way, I don't want to be like a spare prick at a wedding.'

Finn grinned back. 'You bastard. Did you stand outside that door till exactly half seven? You did, didn't you, you cunt that you are? I thought you had shirked me.' Both they and the clientele laughed loudly.

'Did I not tell you Bernadette is bringing a friend for you? I don't know her name or what she looks like so don't ask!'

As they made their way on the bus to the hotel, Tam questioned himself for going. His stomach churned away at the couple of pints he'd just had like an automatic washing machine, whitening his olive skin.

Finn noticed the blank look of dread in Tam's eyes and his constant nail-biting. 'You okay, Tam?'

'Well, I'm not too sure about tonight … I have a bad feeling about going. It's a bit far out is Bridgeburn. What's the chances we both end up with a kicking or

131

even worse? It's the BMB hangout and we must be daft going there.'

'Okay, Tam, if you want to go home, I understand. Don't you worry. I won't hold it against you if you do. I have my doubts too. But we could just see how it goes, and if it's not going too well we can fuck off.'

Fear ran through Tam as he tore up his bus ticket, but he didn't want to let his mate down. Reluctantly he nodded.

On arrival at the venue, the hall shook with loud rock and roll music; the band was playing 'Johnny B. Goode'. Finn and Tam were stopped at the door and frisked for weapons. They looked at each other in confusion and alarm. Finn threw his hands up in the air in protest and said, 'Hey, wait a minute now – you're frisking for tools? What sort of pensioner venue is this?'

'We are just trying to spoil your chances,' said the doorman.

The hall was long and wide, and dimmed with soft, cold lighting. Finn noticed the two doors that led off from the hall were closed. Tables and chairs were hoarded near the entrance door with young women sitting on them, but there was no sign of any men. And the pensioners were nowhere to be seen.

Catching Bernadette's eye, Finn waved. Bernadette quickly looked away and hurried out of sight behind the stage door. Where was she going? And why would she ignore him? Then he realised: Bernadette had set him up. He and Tam were trapped.

'FUCK!' he shouted.

Tam looked at Finn. 'What's going on, Finn?'

'I'm sorry, Tam, but I have been a fucking eejit. Look!' Finn pointed over at the walls where BMB gang members were lining up. They were appearing from the same door that Bernadette had disappeared through. One by one they emerged like a swarm of marching army ants leaving their nest. Six of them went to line the stage wall, the next six lined the left wall, and then the right. They just kept coming.

Finn and Tam looked at each other aghast. It looked like the whole gang had turned up. 'Fuck me, Finn, what are we going to do?'

'Don't you worry, Tam. They are out to get me; I will make sure you are okay.'

The BMB were all standing with their backs to the wall. In unison, over thirty men stood on one foot and back-kicked repeatedly, slamming their feet on the cavity wall and creating a boom that resonated throughout the building. The crystal drops on the chandeliers twinkled and clinked as they vibrated and danced with every kick.

The gang looked over at Finn and drew their fingers in a slashing motion across their throats and cheeks, chanting 'Kill McGill! Kill McGill!' The room thundered with sound. Boom went their kicks, and 'Kill McGill!' was their war cry.

Baz Donaldson appeared from one of the side doors along with one of his sidekicks. He smiled at Finn as he approached. 'Glad you could make it,' he

133

said. 'Our Bernadette has done a grand job and she must be congratulated. Aye, my sister Bernadette. You know her, don't you? Bernadette Donaldson.' Baz laughed.

Rage filled Finn's heart. He stood staring at Baz, his body shaking inside. He wanted to kill him.

'Fuck me, I couldn't believe it when I saw you walk into the hall. You never twigged, did you?' Baz laughed again. 'Oh and by the way, there is only one way out of here and that's the main entrance. And as soon as you step out there, you're dead meat. Don't worry, we won't touch you in here because there are witnesses.

'I am looking forward to seeing you outside. It will be nice to see you sweat. We have a few of the team out there and they will give us the wire if you go near the doors.' Baz laughed his hideous death-scream and shouted, 'Enjoy!'

Finn felt the rush of adrenalin. He couldn't believe he'd been taken in by – of all things – a bit of skirt! He bared his teeth and screwed his whole face up, thrusting it into Baz's. 'I will tell you this, you fucking pock-faced cunt,' he screamed, jabbing his finger at him. 'I fear no one! You are claimed. And you are getting it first. I will make sure of that.'

'Oh aye, and what with?' goaded Baz. 'Nothing! Nothing but your fists. We were all frisked so there's no way you are carrying a chib. You won't get near me anyhow. So, you fucking dick, it's me having you!'

Tam pulled Finn's arm and dragged him away. He knew Finn was angry enough to swing a punch, but he also knew he wasn't thinking straight. They were in a tight corner and the odds were too much against them. 'Fuck's sake,' said Tam. 'We are fucked. What are we going to do, Finn?'

'Don't worry yourself, big man.' Finn pointed to a side door. 'I was here a few years back at a funeral and I remember they used the hall during the day for breakfast and dinners. If I remember right, the cutlery is kept in the adjoining room.' Finn turned the doorknob. 'Come on, Tam, we will look in here. It's our only chance for a chib.'

Baz bent over double with laughter as he watched them open the door. 'All the windows have bars on them!' he shouted. 'Have a look and see for yourselves!' He turned to the others in the room. 'This is so funny! Look at them fuckers running scared!' The hall erupted in laughter.

In the adjoining room, Finn and Tam scurried about like two scared mice, frantically opening all the table-service drawers and cupboards and looking for anything they could use to protect themselves.

'Fuck, Finn, they've cleared all the drawers of anything sharp,' said Tam. 'There's nothing here except a soup ladle.'

'What? A soup ladle?' Finn rushed over and plunged his hand into the drawer. 'You beauty! They must have missed this,' said Finn inspecting the large aluminium ladle closely.

'What fucking use is that going to be?' scoffed Tam. 'Are you going to whack them over the head with it?' Resentment was building up inside him. He'd known coming here was a daft idea. 'I'm telling you, Finn, we are fucked! We need to find a *weapon*, not a bloody soup ladle!'

'Hold on, Tam, I've got an idea. Go and stand at the door in case any of the BMBs try to get in.' Finn held the bowl of the ladle in his left hand and used his right to bend the handle back and forth. Finn could feel the heat from the shaft as he frantically worked – until finally the bowl snapped off. He was left with a 14-inch handle that was wide at the top and tapered down to a chisel-like point at the bottom.

'Right, Tam, this helps our position. We have a weapon.'

'Aye, it might be so – but as soon as they see what it is they will just fucking laugh at us.'

'Thing is, Tam, they won't be seeing it. Well, not all of it, at least.' Finn slipped the handle into his inside pocket. 'Come on, let's get out of here.'

They emerged from the door with all eyes on them, the gang sniggering as they made for the main entrance. It was then that Finn saw Bernadette by the door, clutching her bag with her two hands in front of her.

'Oh, aye, you done a great job setting me up,' Finn said to her. 'My father always told me to never to trust anyone, especially a woman. Well, now I fucking know what he meant.'

'Look, I am so sorry, Finn. Yes, I did set you up, but I immediately regretted it. I ran out the door after you to warn you but you were nowhere to be seen. I am so terribly sorry.'

'You fucking cow. Not only have you set me up, you have set Tam up too. I hope you are fucking happy,' bellowed Finn. 'Now fuck off out of my sight!' His anger overwhelmed him. Because of her he had led his friend into this mess!

The large entrance door was slightly ajar and Tam peered through the opening. He gasped in horror and nudged Finn. 'Look through here. The cunts are all waiting for us outside.' Finn looked. The crowd encircled the bottom of the wide marble steps.

Making a grand exit, Finn yanked open the double doors. Tam stood shaking behind him. The BMB gang slow handclapped them before bursting into shouts of 'Kill McGill! Kill McGill!'

Baz lifted his arms in the air to quell the baying mob. 'Come on down, Finn. Come on and meet the boys.'

'I will. But only if you let Tam go. It's me you're after anyway.'

Baz thought for a moment. 'Aye, Finn, you are right, it is you we are after. And we will get Tam another time. Right, lads, open up and let him through.'

Tam looked at Finn. 'Let's get fucking into them. At least we will save our pride.'

'Come on now, Tam, don't you worry yourself about me. I will sort this. Thanks for the offer but I will be all right on my own.' Finn placed his hand on Tam's lower back and gave him a push towards the baying crowd. He stepped down on to the next step behind Tam.

Baz shouted, 'Let him through, lads!' and, like the biblical parting of the sea for Moses, the group opened up for Tam to pass through.

'Run like fuck through the bastards, Tam, and don't stop for nothing,' Finn urged. 'I will see you soon.'

'But I cannae just leave you!' Finn gave him a final push of encouragement and Tam set off running down the steps and through the parted gang. He ran so fast his legs left his torso behind them. He kept on running and never looked back.

'Right, Tam is out the way. We made a deal – now you need to come through,' demanded Baz.

Finn stood with his left foot resting on the second step down, and his right foot on the one above. In one fell swoop, he slipped his hand into his inside pocket and drew out the handle of the soup ladle. Like a swordsman, Finn waved it about so fast that only a glint of metal and length could be seen. 'The first one of you bastards to come near me will get this fucker run through them!' he yelled, returning the handle back under his jacket.

Outraged and seemingly outwitted, Baz showed him his fists. 'Where the fuck did you get that?'

'I'm not daft and will always be one step ahead of you lot!'

At speed, he pulled the handle back out from his pocket, swooping it at arm's length from left to right in a semi-circle in front of him as though it were a cutlass. Stepping down to the next step, Finn slowly moved forward. He whooshed the ladle in front of him, keeping the gang at bay.

'Move over! I said fucking move!' he shouted, demanding respect. Finn now had the advantage: he was on the upper part of the stairs and above everyone. He swished the handle from side to side as he continued to step down. The BMB gang – including Baz – backed off, and with every sweep of Finn's blade they parted like a shoal of herring attacked by a seal. No one dared challenge him.

Walking smugly through the crowd now, Finn neared the middle of the opening and took on a swagger of confidence. 'You lot are a fucking pile of fucking wankers!' he shouted. As the last row opened, Finn dropped the ladle handle and ran. Baz saw the 'weapon' and was incensed. 'Get the bastard!' he yelled, and the gang chased after Finn like a pack of hungry wolves, but they were no match for Finn and he quickly pulled away from them.

Way up ahead and still running was Tam. Finn caught up with him and only then did he look back. The gang had given up the chase. 'Slow down, Tam. They're not coming after us.'

Tam slowed to a canter and looked at Finn in disbelief. 'How the fuck did you manage to get away from them fuckers without a scratch?'

'Easy,' said Finn. 'I'm a lot smarter than those stupid cunts.'

Tam grinned. 'I would give my right arm to have seen their faces when they realised it was just the handle off a soup ladle.'

Relief flooded through them and Finn patted Tam on his shoulder. 'There is a pint or two waiting for you at the pub. We will have a drink to us outwitting that fucker Baz!' They laughed and made their way to the Clachan.

Mrs O'Connor

In the spring of 1969, Finn pulled up outside Tam's house and sat his motorcycle on its side stand. He took off his black leather gloves, pushed them into the back pocket of his jeans and patted the black petrol tank as though he had just dismounted a horse. Tam's mother was in the back green unpegging her dry washing from the line, and through a mouthful of pegs she said, 'Hi Finn. If you're looking for our Thomas, he's at work.'

'At work! It's Saturday. He doesn't normally work Saturday.'

'Aye, he does now. He started down in the shipyard on Monday.'

'How did he get in there?' he quizzed.

'You know old Mrs O'Conner from Copeland Street?'

Finn shook his head. 'No, I am not sure if I do.'

'Ach, you do! You and our Tam used to run for her messages not that long ago.'

'Oh, aye, a nice old woman. She was good to us and gave us thruppence each just to get her messages.'

'Well, she works in the offices at the shipyard and carries plenty of clout. Her family have something to do with steel stockholding or something like that. Anyway, she got our Tam a job in at the yard doing bench-drilling. Oh and that's not all. There's a job for a trainee crane driver going. You being eighteen on your last birthday, I'm sure if you went round and seen her you would have a good chance. Aye, that woman always liked the two of you. I bet you would get it. Besides, it's a lot better than humping coal, is it not?'

Rubbing his chin, Finn thought deeply. He realised he was excited at the prospect. 'Aye, you are right, Mrs Fleming. I am fed up humping coal. And me being a crane driver, eh? Aye, that sounds good to me. Thanks very much for the tip! I am going over there now.'

'You do that and good luck, son. I hope you get it!'

Kicking up his Triumph, Finn sped off, soon reaching Mrs O'Connor's house. The grand Georgian house was built of red sandstone. A high wall of the same stone surrounded the garden, and fruit trees trained flat against it were in full bloom. The entire garden was an explosion of colour, though yellows and whites dominated. Finn walked the path to the front door and saw Mrs O'Connor kneeling to tend her garden. Her slim figure was bent over some French marigolds as she reached to trowel a weed.

'Hiya,' said Finn.

'Who's that? Do I know you?' she asked.

'Hi Mrs O'Connor. You should do – it's me, Finlay McGill, who used to go for your messages.'

She turned and bent the rim of her straw hat, seeing only a faint silhouette as her blue eyes squinted against the morning sun. Finn moved his shadow over her face, and her eyes lit up as she recognised him. 'Oh my oh my, Finlay McGill! I am so sorry I didn't recognise you. Oh my, how you have grown! And into a handsome young man, too!'

'Aye, I sure have grown,' he said, 'but maybe not so handsome.'

Finn knew Mrs O'Connor was keen on gardening from when he used to call round on Saturday mornings to run her errands. But today he could see she had more than just a liking; it was something of an obsession. Finn decided to try a bit of his charm. 'The flowers look magnificent,' he said.

Mrs O'Connor smiled, pulling off her leather gloves and pushing them into her green apron. 'Do you thinks so, Finlay?'

'Och aye.' Finn swivelled his head and took a long sniff as though to savour the scented garden air. The smell of the flowers and newly dug soil took him aback, and he took another deep pull at the fragrant air.

143

'Well, I can honestly say I haven't smelled anything like this before,' he said. 'Absolutely amazing.'

Pleased, Mrs O'Conner shot her hand out and pointed to a flower head. 'That there,' she said, 'that's astrantia. They have beautiful, scented roots and the flowers attract all sorts of bees into my garden. That one with the purple heads as big as your fist is allium, which is Latin for garlic. They're a relative of the leek and the rats and mice don't come in your garden when you grow them. That's aster. They are a relative of the daisy and grow well through the summer. That one there—'

Realising this could be a lengthy conversation, Finn quickly interrupted. 'Brilliant colours too, Mrs O'Connor!'

'Och aye, I like to grow bright colours. Besides, all the insects love them too,' she beamed.

'Yes. I've learned a lot about flowers that I never knew,' said Finn.

Mrs O'Connor looked at Finn from head to toe. 'It's so lovely to see you, Finlay. It looks like you are now old enough to call me Maisie.'

'That's a lovely name, Mrs O'Connor.'

She wagged her finger at him. 'Now, now.'

Finn smiled. 'Okay, Maisie it is.'

'This one here—'

'Eh, Maisie,' Finn interrupted again. She was a nice woman but enough was enough. It was Saturday morning and he wanted to get off on his motorbike for a blast down the road, then go for a pint or two in the Clachan with the boys. 'Sorry to butt in, but I have just had a thought. Would it please be possible to have a couple of heads off that one over there for my mam? She would love a nice wee bunch for her kitchen windowsill.'

'What, that? That's a butterfly bush. It's called that because it has a sweet nectar that attracts butterflies and other plant-friendly insects. And may I say it's an exceptionally good choice. Of course! That would be no bother at all. I will make a wee posy for your mother. You will be her best friend when you give her these!' She dipped her hand into her apron and pulled out a pair of secateurs, eagerly pushing the flower heads to the side before snipping away at the stems.

'Eh, Maisie, I heard there is a crane-driving job going at the yard. Is that true?'

Maisie's brows knitted together and her thin top lip took a downward turn and covered her lower lip. She was confused by the sudden change of subject. 'Is, eh, what? The crane driver's job …' she murmured.

'Aye. I am interested in the job if it's still available.'

'Oh yes, the crane driver's job. Yes, I see. Yes, it's still available. Tell you what, just go down first thing on Monday morning and see the foreman in fabrication. It's the big unit up on the right-hand side as you go through the main gate – shop number twenty-one. Ask for Andy Monahan and tell him Mrs O'Connor sent you.'

Handing Finn the flowers, she smiled and said, 'Good luck with your new job, Finlay. You best take some work clothes with you on Monday, too.'

'Call me Finn, Maisie. Just call me Finn,' he smiled back.

'Aye, okay, Finn it is.' They both chuckled.

'Thank you very much, Maisie. I will not let you down!'

'Well, I have always known that. When I sent you down to the shops for my messages with a ten-shilling note, you always came back with the change. Cheerio now and shut the gate behind you. Remember: shop number twenty-one, Andy Monahan.'

The crane driver's job was in the bag, and Finn was excited. Not only would he be getting a chance at skilled work, but he could give up his low-paid coalman's job. Now he would be doing a man's job. Before heading for home, Finn stuffed the flowers into the inside of his partly zipped black leather biker jacket. Their fragrant heads sat under his chin and made him sneeze. He hoped none of the Executioners would see him with these flowers. He'd be the laughing stock of Gallows Hill.

My mother does not deserve these flowers, he thought. *I would rather bin them than give them to her.* Finn turned the corner and saw a sign ahead of him: Clyde Care Home for the Elderly. He screeched to a halt outside, dismounted, walked up the paved path and rang the doorbell. It seemed an eternity before the door was opened by a woman in a blue uniform with a 'Staff Nurse' badge pinned to her top.

'Here!' he said, thrusting the flowers out towards her. 'I brought you these because you really do an excellent job looking after the ex-shipyard workers.'

The woman stood rigid for a moment, startled. Then she put her hand out and gently grasped the flowers, thanking him. 'What's your name?' she asked.

'Finn.'

'Well, thanks again, Finn. That's truly a lovely thing to do. It is so nice to know there are still kind and caring young folks about.'

'It's nae bother.' Finn turned away smiling to himself. He was glad to have rid himself of potential embarrassment. He jumped on the kickstart to fire up his motorcycle. As he sped away, Finn felt excitement flood through him. Life was just getting better and better. He let the handlebars go, stood up on the foot pegs and, like a victorious racer, punched the air with both his fists and whooped with delight. Then he made straight for the Clachan Bar.

The shipyard

Monday morning soon came around. Finn rode his Triumph bike to the shipyard and then along the road beside a gigantic ship being built on the dry dock. *Thank God I have this bike*, he thought. *This place is massive.* He had only reached shop number fifteen and still had six more workshops to go. Finally, he saw the yellow-painted 'Number 21' sign above huge steel doors, and he walked into the dark steel-fabricating shop. It was as big as ten football pitches.

Looking all around the shop floor, Finn spotted the distinctive collar and brown coat of a foreman and knew it must be his new gaffer, Andy. He was a tall and balding potbellied man, and his cheeks shook like a British bulldog as he spoke.

'I guess you are Finlay McGill? Maisie told me to expect you. Have you informed your last work that you are leaving?'

This was a new start for Finn at the shipyard and he was determined to leave his old name behind. 'Hi Andy. They call me Finn. And, aye, I told them Saturday afternoon I was leaving and they were fine about it. In fact, they wished me all the best, so I am all sorted and ready to start.'

After filling in some paperwork, Andy took Finn over to the bottom of the crane ladders and introduced him to Tommy Boyde, the crane-driving instructor. 'This is Finn. Look after this young man. He's going to be your new project.'

Tommy drank down the last dregs of black tea from his billycan and hung it on the end of a steam pipe. Talking very fast, he said, 'Aye, Finn, we are a wee bit antiquated here – we still use steam for some things. Besides, the hot pipe is handy for keeping your tea warm!'

Tommy's workmates nicknamed him Tommy Gun as he could rattle his words out faster than speeding bullets.

'C'mon with me, son,' he urged. 'I will tell you a wee bit of what we do here. We make multiple steel-fabricated sections: some are riveted together and some welded, and most of the intricate and complex patterns are made here in shop twenty-one. All the finished segments are sent up the yard to the shipwright who will see that it is welded or riveted into place on the ship.

'Now, Finn, your job is mainly to lift and turn these sections so that they are welded on both sides. It can be boring at times as there can be quite a lull when everyone else is working. A wee tip for you is to take that time to do a crossword or read something.

'This morning I will show you the controls and we will have a wee play on the crane and then we can have our sandwiches. Have you brought something with you? Because we usually just eat it up there in the crane; by the time you climb down and back up it's just not worth it for a fifteen-minute break.'

Finn slapped his haversack. 'Aye, I have some cheese sandwiches in here.'

They made their way over to the gantry ladder and started to climb up to the top. Finn looked over his shoulder as he climbed. He just couldn't comprehend the vastness of the place. He looked up at the clear corrugated polypropylene roof that let sunlight in. He had heard people talk in the Clachan about how this material had lit up their once-dismal workshops.

'Never forget, Finn, the golden rule: safety first. Think of your safety, and the safety of everyone else who works here, at all times.'

Tommy was a rather large and weighty man and his over-washed dungarees were tight around his bulky frame, emphasising his girth. His folded tweed cap sat inside his chest pocket. He always wore a collar and tie, and would often say, 'Just because you work in the shipyard, it does not mean you have to be untidy'.

They reached halfway up the ladder. Breathless, Tommy paused on the middle rung with his back against the safety hoop while he puffed and panted.

He took his hanky from his pocket and wiped his sweat-peppered brow before blowing his blobby nose. His round face was almost purple.

'See that glazed building over there in the middle of the shop? Well, that's Big Andy's office. We call him the Goldfish because he has a 360-degree view – the tall windows go all the way round without a break. But now his nickname's shortened to Goldie. For God's sake, don't let on or call him that – he would go off his nut! We reckon he suspects we have a nickname for him but he's not sure.'

Finn laughed. 'Goldie Monahan. There is something fishy about that!'

They reached the top and walked the rail line of the gantry. Finn could hardly believe the length of the gantry rails: the parallel rail on the other side was almost fifty feet away and seemed to go on for miles. The crane itself was suspended between the gantry rails. He shook his head at the enormity of it all. As they approached the crane, Tommy stopped for a short breather before climbing down the few steps into the cabin.

'Right, Finn, we have three levers at the front of the cabin: one for moving the crane left and right, one for sending the jib out, and the other is for lowering the jig and hoisting. There is a break for slowing the crane down on this one …'

After nearly three weeks of intensive training, Finn passed his crane test. He punched the air in delight. His wage would now increase considerably.

'Hey, Tommy, how do you put up with this bloody noise in here?' asked Finn, putting his fingers in his ears. 'It just drives me daft.'

'Ach, you will soon get used to it, Finn. In time you won't even notice it. And that's why we use hand signals most of the time. But never mind that – there has been a lot of talk about lay-offs. You're dead lucky you got the chance of this job and that you got started when you did.'

Finn thought it was about time his luck changed and he was thankful for it. 'Aye, I suppose I am dead lucky.'

Yes, his luck was changing. He had a nice status in the gang and many friends, and now he had this job. But he was aware that there was something still missing in his life. He felt a sadness that he didn't understand.

'Now that you are a licensed crane driver, Goldie wants you up on the crane on gantry twelve. That's where they do all the heavy welding. Take your time up there because head office don't want any more accidents in this place. Just ask for Jimmy Baird – he's the first-hand slinger.'

Looking Finn straight in the eye, Tommy shook his head from side to side. He hung both his thumbs through his dungaree straps and screwed his face up in a frown.

'Another thing, son. Just to let you know, Jimmy does have a bit of a reputation for being a hard man. He's the leader of the Clydeside gang the Razors. Between you and me, he is a right bastard. He has all the shop workers walking on eggshells and jumping through hoops – and that includes Goldie. I got to tell you, Jimmy is not too keen on crane drivers since he nearly lost his thumb to a young rooky. I'm sorry, son. But that's where Goldie wants you to go. Good luck. It's been a pleasure training you.'

Man against boy

Making his way towards the gantry, Finn felt a slap on the back of his head. Turning around quickly, he saw it was a smiling Tam. 'Congratulations! I heard you passed your test!'

'Thanks, Tam. I better get up to my new crane. It's my first shift on my own and I am late. It will take me a few minutes to get there. This place is massive!'

'Aye. This yard employs over thirteen thousand workers alone. What crane will you be on?'

'Gantry number twelve.'

Tam jolted and straightened. 'Oh, fuck! Finn, that's Jimmy Baird's gantry. He is that bastard who greased wee Joe Davies' balls! Joe was his crane driver for less than a week before Jimmy tied him with rope to the crane hook. Can you believe the bastard hoisted him thirty foot in the air and left him dangling there during dinner break? All because he hoisted the crane hook too early!'

Finn shuddered. 'Shit! What a cunt.'

'Not only that, before he hoisted him up, he pulled the poor bastard's boilersuit down around his ankles and then hung him fully naked. He slapped black roller grease on his balls. Left him hung up and dripping grease. Now everyone refers to Jimmy as the wee black fairy!' Tam smiled at this image of Jimmy. 'Aye, but what an awful thing to happen to Joe. And what would have happened if the rope had slipped? Though the only good thing about that would be he is one of the Toonies gang.'

They both looked at each other and grinned, and then burst out laughing.

'Fuck me! Are you sure it's Jimmy Baird?' asked Tam.

'Aye. That's who Tommy said I must report to. What did the gaffer, Andy, do about Jimmy hoisting Joe up?'

Tam put a hand on Finn's shoulder and moved in closer to his ear. Finn needed to hear this and take heed.

'That's the thing – he done nothing. He did fuck all because he is shit scared of Jimmy and he always turns a blind eye to everything he does. Jimmy's a pure evil bastard. You will be the fifth crane driver who has worked with him in just the four weeks I've been here.'

Finn was aghast. He had to work with this madman. 'Ah well, he will not fucking push me about or bully me out the job, hard man or not. I won't let him.'

'For your sake, I do hope he doesn't,' said Tam, walking off. 'Anyway, I will see you at dinner break. You can let me know how you got on. And for fuck's sake, Finn, watch your back!'

Fuck, what am I going to do? Finn started to tremble. 'Pull yourself together, man!' he muttered to himself. With trepidation, he headed for gantry twelve. Stopped in his tracks by a long train going past, he noticed the raw materials it carried: heavy steel plate, wide-flange steel beams, T-bar, I-beam and channel. It was also heading into gantry twelve and it took the train a few minutes to pass before Finn could enter.

Walking deep into the shop, Finn saw people strewn all over the place and all hard at work. Giant machines shaped and bent the steel plate, while workers busied themselves welding, drilling and riveting the plate together. The flash of blue light from the welding rods illuminated the heavy orange-brown rust cloud that hovered above the riveters' bench and swirled around their heads like a swarm of orange midges. Most of the steel was covered in a light dusting of this fine rust. Finn tilted his head back and saw the roof far above him. Orange and grey clouds could also be seen floating and twinkling in the sunbeams far above the workshop, stirring around like slow-churning volcanic lava.

A large yellow crane labelled 'Gantry 12' was suspended above him and Finn felt daunted. The whole place was vast and much bigger than the bay he was trained in.

He noticed a tall, muscular man kneeling on a wide universal beam, welding it on to an enormous steel plate. Finn ran his eye over him as he approached and reckoned he was maybe in his early thirties. A dirty, blackened flat cap sat on his head with its peak pointing backwards, and a welding helmet lay snugly on top of it. The top half of his one-piece boilersuit was wrapped around his waist, secured with the loose sleeves, and a heavy, brown, grease-smeared leather apron hung down over the top of a sweat-soaked navy-blue T-shirt that clung to his chest like a limpet.

Finn went and stood patiently by his side until he paused his welding. Still bent over the metal, the man lifted his black visor from his face and stared at Finn. 'What? What are you after?'

Finn noticed his sharp Roman nose and a two-inch scar on the corner of his unshaven mouth that gave him an evil-looking appearance.

'Hi there. I'm looking for Jimmy Baird.'

'That's me! I'm Jimmy Baird. What do you want with me?'

'I'm Finn, the new crane driver. I was told to report to you.'

Jimmy's eyebrows lifted. He looked Finn up and down and walked all the way around him, scrunching his face up into a scowl. It was obvious he didn't like what he was seeing. He had been sent another youngster.

'Fuck me!' he shouted for the benefit of all the ears in the vicinity. 'They keep sending me fucking wankers. Have you seen what has just turned up?' Jimmy gestured towards Finn, moving his hand slowly downwards just inches from Finn's face and body. 'Look at this! This is what they send you! And they expect us to meet targets. Fucking diabolical it is.' Jimmy was still circling Finn, shaking his head from side to side in disapproval. 'Fucking diabolical!' he screamed. 'How long have you had your fucking licence?'

Finn fumed. His heart was busy pumping adrenalin around his body and he wanted to punch Jimmy. But he also wanted the job. He calmed himself before saying, 'I passed my test and got my licence this morning.'

'Oh, fuck, I knew it. I knew they would send me another fucking waste of time. That's my piecework fucked now.'

Jimmy spoke with a rough voice that sounded like sandpaper running over metal. He chain-smoked Capstan Full Strength, lighting his next cigarette from the one he'd nearly finished. He'd stick a pin – kept embedded in his T-shirt collar – into the lit half-inch butt and hold it against a fresh cigarette; the butt would disappear as he drew on the new cigarette to light it. He smoked all day. Even through his dinner break a cigarette burned by his side, and Jimmy would pull on it between chewing and swallowing his food.

Jimmy blew smoke into Finn's face. 'Right, bawbags, that is your crane up there. Get yourself up there like the good wee boy that you are. Fucking move it! And do not dare come down until I tell you. Is that clear?'

Finn filled with resentment, humiliation and dismay. He knew in his heart he would not be able put up with Jimmy's dominance and there was bound to be trouble between the two of them eventually. But at this point, he refused to be drawn in by his aggressor for fear of losing his job. He would see how it went and he would keep his head down for the time being. He nodded at Jimmy. 'Aye, that's clear all right.'

Finn climbed to the top of the metal ladder until he was thirty-nine feet off the ground. Blue light from the electric welding cast an eerie shimmering shadow on the ceiling, like blue ghosts dancing in the night sky. Finn flicked the large fuse-box switch and made his way down the small cab ladder and into the main cabin. He familiarised himself with the new crane and its different control layout. Though the cranes were mostly the same style, Finn would make absolutely sure that he knew this type inside out before operating it. He remembered Tommy's maxim of safety first and knew he had been trained well. He knew he had to be careful and hoist his load high enough to make sure it cleared any machinery.

As he looked over the hand controls on the ledge of the open cab, the noise in the fabrication shop became overwhelming; it seemed even worse up in the crane. From up there, he had an all-round aerial view of the workshop and could see how all the huge machinery – scattered across the shop floor like marching tyrannosauruses – created such a deafening cacophony. Large plate-bending rollers rumbled as they shaped the heavy steel. Tall upright drilling machines squealed as they drilled the holes for the riveters. The screech of the high-speed saw as it cut through cold steel shrieked through Finn's skull and embedded itself there so deeply that he would still hear it in his bed at night.

Finn loved this job but not the noise. It hurt his ears and gave him a headache. It was so hard to bear that he quickly used his penknife to cut two small pieces from a clean white cotton cleaning rag and placed them into each ear canal to try and dampen the sound.

He'd barely had a few minutes to familiarise himself with the cab and its controls before he heard the faint sound of Jimmy screaming. Jimmy was looking up at him, pointing towards the rear of the shop unit.

'Right, bawbags, I have been shouting you for the last ten minutes! Are you fucking deaf? Down the fucking shop!'

Finn's heart thumped with anger as he pulled the rags out of his ears. He'd only been on the job for half an hour and had already withstood a barrage of abuse from Jimmy. He would not take much more of this.

Looking over to his trolley, Finn moved the hook out and hoisted it high to miss the machinery below. Jimmy walked across the shop and was pointing and beckoning for Finn to follow.

Finn's nerves took a hold and he shook on his feet as he turned the lever of the crane to his right. The crane jerked and started to move but, to Finn's dismay, he had flicked the lever in the wrong direction. He quickly turned the lever the other way and the crane stopped momentarily before lurching back in the opposite direction, causing the hook to swing violently like the pendulum of a grandfather clock.

'Fuck. Did you see that, everybody?' Jimmy shouted at the top of his voice. 'What did I say! Another useless fucker they have sent me. Bawbags, lift that fucking hook higher before you kill someone!'

Body tensed and almost rigid, Finn knew he had the hook high enough; he had made sure that it was. Jimmy had made him feel stupid, and he was angry with himself. He clenched his fist and, taking one almighty swing, punched the woodwork of the crane, hitting it with such force that it split his knuckle painfully. 'Fuck off, Jimmy!' he muttered to himself.

Jimmy's intimidating voice came again and Finn's legs began to feel weak at the joints. He tried to calm himself and began massaging his legs but another shout came. 'Fucking move that crane, bawbags! Or else I will come up there and teach you a lesson you will never forget!'

Determined not to make any more mistakes, Finn made sure he was using the right lever, lifted the hook up all the way to the top and followed Jimmy down the shop. Jimmy pointed to a large sheet of two-inch steel plate. 'That one there. Pick that one up,' he ordered.

Positioning himself over the plate, Finn concentrated hard and was relieved that the trolley moved the hook all the way over and above the sheet that Jimmy had pointed at. He then began to lower the hook – but was startled by more aggressive screaming.

'For fuck's sake! What the fuck are you doing? I said that one over there. Aye, that three-quarter plate over there!' Jimmy was pointing to an entirely different steel plate, more than twenty feet away from where he had first pointed.

Growling to himself now, Finn's face whitened with anger. He knew Jimmy was deliberately making a fool of him in front of the other workers, and so he screamed back. 'No, you never asked me to lift that sheet! You pointed to the one the hook is above!'

'Bawbags, are you calling me a fucking liar then, eh? Well, are you?'

Finn thought better of arguing with Jimmy on his first day. There might well be retaliation if he answered back, and his job was on the line. He backed down. 'Aye, right, maybe I am mistaken.'

Satisfaction gleamed on Jimmy's face as he laughed. He'd got the better of him. With a heavy frown, Finn kicked the cabin. His stomach churned. Jimmy grinned up at him before marching away in an exaggerated gallus swagger. Finn knew Jimmy was savouring having the upper hand.

'Pick that fucking sheet up, now!' Jimmy demanded.

Finn's nerves were stinging. They were like tiny fireworks exploding everywhere in his body, leaving a tingling sensation behind. He had to concentrate hard before he could lift the sheet and place it on Jimmy's bench. The moment he succeeded, Jimmy began his welding. *Thank goodness*, Finn thought. Jimmy would be welding constantly for a good couple of hours now, earning his piecework money, and that would give Finn some reprieve.

While Jimmy was busy, Finn was regularly called over by other workers to turn over their work, and he worked hard hoisting and unloading the girders and plate from the train that had pulled up earlier. He managed to work at a steady pace and without incident for the rest of the morning, and enjoyed the couple of hours without Jimmy berating him. Feeling pleased, Finn patted his left shoulder, congratulating himself on completing his first shift alone. He had driven the crane perfectly for all the other welders and slingers.

But the feeling of uneasiness that Jimmy had cast upon him lingered nevertheless. Finn's blood boiled with anger at Jimmy's humiliation of him in front of the other workers. He couldn't bear the thought that he had backed down from him. Stewing on these thoughts, Finn shuffled about in the small cab, clearly agitated. He grabbed hold of the wooden door post of the crane and headbutted it. Jimmy had made him feel like a coward – and that was not Finn at all. He had vowed to himself ever since the ice-cream van incident that he would always fight back, no matter the outcome – even if it meant death.

He worked himself up into a rage, his face turning the colour of a freshly pulled beetroot as he visualised beating the hell out of Jimmy. Then he sat down in the cab and tried to calm himself with deep breaths. But, as he waited to be called, his thoughts flashed back to his uncle's abuse. It was always there, always sitting in the corner of his mind, always ready to pop up when he was most vulnerable. Finn fought hard to dismiss these demonic thoughts, but the morning's traumatic events with Jimmy just triggered more difficult memories, this time of his mother.

Then the connection struck him. Thanks to Jimmy, he was experiencing the same feelings of humiliation that he'd suffered at the hands of his mother. It was the same embarrassment, the same put-downs that had taken away his confidence before, piece by piece.

Stamping the floor of the crane in anger and contempt, Finn felt a familiar panic rush through his body. He felt sick. His stomach brutally lurched upwards as it wrenched and bulged towards his throat. He stood startled and breathless. His whole body quaked.

'The bastard!' he said to himself. 'I don't, and I will not, take shit from anyone, no matter who they are—'

A large six-inch steel rivet came flying through the opening of his cabin passing close to Finn's face, before rebounding off the cabin roof and hitting him on the top of his head. Instantly, a large split opened up on his scalp and began to bleed profusely. The pain stunned him for a moment.

Jimmy was looking up at the cab. 'Hey, bawbags, are you fucking sleeping in there?' he shouted. 'Move it up the shop, now!'

Finn ignored him and reached for the first-aid box that was attached to the cabin wall, but before he had the chance to open it, another large rivet bounced off the wall, narrowly missing him.

Jimmy was pacing about below, frustrated that Finn hadn't moved the crane. 'I said up the shop, you lazy bastard!'

As Finn looked out and down at Jimmy, blood gushed from his head and poured over the side of the cab. Bloody rain splattered over Jimmy's face and clothes. 'You did that deliberately!' Jimmy shouted angrily.

Finn's face knotted and contorted uncontrollably with anger. 'Look at me! Look what you done. You could have killed me! You are a fucking idiot.'

'You deserved it, you lazy bastard!'

Things were not going the way Jimmy expected. He knew his piecework would be interrupted if he didn't get another job on his bench soon. 'Move it up the shop!' he demanded, trying to reassert himself. 'Just be sure I will see you later. You will never call me an idiot again after I am finished with you, I can assure of you that.'

Finn felt every muscle in his body tense. He was trembling with rage and, by now, he couldn't care less who Jimmy was. He held himself tight with his feet under the cabin's back shelf and, gripping the front of the cabin ledge, he leaned out as far down as he dared just to get as near as possible to Jimmy's face.

'You can fuck off! I am not moving this crane anywhere until I have stopped the bleeding from my head. And, aye, you *are* a fucking idiot.'

'You better move it, bawbags, or else!'

Finn ignored him and tended to his wound. Jimmy kept screaming at the top of his voice, and Finn continued to hold a clean rag to his cut to stem the blood flow. But all the while, Finn's temper gripped him by the throat and shook his body like a rag doll.

'Fuck off! Go take a fucking run and jump into the Clyde, you cunt,' he yelled back at Jimmy. 'Can you not understand English? I am going nowhere until I see to this cut.'

Dead man walking

A showdown was inevitable. Standing on his toes, Jimmy glared upwards at Finn. He rocked and snapped his body backwards and forwards, snarling and physically foaming at the mouth.

'Tell me to fuck off, would you! You think you are safe up there, but when you eventually come down off that crane, I will be waiting. You are a dead man walking!'

Within minutes, the news had spread and everyone in the fabrication shop feared for the new boy – but not one person said anything to Jimmy. Jimmy sure had bay twenty-one sewn up: he controlled everyone with fear. His Clydeside gang were the same, cruelly intimidating young and old through violence and terror.

Remembering what Tommy and Tam had told him about what Jimmy had done to others in the past, Finn knew he meant every word. He felt his stomach knotting and his heart pounding with those very same feelings of helplessness and sickening fear that he'd endured as a child. Frantically, he searched high and low around the cab for anything he could use as a weapon. To his despair, he found nothing – not even a spanner – to defend himself with. He resigned himself to his looming fate.

His head wound had stopped bleeding and he took the bloodied rag away before shouting down to everyone below. 'I'm back on my shift now if you need me.' He was immediately called over by a drill operator to turn an H beam.

'Hoy bawbags, are you trying to wind me up even more? Or have you forgot I am still waiting?' said Jimmy.

Finn knew how to hit back at him right away and without any more confrontation. For Jimmy, time off his piecework meant less money for him. So Finn moved plating for another job and then carried the H beam over and past Jimmy's bench.

Jimmy blew a cloud of cigarette smoke upwards and called up to Finn. Holding four fingers up and pointing at his watch, he said, 'Four o'clock.' Then he crossed his arms over his chest as if he were a corpse. 'Remember: you are a dead man,' he laughed. 'I will be waiting.'

Dinner break arrived without incident. Though Finn had said he would meet Tam, he was afraid Jimmy would attack him if he climbed down to the shop floor. If he could stay well out of his way, then Jimmy might just calm down and forget about it all.

He spent twenty minutes trying to unwind before he opened his sandwiches. He took a bite and started to chew but the morning had taken its toll and that sickly rumbling feeling still lay deep in his stomach. He couldn't face eating anything and spat the half-chewed bread into the empty axle-grease can that was used as a bin. Then he stood up and threw his sandwiches with such force that he bowled the can over. He was taken aback by his own strength. *If I could only get one or two punches into Jimmy as hard as that, I might just make my mark*, he thought to himself. Spotting an old newspaper, he grabbed it and began to read in an effort to calm himself down.

A torrent of water suddenly exploded into the cab, immediately saturating Finn. Startled, he jumped up and noticed thick smoke and sparks bouncing out of the fuse box. Frightened he might be electrocuted, he grabbed his leather work glove and used it to slam the fuse-box lever switch up and off.

Water continued to pour into the cabin. Blinded by the torrent, and anxious and confused, Finn began to panic. 'Come on now,' he said to himself. 'The electric is switched off. Deal with the water.' It seemed to be coming from the roof of the cabin. He held his hand out to divert the flow away from his face and tried to see. The water was in fact coming through the open side of the cabin in a jet that then bounced off the ceiling.

There was loud laughter below him and Finn looked down over the ledge. Jimmy held a high-pressure water hose, used for blasting metal clear of grease before welding, and he was deliberately aiming the jet into Finn's cabin. The large factory lights shone down on Jimmy's head. His face looked crazed and was almost halved by a wide grin that revealed rotting teeth and a missing incisor.

Leaning over the side, Finn shouted down, 'You fucking idiotic lunatic! You are not right in the fucking head. You need locking up!'

Taken aback, Jimmy did an angry jump towards the cabin. 'Not right in the head, am I?' he said through gritted teeth. 'We will see at four o'clock.'

'Fuck you! You should be in a straitjacket!'

Jimmy was laughing again now. 'I knew I would flush you out. Just like a fucking rat from a sewer.'

Glancing over at the fish tank, Finn saw his boss Andy sneak into his office, but his heart sank when he made eye contact with him. Andy quickly ducked his head behind a blueprint, choosing to leave Finn to his fate.

Putting both his hands out to stop the flow of water hitting him, Finn shouted, 'Stop that! Stop it now!'

One of the older workers, Old Bert, who was well-liked, approached Jimmy and said in a soft voice, 'Come on, Jimmy, that's enough now!' He made his way over to the tap and turned it off. The flow of water subsided. Bert placed his hand on Jimmy's shoulder. 'Come on, Jimmy, give the laddie a break. Leave him alone now. He's not worth it. Besides, he's only a young laddie.'

'No, Bert. There is no fucking way I will leave that bastard alone! I cannae just let someone call me an idiot and not right in the head, and let the cunt get away with it. Well, can I? A young laddie or not, I cannae let him get away with saying that in front of everyone.'

The clock was ticking ever closer to 4 o'clock. The flood of blood to Finn's head was overwhelming. Thoughts of his mother's abuse rushed back at him like a flying demon. *I can't go through this again. I can't. I just can't.* Within the chaos of his thoughts, the ice cream van incident fought its way to the front of his mind. He had been frightened back then too. Just like then, the only thing left for him to do was hit back. He just had to psych himself up. He might get a sore face but he could get one or two punches in and give as good as he got before Jimmy overpowered him.

'Hoy, bawbags!' Finn's shift was nearly over and Jimmy was pointing to his watch again, turning the side of his head level to the ceiling and cupping his ear with his hand in anticipation of the four o'clock siren.

As the siren finally blasted, a shiver shot down Finn's spine. Jimmy was jogging on the spot as if he were limbering up, and putting on a show for the onlookers. He began to shrug his shoulders from side to side whilst moving his head in a circular motion. Then all at once he stopped and pointed at the shop floor. 'Right, bawbags, you come down here, now!'

Finn was hit with another flashback: his mother doing the very same thing, pointing to the floor, demanding he come nearer to her bed so she could reach him with a slap. The same sickly feeling from those unbearable days bubbled away in his stomach like a witch's cauldron. There was the familiar and overwhelming feeling of despair. Finn tried to compose himself. He stood up, only for his knees to buckle and shake and knock together. His legs just would not follow his mind's instructions, and he was thankful that the gathering crowd beneath him were unable to see.

Workers from some of the other shops had now got word and were also assembling at the bottom of the gantry ladder. The crowds were dotted around it in a wide semi-circle, their heads tilted back, looking skyward to his cab. They could have been a medieval baying crowd waiting in eagerness for a forthcoming hanging.

With chest out and arms back, Jimmy strutted over towards the ladder and, just like a prize fighter entering a ring, the crowd opened up for him. He stopped and stood at the bottom of the crane ladder; the crane was about twenty yards away. Jimmy stood repeatedly slapping the palm of his hand with a long club-sized piece of two-inch pipe. 'I am waiting ...'

Just a short turn of the lever was necessary to position the crane alongside the ladder, but Finn felt dizzy and couldn't concentrate. His muscles were tense and his mouth dry. It was as if every drop of moisture had evaporated from his entire body. He tried to swallow but couldn't.

'Yesss!' he hissed as he grabbed his billycan: it had filled with the water from Jimmy's hose. He took a slug gratefully and swilled it around his mouth. The cold water felt good. He could feel his head clearing a little. Emptying the last dregs into his mouth, he slammed the can down on to the ledge.

Now what? One moment he could see himself fighting back and winning; the next, he saw himself beaten to a pulp. He toyed with leaving the crane where it was. If he didn't position himself over the ladder, he would be safe up in the crane until everyone went away.

But Finn soon dismissed that thought. 'No!' he said out loud to himself. 'What am I thinking? I have got to hit back and fight with all my heart. I am who I am, and I am worth more than this trembling wreck standing here.' He tried to psych himself up. 'Come on now, Finn. You need to fight back.' If he had learned nothing more from his mother, he had at least learned that.

Finn peered down. Dozens of excited faces looked back at him. Among the clamour of hostile voices and distinctive shouts, he heard, 'There he is, Jimmy, look! He's shit scared!' In acceptance of his impending fate, Finn again spoke quietly to himself. 'Well, it's only a sore face.' And he hoped that it all would be over quickly.

But within seconds, an effervescent anger bubbled up through his blood once more. All he could feel was hatred and intense fury. Finn clenched his jaw and bared his teeth. And then he was screaming, 'Go

173

and kill the bastard!' He was wound up and ready for the showdown. With excessive force, he threw the crane's lever. The crane screamed back at him as its iron wheels skidded and smoked on the rail. It jerked and rumbled as it made its way towards the ladder.

Enraged and ready to fight, Jimmy stood waiting at the bottom. A visible sweat sat upon his brow. 'Come on down!' he bellowed up at Finn. 'You will have to come down sometime so don't fucking keep me waiting. It will only be worse for you.'

Taking slow, deep breaths, Finn tried to regain his composure. He knew he couldn't go down the ladder feeling so much rage; he needed to think tactically. *Who dares wins*, he thought to himself. He was about to climb out on to the steps that would take him from the cab to the gantry when he noticed the large mushroom-shaped rivet that had hit him on the head. It was still covered in blood. He picked it up and tossed it up and down in his hand, feeling its weight. He guessed it was about half a pound, at least. He was surprised how snugly it fitted into his shaking hand. He curled his fingers around it and gripped it so tight his knuckles whitened.

He grinned and nodded to himself. Now he had a weapon.

Do or die

Trembling inside, Finn made his way out of the cab towards the crane's guard rail. Slowly, he continued along the gantry to the steel ladder. He looked down. A multitude of excited mouths opened with intermingled voices, and from someone in the crowd he clearly heard, 'Fuck, it's his first day on the crane and now it's going to be his last. Poor Finn. What a shame!'

Finn's blood stewed at this flippant remark. How dare they all write him off! He was Finn McGill, the leader of the Gallows Hill Executioners! Adrenalin pushed his anticipation of a win over Jimmy to a peak. Darting his eyes from left to right over the crowd, he spotted Jimmy swaying at the bottom of the ladder like a foxhound baying for blood.

All eyes followed Finn as he continued to the top of the ladder. It was thirty-nine feet high with metal hoops every few feet to protect the user from falling off. Though he did not know it yet, those safety hoops were to be Finn's saving grace.

Finn placed his foot on the top rung. To his amazement, his nervous trembling subsided and a surreal calm settled over him. He felt as if he were floating in mid-air, looking down upon himself, watching his anxiety and fear evaporate like methane from a bog.

He had resigned himself to his fate, but his mother's words rang in his head: *hit the fucker back!* If he could not beat Jimmy, he could at least give him something to remember Finn by. He clenched the rivet tighter. With his fear fading, he felt more able to focus. His body was now running on pure adrenalin. It was do or die. He started to descend the ladder.

Almost halfway down, he glimpsed Jimmy's face contorted with rage. His lips were drawn back, displaying his ugly, rotten teeth, and he was snarling like a wolf at the bottom of a tree, its prey trapped in the branches above.

Finn realised his back would become vulnerable as he climbed further down. Holding on to a hoop, he swung his body round so that his back was now against the rungs and, using the hoops to steady himself, he carefully dug his heels into each rung as he descended. As he neared the last ten foot, Jimmy started jumping up in an effort to grab his feet.

'Ha, bawbags! I'm going to fucking kill you!'

Finn stopped and climbed back to the next rung up. Sure that Jimmy couldn't reach his legs, he crouched down and gripped the bottom hoop. Now in an advantageous position, he sat on his hunkers and watched as Jimmy stopped jumping and stared up at him, still screaming at the top of his voice. An unnatural calm still enveloped Finn's body and he waited for the right moment to make his move.

Jimmy took his eyes off Finn for a moment to turn to the baying crowd. 'What a shit bag, eh!'

Taking his chance, Finn dropped his legs and kicked out at Jimmy, taking him completely by surprise. There was in an almighty crack, like a tree branch breaking, as Finn's steel-toe boot made contact with Jimmy's jaw. It hit him with such force that Jimmy dropped straight to the floor. He lay, like an effigy of Jesus on the cross, flat on his back with his arms outstretched.

Finn was now the one screaming like a madman. He was still swinging from the ladder's hoop ten feet off the ground, and as he swung out towards Jimmy's body he lifted his knees upwards towards his chin – and let go. He dropped like a lead balloon, landing squarely on Jimmy's chest. The crowd screamed in horror as Finn's doubled-up knees dug deep into Jimmy's chest, knocking the wind clean out of him. There was the horrific sound of crushing cartilage and breaking bone. Finn was still screaming incoherently. The heavy rivet was still in his hand. He straddled Jimmy and began pounding him squarely on the nose and jaw, his knuckles ploughing deep into Jimmy's face.

'Fucking hard man … Bully young lads, would you?' he yelled as he pummelled. 'Well, you will not fucking bully me, you cunt!'

Jimmy was pinned down and Finn's rivet hand continued the barrage of punches. Fear fed Finn's frenzy; he could not stop until he knew it was over. If Jimmy got back up he would kill Finn for sure. This he knew. The strength of his punches increased with this fear.

Shouts of encouragement from the onlookers echoed throughout the shop. 'That's right, son! Fucking kill the bastard and don't let him get up! You will never get rid of him till you do him over for good.'

It was plain that no one wanted Jimmy to win. And as long as Finn was winning, no one wanted to stop the fight. They all knew what kind of person Jimmy was. He deserved all that he had coming to him.

'Finish the job!' someone shouted again.

Old Bert, good man that he was, tried to intervene and started pulling at Finn's arm. 'Come on now, son, the game's over. He's beat,' he said in a faint voice. 'Can't you see that Jimmy's beat?'

Still in the grip of fear, Finn continued his bombardment, unaware that Jimmy was by now unconscious. Bert lifted his voice to a shout. 'That's enough now, Finn! Enough is enough! You have made your point. Let it go, son. Let it go!'

Finn looked down at Jimmy sprawled out on the ground. It really was over. He was the victor, he realised with pride. He threw the rivet to the side, his heart pounding, and shouted into Jimmy's face.

178

'Fucking bawbags, am I? My name's Finn McGill and I'm leader of the Gallows Hill Executioners! And don't you fucking forget it!'

'Come on now, Finn,' said Bert, prising him off Jimmy. 'You're going to kill him.'

Finn stood up and inspected himself for cuts but, apart from his knuckles and the rivet wound on his head, there was not a scratch on him. It had all happened so fast Jimmy had been unable to get even one blow with his pipe on target. Everyone would now know that Finn was a formidable force to be reckoned with.

Bert and another worker helped Jimmy up off the floor. Slowly and painfully he found his feet. He rocked backwards and held his chest, wincing. His face was bloodied and swollen. But more than that, Jimmy's pride was seriously wounded. He knew he had to make a show of it. Pale and breathless, he tried to stand upright but was too weak. Crouched over and holding his chest, his face both dazed and grimacing, he caught Finn's eye and with his deep rough voice he started to threaten Finn.

'When I see you again, I'm telling you, you are a fucking dead man!' Jimmy pointed his finger at Finn. 'YOU. ARE. A. DEAD. MAN. I will see to that!'

'Aye, that's right. I am a man, and not that vulnerable wee laddie you took me for. And I'm a far better fucking man than you will ever be! Truth is I've heard it all before!' And Finn really had heard it all before.

When Jimmy was safely out of sight, those watching ran over and crowded around Finn, excitedly yelling praise and congratulations. They patted his back and lifted him high into the air. It seemed as if the whole of shop twenty-one was right behind him. Finn smiled to himself. This was what he had always wanted: recognition and popularity. Most of all, he'd just wanted to be liked. It was a sweet ending to Finn's working day.

He left the shop, vaulted on to his Triumph motorcycle like an Argentinian gaucho on to a horse, and patted the petrol tank. With a kick, the bike roared into life. Finn was more than exhausted but adrenalin still pumped through his veins. He had beaten the leader of the Razors! Pure exhilaration filled his body. He revved the bike's engine two or three times and grinned to himself before speeding off in the direction of the Clachan for a well-earned pint.

When he arrived at the bar, Peem and a few of the others were there, including wee Davie.

'Hi Davie, it's so good to see you out and about. Are you all right now?' asked Finn.

'Aye, I'm all right.'

'You all healed up? Let me buy you a pint.'

'Aye, okay. Though I'm out and about, I have still got bandages on. The wee fellow's looking grand as ever, if I say so myself!' The lads all laughed.

'That's my man!' declared Finn.

'How was your first day at the yard?' asked Peem.

'Aye, all right.'

Just at that moment, the door swung open and Tam hurried over to them.

'Finn! I was wondering where you were at dinner time – well, now I know!' he said excitedly. 'Wee Eric McNally told me about you and Jimmy Baird – is it really true you beat the shit out of him and sent him to hospital?'

Sitting slouched at the pub table, his legs straight out in front of him, Finn relaxed as he sipped his beer. 'Aye, I did,' he replied nonchalantly.

'There you go, boys! The leader of the Executioners takes on the leader of the ClydesideRazors and knocks the fuck out of him!'

The gang all whooped and congratulated Finn. Finn found comfort in this and a warm feeling engulfed him. He smacked his lips, smiled and closed his eyes as he took a long drink from his glass. It seemed to him that the more he stood up for himself and for others, the more he was accepted. And he savoured this special moment. Slowly but surely, all that he'd ever yearned for was coming his way.

That night in his bed, Finn mulled over the traumatising events of the day. Yes, he felt proud of what he'd achieved by beating Jimmy, and he loved the fact that all the gang had cheered his success. It had felt great. But he still felt lonely, and he could not understand why. His true friends were Tam and Davie – the three of them had gone to school and grown up together – but he felt he had never seemed to gel with any of the others in the gang. It was him and them.

Though he had felt the warmth from the gang today, Finn wanted to be liked for who he was rather than what he could do for them. He still doubted himself, and instead of his confidence increasing, it waned.

Things had definitely got better in his life since all the abuse had ended, and he was now the leader of the Executioners and their hero. The gang all looked to him for direction. Why then should he feel something was amiss? Finn pulled the bed covers up and curled his knees up to his stomach, inserting his clasped hands between his closed thighs. He gazed into the darkness and an old, familiar thought reared its ugly head: maybe he'd be better off dead.

Returning to work the following day was daunting. Finn had no idea what might be in store, and his heart pounded like a Hopi Indian's war drum. Looking over his shoulder, he flicked his eyes left to right, scanning the workshop for Jimmy, as he walked up towards his crane.

A voice rang out as he passed the fish tank. 'Hiya, Finn,' said Andy. 'How are you doing after yesterday?'

'Well, it's no thanks to you that I'm all right!' he said in annoyance. 'Don't think for a minute that I never noticed you cower away in your office. And I tell you this, Andy, I won't forget that!'

'Don't be like that, Finn. What could I have done to help your situation? I'm sorry that I left you to fight your own battle, but I've already been at the end of one or two punches off Jimmy.'

'What! That bastard punched you and you never done anything about it?' Finn was incredulous.

'No, never. Between you and me, he threatened to do me over. Aye, he said he'd knife me if I didn't feed him some easy piecework jobs. Now he's out of sight and out of mind, I can offer you a sweetener to say how sorry I am. I can get you training on oxyacetylene profile burning. It carries extra money on your hourly wage.'

Andy seemed genuinely remorseful, and Finn's heart melted a bit at his explanation.

'Andy, if you really want to come good by me, then put me down for a trainee welder. That's where I can earn some decent money.'

'Aye, I will, but it might be a month or two before anything comes about.'

'That's great, just make sure you see that you do,' said Finn. 'Where is Jimmy anyway?'

'I got a phone call this morning – he's in hospital and he won't be in at work. You managed to break his jaw in several places. Goodness me, that was some kick you gave him! It's a wonder you never killed him. I heard the crack from his jaw through the office door – and it was shut!'

'Go on, you were saying?' urged Finn.

'You also broke five of his ribs. One of the workers tells me Jimmy had no chance – you were on him like a whippet on a hare! He was very impressed with your stance. To tell you the truth, Finn, I don't think

Jimmy will be back. He'll be too embarrassed that a youth of your age done him over. He won't want to show his face in here again.'

'Oh, so that's why you offered me the training!'

'Aye, that's right. Thanks to you, we should have seen the last of him. But you best watch your back for a while!' warned Andy. 'I'm glad he's out of all our hair. This workshop will be a happier place for everyone now that cunt has gone.'

Though Finn did not like himself, the genuine recognition and respect he received from Andy and the boys in the workshop tasted sweet, and he wanted more.

Alone on the bus

Finn was now twenty years of age. He continued to make a name for himself and was enjoying the popularity he'd always dreamed of.

One evening, when the gang were messing about at their Gallows Hill hangout, the Toonie gang passed by on a double-decker bus. Some stood at the narrow crack of the bus's sliding windows, shouting abuse at the Executioners whilst giving them the V sign.

'Come on, lads,' shouted Finn. 'Let's get them bastards!'

He ran off, leaving the others to follow, and as the bus slowed to a stop, Finn jumped aboard. The driver saw the rest of the gang running toward the bus in his mirror and quickly pulled away. Finn made his way up the winding stairs and only then when he checked to see behind him did he realise he was on his own.

'It's a well-known fact, Finn McGill, that you are far too fast a runner for your own good,' said one of the gang, Tosh MacAlister. 'Now you belong to us!' The Toonies stood up and advanced towards their prey.

Finn could see the Executioners through the back window running full pelt after the bus, but it was pulling away from them. It was a bad situation he'd got himself into, and he'd have to think on his feet.

Grabbing the steady pole at the top of the stairs, he swung himself on it and stepped up on to the seats with a foot either side of the aisle, and took out his knife. Just like Achilles, poised to slay Hector outside the gates of Troy, Finn stood high. From here, he had the advantage and could defend himself: they would either have to climb over the seats in front of him or come down the aisle one by one and face his knife.

'Come on then,' he said. 'Who wants it first? You just might get to me, but I will make sure I get a few of you before you do.'

Finn could see that none of the Toonies was prepared to approach him. Confident that they wouldn't, he said again, 'Come on then, who's first?'

The bus stopped further up the road and the clippie was frantic, shouting up at Finn, 'Get off my bus, you! I don't want any trouble on the 44-route. Come on down now.'

Finn thrust the knife blade at his adversaries. 'Are you going to be first, Tosh? Or you, Pete Morrison? Will it be you?'

The gang all stayed where they were. 'I fucking thought so.' Finn slowly backed away to the stairwell, only turning at the very last moment to make his way downstairs.

The Executioners were almost upon the now stationary bus, and the clippie, frightened they would climb on board, quickly rang the bell for the driver to move off. Finn jumped off as the bus sped up the road, with the Toonies banging at the windows and shouting obscenities until out of sight.

'What happened?' asked Jed.

'I will tell you what happened – that lot shat themselves! Especially that Tosh MacAlister. Nobody dared tackle me.'

'Aye, that was because they saw us running towards the bus,' said Davie.

'Shut up, Davie! If you believe that, then you are an idiot,' said Jed.

There was a buzz about the gang as everyone talked about what had just happened.

'You are a mad fucker!' Tam told Finn. 'Why didn't you wait on us? You could have got yourself stabbed!'

'To tell you the truth, Tam, I thought you were all right behind me. Once I was on board and up the stairs, there was no turning back for me. I had to play the big man.'

Finn and the gang turned and walked back down the road, stopping at the chip shop. As they waited for their chips, a guy wearing a short flying jacket and jeans walked straight towards them. When he reached them, he pulled out a World War II bayonet

187

and slapped the flat of blade repeatedly against his palm.

'You bastards are always hanging about this area,' he said. 'My mother uses this chip shop on a night, and if I see you hanging about here again, I will run this bayonet through you. I have heard about yous hitting old men and taking their money and intimidating old ladies. Why don't you try and intimidate me? Go on then, you're all big men!'

'That is a lot of fucking nonsense,' responded Finn. 'Who told you that? We look after our kind in this area. Everybody is safer with us around here.

'Fucking shut up!' snarled the guy, pushing the bayonet towards Finn. Then he pointed it down the road. 'Right, move out of here!' he ordered. 'And if I see so much as one of you going in this chip shop, you will cop this!'

The gang all looked at Finn for direction. The man was turning to point the bayonet at another member of the gang, and Finn saw his chance. Without thinking, he ran and kicked the bayonet out of his hand. The knife flew into the air, then dropped like a stone and embedded itself in the bottom of the chippy's door. Finn followed through with an almighty punch to the man's jaw that knocked him clean off his feet.

The gang then joined in, sticking the boot into the stranger until he lay motionless on the floor. As Finn ordered everyone to stop, Davie appeared with the chips and a bottle of IRN-BRU. Finn grabbed the bottle off Davie, took a swig and then poured some of it over the stranger's face.

Finn then sat the man up. 'Right, Jed, give me a hand getting this one on to his feet.' They struggled with his dead weight but managed to get the stranger upright. Finn brushed him down with the back of his hand.

'Pass me that bayonet, Peem,' said Finn. He grabbed the groggy stranger by the hair and spoke quietly. 'My name is Finn McGill and we are the Gallows Hill Executioners. If any of us see you within a quarter of a mile of this chip shop, I personally will run this through you.' He grabbed the man by the arm and led him down the road a yard or two before putting his foot on to his back and pushing him with a flick of his boot. 'Now fuck off!'

The gang were ecstatic, whooping and chanting his name. Fill felt invincible. Tonight, between the Toonies on the bus and the bayonet man at the chippy, he had proved himself a hard man twice. His popularity moved up another notch.

The Argentine tango

The jumping sparks faded like dying fireworks as Finn lifted his electric welding rod from the glowing metal before him. He flipped open his helmet and peeled it away from his face, and wiped his sweat-beaded brow with the back of his boiler-suit sleeve. Content that he'd finished his piecework job a lot earlier than predicted, he looked down at his work and examined it. It was a clean weld with no spatter, and a nice bevel and flow. He knew it was a professional job, worthy of any inspection; his weld had a better finish than most of the chancers in here could manage.

Finn took a long drag on his cigarette, holding the smoke in his chest before blowing it out and smiling to himself. He felt fulfilled. *Aye, that's a good bit of piecework money to add to my holiday savings. Soon, I will be in Manhattan, New York City, living it up!*

It was always his ambition to travel. He wanted to go around the world to as many places as he could. It was one of his four goals in life, after being liked and accepted for who he was, being happy, and being married with children of his own. He promised himself he would achieve these goals, and he pushed himself to get the money for his first expedition, to the Big Apple.

Finn folded his paperwork and blueprint, tucked them under his arm and headed up to the office for another piecework job. Peering through the windows of the fish tank, Finn saw piles and piles of blueprints strewn around the office. Specialist welding rods lay along the dust-covered grey shelving, and a picture of Andy's wife and children sat on his oxblood leather-topped desk. Steam was rising from the kettle on top of a green two-drawer filing cabinet. The swing of a 1970 Pirelli calendar suddenly caught his eye as the rear door opened and a slim young woman entered and sat at the desk. Finn watched as she took a long sip of her coffee, her eyes glued to her paperwork.

Unnoticed, Finn continued to stare through the window at her. Wire-rimmed glasses sat on her dainty nose, their arms protruding through long brown ringlets that hung either side of her face. The rest of her hair sat lightly on the collar of her white satin blouse. Finn's heart missed a beat. She was so beautiful. He stood dumbstruck with his mouth agape, noticing too late that she had lifted her head and caught him staring. Startled, Finn pulled his

191

head away from the window. He hesitated a moment, cracked a sheepish smile and knocked on the open door.

'Hi. Is Andy about?' he said.

She smiled back at him, displaying perfectly formed white teeth. It seemed to Finn that the whole office lit up with that smile.

'No, he's off today. I don't know what's wrong with him,' she replied, softly-spoken. 'Mr McAfee has sent me down from head office with all these new job blueprints.'

'Oh, that's great. I have just finished my job and am due another one. Do you have anything for me?'

'What's the name?'

'Finn McGill.'

She thumbed through the pile of blueprints, murmuring to herself. 'Let me see … ah! Yes, here you are. Finlay McGill. My, you have finished that job quick, Finlay. A fine bonus you should be collecting with Friday's pay packet.'

His face dropped to a frown. He was annoyed and embarrassed that the blueprint said Finlay. He'd asked Andy to get it changed to Finn several times but nothing had been done about it. 'Wait a minute!' he barked. 'Before we go any further, call me Finn. Just Finn. Okay?'

She raised an eyebrow. 'Okay, righty-ho. Finn it is,' she said, squaring up his paperwork on the desk. 'Just so you know, it's only Andrew who can sign you off for your piecework. But I will make sure he knows you have finished your job. First thing Monday morning, I promise.'

Finn smiled wide and, moving the blueprints on the desk aside, sat on the leather top and crossed his legs. He held steady eye contact with her, leant forward and winked. 'Thanks very much, I appreciate it.'

There was a lot of eye movement between them then as they sussed each other out. Finn felt an immediate and obvious attraction and strongly sensed she felt the same.

She handed him his paperwork. 'Here's your new job.'

Finn looked deep into her eyes. She held his gaze longer than she would normally before cracking a smile and dropping her head off to the side. She fidgeted with the blueprints, embarrassed.

'I have never seen you down here before. Are you a fresh starter then?' he asked.

'No, I started in head office three and a bit years ago.'

'Well, what do you do up in head office?'

'I am a trainee metallurgical engineer.'

'Wow! I'm impressed!' Finn didn't really knew what her job entailed but he dared not ask for fear of looking stupid. It certainly sounded impressive.

He watched as she swept her hair back with her hands and pushed it through a hairband. She threw her head back, her ponytail whipping down her back, and repositioned her long curls on either side.

'What about you, Finn? How many years have you been here?'

'Three.'

'Only three years? I see you have been promoted through the ranks very quickly. Why's that?'

He couldn't take his eyes off her. Finn was smitten. She reminded him of Audrey Hepburn's character Holly Golightly in *Breakfast at Tiffany's*. Her soft accent was so sexy: when she spoke, she pronounced her words properly with barely any slang. She was unlike any of his former hangers-on and one-night stands; this beauty had class and he knew he wanted to be with her. They both paused for a moment as their eyes and minds danced the tango, each staring at the other before quickly snapping their gaze away. It was obvious the attraction was mutual.

'Well, it's not what you know in here; it's who you know,' said Finn finally, breaking the spell. 'Me and Andy do all right together.' Then he worried she might think he'd got his promotion on a plate. He may have had a nudge from Andy but he didn't want her to know that. 'Let me tell you though, I worked really hard for my promotion,' he added quickly. 'And another thing—' He was interrupted by her laughter. 'What are you laughing about?'

Still laughing, she said, 'Nothing! I'm only teasing!'

'Oh, you wee bugger,' he said, smiling. 'Does your boyfriend work here too?'

Her neck reddened slightly as a blush travelled down from her cheeks. 'I don't have a boyfriend. And never have had one either.'

'What! *You* have never had a boyfriend? I don't believe that. A wee stoater like you! I'm surprised you've never been snapped up by someone as handsome as me,' laughed Finn.

Finn found her shyness attractive, and even more so when her face turned a pinky red and then a deep crimson as she lowered her eyes to the floor.

'Well, if you must know, I've been out with one or two guys ...' She quickly touched the back of his hand with hers, stumbling over her words. 'They just weren't for me.'

'What do you mean they weren't for you?' asked Finn.

'Well, don't get me wrong ... They were very decent and good-looking young men or I would not have entertained any of them. But they were simply not my type. They were a wee bit slow on the uptake. Things got a bit awkward at times and, for me, they were, well, um ... I know this might sound awful, but for want of better words, they were, well, too much like a soft-boiled turnip for my liking.'

Finn smiled. 'Ah, a little bit like a soft-boiled turnip, eh? So you want a tough guy, do you?'

'No, not so much a tough guy, but someone who is kind, loves animals, makes me feel safe, has respect for me and treats me like a queen,' she said.

Rubbing his chin, Finn stood thinking for a minute. 'Well, that all sounds just like me. I tick all of them

195

boxes. Though you did forget the ruggedly handsome bit.'

She covered her mouth with her hand and giggled.

Making a fist, he put his hand to his lips as though he were about to play the trumpet, and mouthed musical trumpet sounds: toot-doo-dee-doo-daa-doo. He threw his arms to his side and stood to attention.

'Well, Your Majesty, I'm your very man. For your eyes only stands the Right Honourable Finn McGill at your service!' The freshness of her perfume enveloped his face as he took her hand and kissed it. 'I ask that Your Royal Highness accompany me tomorrow night, that being Saturday 21st June 1970, for a refreshment and a bite to eat.'

She laughed. 'What! You are asking me out and you don't even know my name!'

'Listen, I don't need to know your name because we will have plenty time to get to know each other.' He bowed towards her, looked her in the eye and said, 'Meet me in the Clachan Bar up Gallows Hill tomorrow night. Half past seven. I will see you then!'

'But-but ...' she stuttered, 'I can't—'

'What do you mean you can't? You're my bird now!' He smiled, and her jaw dropped in disbelief as he kissed her on the cheek.

'Hey, wait a minute—'

'Half seven, the Clachan Bar,' he repeated before walking out on to the shop floor, leaving her stunned.

She smiled, her eyes following him as he swaggered away. 'My goodness!' she muttered to herself, intrigued. 'My oh my!' Then her hands, down by her sides, clenched into fists. 'Who does he think he is!' She stood there rooted to the spot, but soon her hand found its way up to her face and caressed her kissed cheek. She grinned again. It was then she noticed he'd left his blueprint on the desk. She picked it up and ran to the door, calling out, 'Hello-o-o!' She elongated the word in a sing-song voice.

Finn turned and was mortified to see the blueprint in her hand. *What a dick!* His face scrunched up in disbelief and he smacked his forehead with the palm of his hand.

With a teasing smile, she pushed the blueprint out towards him. It started to flop and droop. 'Would the Right Honourable Mr McGill care to take the worksheet and blueprint that he came to collect in the first place?'

'Aye, right, you got me there,' said Finn, embarrassed.

They looked at each other and burst out laughing. Finn's face was a picture to behold, and she found his embarrassment endearing. Finn snatched the paperwork from her hand, and jokingly said again, 'The Clachan Bar, Gallows Hill, Saturday at half seven. See you then and don't be late!'

A warm glow engulfed her. It was as if someone had covered her with a heated blanket. She wrapped her arms around herself and hugged her body as she watched him make his way up the shop to bay twelve.

***

When Saturday night came, Finn sat in the bar with the usual gang. He looked at his watch again: quarter past seven. There was still no sign of the young woman.

He didn't know it, but Fiona lived not too far away in Blackwood Gardens, at the bottom of the hill. She lived with her parents in a large detached six-bedroom red-sandstone house that they'd inherited in a rather posh part of the Parkside estate. Her family really wanted for nothing.

Fiona couldn't stop thinking about her encounter with Finn the day before. She had found him extremely attractive in his blue-checked cheesecloth shirt, his jeans and leather apron. She'd liked the way his long, thick black hair framed his handsome cheekbones, and his muscular arms and well-formed body had certainly got her pulse racing. But she was filled with indignation at how he'd ordered her to meet him. She'd thought about it long and hard, and decided in the end that she had better not go.

It was, though, very much an ongoing debate in her head. Looking at her reflection in her dressing-table mirror, she scowled. 'No, I can't go and see him. How dare he!' she told herself out loud. 'Does he really expect me to jump at his beck and call? No, I will not go!'

But as she was telling herself this in the mirror, she was also applying her make-up and getting ready to meet him.

'Oh, Fiona, stop this! You're only kidding yourself … Fiona Blair, just go and see what happens. If you don't like it, then you're off! Right? Is that a deal?' she quietly asked her reflection. 'Okay, a deal it is.'

And yet, the next moment she was back yelling at the mirror, 'Oh and who does he really think he is anyway!'

But she pulled on her new cream cheesecloth blouse before slipping into her floral-embroidered bell-bottom jeans. She winked at herself and sat down at her mirror again to check her make-up.

Fiona had had gone into the city earlier that day with her best friend Linda to shop for new clothes. She'd told Linda all about Finn and how he'd asked her out after little more than fifteen minutes.

'Well! Are you going to meet Mr McGill then or not?' asked Linda.

'No, I don't think so. Eh, what cheek! I can't believe that he thought I'd come at his beck and call,' she scoffed.

'Oh, will you give that a rest, Fiona! That's the third time you have said that.'

'Well, it's true! What does he take me for anyway?'

'Let's just have a nice morning shopping together,' said Linda. 'What are you looking for?'

'Well, I would quite like a pair of the modern-style bell-bottoms, and maybe a light-brown suede leather waistcoat.'

'Wait a minute, Fiona. You don't mean those brown fringed lace-up waistcoats that are just in at the Paris Fashion Boutique, do you?'

'Yes, that's the ones!' said Fiona excitedly.

'But they cost a fortune! Oh. Now I see. It's for your date tonight, is it not?'

Fiona turned and faced Linda. 'Look, I told you, there is no way I am turning up at the Clachan Bar tonight. Besides, it's as rough as they come.'

'Okay, if you say so,' Linda replied knowingly.

On entering the boutique, Fiona headed straight for the jeans and picked up a couple of pairs to try in the changing booth. The first pair fitted her like a glove. Looking in the mirror, she knew she need not try the other pair: these were the ones. She loved the cut and feel of them. They were just what she'd hoped for. She twice clicked her tongue at herself, then opened the swing door. 'What do you think, Linda?'

'Yes, they are okay … but they are a bit too tight, I think.'

Fiona's face fell. Was that a hint of jealousy on Linda's face and in her voice? Fiona knew she looked good in the jeans. She definitely wanted them but maybe she'd return later to buy them so as not to make her friend feel any worse.

Linda was no Mona Lisa. Her blonde bobbed hair washed out her pale, sharp features, though she did have a nice figure. She was a kind and gentle person and was certainly worthy of being Fiona's best friend, but Linda had even less confidence than Fiona. Fiona tried a different tack.

'Linda, you are my best friend and I always tell you everything, don't I?'

'Well, I suppose so.'

'Well, I really am not sure about going to meet Finn tonight. But if I do go, I want to look my best. You have such a great dress sense and always look so cool. What do you think of these really? I know they're tight, but do you think I can get away with it?'

Linda chuckled. 'I knew all along you were going tonight. I just knew it!'

'Well, we'll wait and see,' smiled Fiona. 'So, what do you think then? Do you think I can get away with it?'

Linda looked her up and down approvingly. 'Oh yes, I am sure you will. They certainly do look nice on you.'

'Oh, Linda, that's great. You are a real good friend to me,' Fiona gave her a hug and shrieked with delight. And she purchased the jeans. As they were leaving, a brown suede waistcoat caught her eye.

'Wait a minute, Linda! I want that too!' Fiona looked over at Linda for approval. 'What do you think?'

'Just go for it! A few pounds more won't break the bank.'

'Yessss!' Fiona hissed. 'I was hoping you would say that!'

Linda smiled to herself, happy she'd played an important part in helping Fiona get ready for her date.

A good night in the Clachan

Back home, Fiona was startled from experimenting with her new brown and beige eyeshadow by her mother's barking voice.

'Oh, and where do you think you are going, young lady?'

She swivelled around quickly and sat rigid with her hands on her knees, visibly annoyed at her mother's nosiness. 'I am meeting a guy later, Mam, and I am going to be late if I don't hurry.'

Astonished, Fiona's mother shuffled hurriedly over to her daughter. 'A guy! What guy?' she demanded, her voice raised.

Fiona stood up from the chair and made her way over to the door. In a calm voice that hid her agitation, she said, 'Mam, please don't start! He's a nice boy. I met him at work.'

Fiona's mother scowled. She wanted her only daughter to meet a nice, respectable man and certainly not any working-class reprobate. 'At work!' she snapped. 'Oh, now I see. A working-class boy, a no-gooder, I suppose?'

'Look, Mam, it's only a first date. I'm not going to marry him! I just need to get out of this house before I turn to stone. So, please, let me go, and if you can, give me your blessing.'

'What's his name then?'

'Well, if you really need to know, his name is Finlay McGill.'

'And what does he do at your work?'

'He is a welder fabricator.'

'Huh! A welder! What about that Victor MacBride? Now, there's a fine, bright, young boy. He's just qualified as an accountant and is now working for his father's firm.'

'Well, what about Victor MacBride?'

'He has asked you out umpteen times and you keep putting him off, and for the love in me, I don't know why you always say no.'

'Well, Mam, the answer to that is simple. I won't go out with him because I just don't fancy him. That's why. Besides, I am well able to pick my own man.'

'You go with that welder if you must, but go at your own peril! And don't you come running to me when he mistreats you and beats you about the face. Because I know the likes of them yard workers and what they get up to. Your dad was forever fighting court cases for the likes of them and none of it makes very good reading.'

Her mother's constant questions and put-downs always made Fiona feel like a scolded child. Frustrated, she paused and thought about her reply. 'Okay, Mam, I won't,' she said in a quiet voice.

'You won't what?'

'I won't come running to you when he beats me about the face. That's what.' Fiona turned her back on her mother. 'Now let me get ready.'

A final check in the mirror and Fiona applied her strawberry-flavour lipstick. *You never know*, she thought. She checked her teeth and smacked her lips. She liked what she saw. She smiled and winked at her reflection. 'There! All done. Perfect.'

Her mother stood in the background, arms folded in front of her. She was still ranting on about commoners, shipyard labourers and steel workers. 'Welder … huh! Why don't you find yourself a nice boy …'

A sickening flair of exasperation hit Fiona's stomach. She stood up and snapped her purse closed in an exaggerated fashion. Without looking back, she walked out, slamming the bedroom door behind her. At the top of the stairs, she checked her watch and squealed when she saw the time. 'My goodness, it's seven thirty-five and it will take me at least fifteen minutes to get there. What if he won't wait for me?' she muttered to herself. 'Dad! Dad, where are you?'

'He's downstairs having a nap in the study,' said her mother behind her. 'Why do you want him?'

'A lift!' Fiona turned on her heels and ran downstairs to the study.

Her father, in his usual tweed suit, with his brown brogues splayed on the floor and a golfing magazine covering his eyes, was indeed fast asleep. His favourite green leather Chesterfield chair engulfed him like the mouth of a toad about to swallow him up. A part-empty whisky glass was at his side on a small green baize card table, and he was snoring like a snorting pig.

So as not to frighten him, Fiona pulled back the magazine and tickled his pencil moustache, gently pulling at his whiskers. 'Dad!' she whispered. 'Dad! Could you do me a favour?'

He was just barely awake, and he cleared his throat with a cough. 'Anything for my little angel,' he murmured.

'Thank you! Could you run me to Gallows Hill? I have a date and I am late.'

He heard the urgency in his daughter's voice. 'What, now?'

Fiona put on her 'I can twist my daddy around my little finger' voice. 'Yes please, Daddy. Now.'

'Darling, I er—'

Fiona quickly interrupted. 'Dad I am holding you to that. Please, Daddy, you promised! You said anything for your little angel.'

'Okay. Give me a minute or two to come round,' he said finally. Fiona kissed her father on the cheek with a loud smacking 'mwah'.

'Thank you, Daddy! I will get the car keys and wait in the car.' Fretting that her father would do his usual slow shuffle, she attempted to spur him on. 'Daddy, please hurry. This is important to me.'

'Yes, darling. Be there soon.'

Fiona's mother was by now at the bottom of the stairs, immaculately dressed in a bright floral evening gown. She was going with Fiona's father to a friend's house for dinner, and she stood nervously playing with her pearl necklace. Though small, slender-framed and frail-looking, she was a bit of a nag and had the bark of an angry wolf. She looked meaningfully at Fiona. 'Just remember what I said.'

Grabbing the keys for her father's Jaguar, Fiona went to the car and waited. Its red leather seats felt cold through her jeans. She anxiously twisted her index finger through her ringlets and tapped her feet as she tutted to herself. 'This is so annoying!' she said out loud. 'Good God, I would have been there by now if I had walked it! Where is he?' Just at that moment, the front door opened. 'Hallelujah!' she cried.

Her father got in the car and gave Fiona a side glance. He'd had this Jaguar MK II, 2.4L manual, 1968, from new, and he kept it immaculately clean, polishing it without fail every Sunday morning. But the smell of stale smoke from his pipe clung to the seats, and an immovable layer of nicotine had

206

stained them a dirty pink. He did not care; it was his little vice. An escape from Jean's nagging. He just loved the freedom and the solitude of cruising down the road in overdrive whilst puffing on his pipe. He was adamant that the smoke gave a certain patina to the car.

Speaking in his usual soft and low voice, her father asked, 'Now, my dear, where to?'

'Gallows Hill, please Daddy.'

Startled, his eyes sprang wide open. 'Gallows Hill?' he coughed, nearly stopping the car. He gave her a frowning glance. 'Well, that's one place we have always warned you about going to. It's certainly not a suitable place to go on a Saturday night, is it? Or on any night, in fact. I'm not happy that's where you are wanting me to take you.'

Fiona pulled a hardened face at her father's concern. 'Oh Daddy! I've already had the full Spanish Inquisition from Mam. To tell you the truth, I have had enough for tonight!'

Her father grunted as he stopped at the traffic lights. 'Now where is my pipe?' he mumbled to himself, plunging his hand into his pocket and pulling out his briar pipe.

'Oh no you don't! Don't you dare light that up and send me on my date smelling like a smoked kipper. Put it away! I mean it, Daddy. Put it away.'

'Okay, darling, as you wish. Now, whereabouts on the hill?' he asked.

'The Clachan Bar. It's just off Clyde Street.'

Shocked by her request, Richard pressed his lips together and placed his hand over hers. 'Fiona, I can't let you go there. Your mother would crucify me. That place is like the devil's porridge, bubbling away inside with wrongdoers. And it's full of—'

Fiona pulled her hand away. 'Dad!' she shouted in frustration. She swung open the car door as her father was still driving along the road. 'Stop the car, Daddy! I will throw myself out if you don't let me out!'

Surprise showed in her father's face. He had never heard her being so assertive; this was the first time he'd heard her even raise her voice. He could see in her expression that she was determined, and so, reluctantly, he gave in. The tyres on the wire wheels dug into the tarmac as the car screeched to a halt. Fiona climbed out and walked round to the driver's side. Her father looked straight at her, his brows meeting in the middle in visible concern. He rolled down the window.

'Look, Dad, the pub has a payphone. If there's any trouble about to start or if I feel uncomfortable, I will ring you to come and pick me up. I promise,' Fiona whispered, crossing her chest with her index finger. 'Cross my heart and hope to die. Please don't worry.' She lifted his tweed cap and kissed him softly on his forehead. 'Thanks for the lift.'

'Bye, darling. Do please ring if you need me.'

Finn had walked outside the Clachan Bar and stood smoking as he waited for his date. The weather was sticky and close, and the streets were quiet and empty. The only sign of life was the glistering light that edged through the cracks in the curtains of the tenement-lined street. He looked at his watch: it was seven forty-five. She wasn't coming. *Ah, well, it's pontoon I will be playing again tonight*. He turned to go back into the bar but heard a faint voice.

'Hello, tough guy.' His heart missed a beat. He had never really bet on her turning up. Why would someone with her class want to see the likes of him? Why would she like him? But here she was. He ran his eye over her and gasped at her beauty. 'Wow. You look amazing! So trendy. And I love your eyes.'

She was pleased, though a little embarrassed, and her neck reddened. But she felt a warm boost of confidence that made all the running around town with Linda worthwhile.

Playing the charmer, Finn went on, 'Your Majesty, I stand before you and offer you my arm.' Smiling back, Fiona took his proffered arm, but her smile suddenly faded and her forehead creased. The intense look on her face stopped him in his tracks.

'Before we go in, I need to tell you something,' she said.

Finn's face paled.

'Just to let you know …' She hesitated for a second or two.

Finn looked straight into her eyes, frowning, eager and impatient to know what she was about to say. 'What is it?'

She leant backwards slightly and laughed. 'My name's Fiona,' she said. 'It's Fiona! I don't want you to walk me in there and not even know my name!'

His frown turned into a relieved smile. She'd been teasing him. 'Oh, I see. You wee bugger! I didn't know what you were about to say then!' He joined her in laughter. 'I can see you and I are going to get on, you wee bugger that you are!'

Feeling proud with Fiona on his arm, Finn opened the door to the pub. Thick smoke rushed out at them like a ghostly demon leaving a grave, and the clagging taste of tar caught in her throat. Coughing heavily, she clung on to Finn as they walked in through the blue haze. The Clachan Bar was busting at the seams as usual, and Finn noticed all eyes turn and look at Fiona.

Walking towards Finn was Wee Davie, who was wolf-whistling at Fiona. 'She's a bit of a stoater, Finn.' He turned to Fiona. 'You are too good for the likes of him!'

'Ah, this here is Davie Fleming,' Finn explained to Fiona. 'He thinks he's God's gift to women, ever since his first girlfriend Aggie fell in love with him.'

The bar erupted in laughter, leaving Davie red-faced.

'Where's your other half then, Davie?' asked Finn.

'Tam is picking her and Bridget up and dropping them both off here later.'

'That's great, Fiona can meet them later. Right, lads, this is Fiona.' A barrage of wolf-whistles came hurtling towards her. Her face was noticeably turning pink with embarrassment. Finn came to her rescue. 'Right, you lot, settle down. Have you never been in the company of a classy woman before? Now leave her be. Come on, Fiona, what do you want to drink?'

'Dry martini and lemonade, please Finn.'

'Dry Martini, Keeno!' ordered Finn.

Keeno was the owner of the pub. He put his two hands on to the bar and looked Finn in the eye as he leant forward. 'Are you taking the mick? What do you mean dry Martini? Come on now, Finn, you should know better than most. We just sell whisky and ale to make the locals drunk. You know this is a rough and ready pub.'

'Aye, rough around the edges and ready for demolition,' Finn retorted.

'Funny ha! The old ones are the best. The cocktail bars are in the town. So it's Bacardi, vodka, Lanny or Buckfast for the young lady, I'm afraid – unless she would like a single malt? What's it to be?'

'Lanny? What's that?' asked Fiona.

Keeno, not too sure what to say, stuttered, 'Ah, em, it's a fortified wine … almost like a sherry. Extremely popular with the locals.'

'My mam likes a sherry or two. I will try one of them.'

Finn knew it was the cheap drink of the locals and didn't want his date to be seen drinking that. 'Wait a minute now!' he said quickly. 'I want only the finest and purest alcohol for my Fiona! Believe you me, that stuff is firewater and would strip the paint off a church door. It certainly is not for the likes of you.'

Fiona scowled at the very thought of the drink taking paint off a church door. 'Righty-ho! In that case, could I have a Bacardi and coke, please?'

Drinks in hand, they went to sit down. Fiona noticed the tartan-covered bench seats were limp and distressed with knife cuts all over them so that the stuffing hung out like a bursting haggis. She pointed to the juke box. 'Let's play some music, Finn.' Walking over to it, she felt her feet stick on the tacky beer-sodden carpet and wondered what she was doing here in this hovel. *I will finish this drink and phone my dad*, she thought to herself.

Finn noticed a large poster on the wall.

CLACHAN ANNUAL DAY TRIP TO SALTPORT
SATURDAY 23 JULY

BUS LEAVES HERE 9AM PROMPT

SOFT DRINKS AND TUNNOCK'S PURVEY
WILL BE PROVIDED AT
SALTPORT GREEN BOWLING CLUB

THREE KIDS TO A SEAT
LIMITED TICKETS AVAILABLE – SEE KEENO

'There you go, Fiona,' Finn said, pointing at the poster with his pint. 'Just the thing for us two, if you fancy it?'

Fiona was taken aback. *What a bunch of characters to go to the seaside on a bus trip*, she thought to herself. 'Sorry, but there is no way at the moment, Finn. I just met you yesterday and, well, I am not too sure. Let's just see how tonight goes.'

'Aye, okay then, but let me know one way or the other so I can make other arrangements.'

Fiona assumed this meant that if she didn't go he would find himself another date, and she felt a momentary twinge of jealousy.

'I am sure Davie and Tam will be taking their women too,' added Finn. 'But no pressure if you don't want to go.'

Sitting chatting to the lads, Fiona was already becoming popular. Like Finn, it was her warm smile that they all reacted to. Davie asked her, 'What do you work as?'

'I am a trainee metallurgist,' she said.

'Wow. I love the stars too. And if I look out my window on a clear night, I can see Venus. Did you know it's named after the Roman god of love?'

Finn laughed. 'Davie! What the hell are you yapping on about? She's a metallurgist and has nothing to do with any stars or meteors!' The rest joined in the laughter, but Fiona smiled nervously, cringing for Davie in his embarrassment. Tapping him on his leg, she said, 'Never mind, Davie, I knew what you meant. Besides, not many people know where Venus is in the sky.'

Davie felt a sense of relief when he heard that. 'Laugh all you want. There you go,' he said. 'A few of you lot would have thought Venus was some chick in blue jeans.' More laughter ensued.

At closing time, Finn walked Fiona home. 'God, that was fun tonight! I really enjoyed it. It was funny with all your mates! They all think the world of you, Finn.'

'I enjoyed it too. Do you fancy a fish supper?'

'No, I am too tired. I'm off to bed when I get in. But thank you for a great night!'

Finn cupped Fiona's face in his hands and held her gaze as he gave her slow, gentle kisses. Her heart was pounding so fast it skipped beats just to keep up with itself. 'Goodnight, Fee. See you at work on Monday,' he said softly.

Fiona looked at him. 'Why do you call me Fee?'

'You're my bird, and to me you're my Fee. No one else will call you that except me. Sleep well, Fee.' She smiled. It was endearing of him, and she liked it. Finn left her at the bottom of the path to her house and watched her make her way up and open the front door before he headed on to the chippy.

Closing the large door gently so as not to waken her parents, Fiona was startled to see her father come out of his study with a worried frown on his face. 'How did it go tonight, sweetheart? Are you okay?' he asked.

'You and Mam will be surprised to hear it but yes, I'm okay! It did go well. And no, he did not mistreat me, if that was going to be your next question. On the contrary – he could not have been any more of a gentleman if he were royalty himself. Before I go to bed, I will answer your next question, which I can see is on the tip of your tongue: yes, I am going to see him again!' She took her shoes off, kissed her father's cheek and ran towards the stairs.

As she started to climb upstairs, she called back to her father, 'Thanks for waiting up for me, Daddy. There was no need, but I know you worry about me. I do love you, Daddy.'

Trouble at the chippy

The streets were empty. The cool of the evening had chilled the summer air and it felt good as it blanketed Finn's skin. He was happy that his first night with Fiona had been a success and was looking forward to seeing her again at work on Monday morning.

Walking along the wide Gallowgate, hands in pockets, Finn kicked a Tennent's lager tin high into the air. It rolled and rattled along the wide pavement, awakening seemingly all the dogs in the neighbourhood, and a cacophony of growls, howls and barks filled the night. He laughed out loud to himself as he saw the bedroom lights along the street illuminate one by one.

Turning the corner, the chippy in sight, Finn spotted the white-coated owner, Orlando, running the window shutters down as if he were about to close. Orlando had lived in this area all Finn's life. As an Italian prisoner of war, he had worked on a local farm and had loved the place so much, he'd stayed and married a Scottish woman. Tall and some would say handsome with his dark olive skin and blonde, wavy hair, he was a very friendly man who liked to keep on the right side of the Executioners – though he'd never had any trouble from them. They had all grown up respecting him and eating his food.

Taking on a bit of a trot, Finn reached the door just as Orlando finished lowering the last shutter. He quickly grabbed hold of the open door frame and swung himself into the shop. 'Can you do me a fish, Orlando? I'm starving.'

'Mamma mia! Feen, you gave-a me the frights! But it's-a so good-a to see you. You been-a having a good-a night-a?'

'Aye, I have. I have had the best night in ages, with my wee stoater of a bird, Fiona.' Finn did a drum roll on the counter and then did a take of Orlando's accent. 'Now-a to finish a great-a night-a, I will have-a one of Orlando's famosio Italiano fish-a and chip-as.'

Orlando laughed as he looked over the fryer and shook his head. 'You're not-a right-a in the head, Feen!'

Taking out a five-pound note to pay for his fish supper, Finn didn't notice the tall, dark figure dressed in green army fatigues standing in the corner, listening in on the conversation.

'How are you doing, my man?' said Finn to Orlando. 'Have you been busy?'

'No, not a great-a night, Feen—'

217

'Hey, are you Finn McGill, the leader of the Gallows Hill Executioners?' the stranger broke in aggressively.

'What if I am? And who's asking?'

Letting Finn know he was serious, the stranger pulled out and brandished a long-bladed knife. He tossed it from one hand to the other and stepped forward. '*I* am asking!'

'Who the fuck wants to know?' demanded Finn, masking his anxiety at the sight of the blade.

The stranger continued to walk forward, the knife gripped tight in his hand and pointed at Finn.

'I am Larry Broon from the Green, and I have heard your name mentioned more than once. You're that cunt that booted the fuck out of Jimmy Baird and put him in hospital.'

Finn had been expecting reprisals from the Razors gang over the years but it had never happened – and he never thought it would happen in his local chippy. He was stunned for a moment. 'Aye, that's me. What about it?'

'What about it!' said Larry, holding the knife out in front of him and prodding it towards Finn.

Finn's stomach knotted and he began a slow retreat.

'I'll tell you what about it,' continued Larry. 'He's my cousin. And I don't like people fucking with my relatives, especially any cunt from the Executioners. Oh and by the way, my friends call me Mad Mental Larry.'

Finn knew he must do something fast, but he still had the five-pound note in his hand and didn't want to lose it in a fight – he'd worked hard for it and it was nigh on a good day's piecework money. To make it safe, he made a motion to put it into his inside suit pocket.

Larry, though, seemed to assume Finn was going for a knife. 'Hey, wait a minute now!' he cried out. He was suddenly shaking like an alcoholic and frozen to the spot with fear. In the background, Orlando was shouting pleadingly at them. 'Come on-a, boys, please-a! No trobble in-a here!'

Finn could see the fear in Larry's eyes and the tremble of his hand. The man had clearly recoiled. Finn was almost certain that he had no intention of actually using the knife and had merely been trying to frighten him. He pushed the five-pound note deep into his pocket, and taking the advantage of surprise, let Larry have a barrage of punches to the face.

Larry dropped to the floor, and with one fell swoop, Finn stood on his weapon-wielding hand, pinning it to the ground. 'You bastard!' he cried, before swiftly bending down to prise the knife from Larry's hand.

Kneeling on Larry's chest, Finn held the knife close to the man's face. 'Big fucking hard man with a knife, eh!' Finn said menacingly. 'You want a fucking Glasgow smile?'

Larry lay on the floor shaking with fear. He was petrified. The thought of being slashed chilled his soul. This was the man who'd put his cousin, the Clydeside hardman Jimmy Baird, in hospital. Larry shook his head from side to side and crossed himself, mumbling, 'In the name of the F-Father …' He hesitated before pleading with Finn through tears. 'Please, d-do-don't,' he stuttered. 'I'm sorry, it all got out of h-hand. I was only trying to scare you in case you recognised I wasn't from around. Please don't!'

'Funny that! I thought you wouldn't want the smile,' said Finn. 'Now get fucking up. Mad Mental Larry, my fucking arse! Fuck off back to where you belong and think yourself lucky that Finn McGill – aye, me! – never ran your own chib through you. And if I do see you round here again, you will never see the Green ever again. Now fucking scarper!'

Larry ran out of the chip shop like a scorned cat. Finn watched his tail end sweep round the corner of the road and smiled to himself, adrenalin still pumping hard through his body. He inspected the knife in his hand with interest: he'd never seen one like it other than in old gangster movies. He pushed a button on it and the blade shot back into the handle. His mouth fell open and his eyes widened and sparkled. 'Wow,' he said to himself. He pushed the button again and the blade shot out from the front and locked. It was, in fact, an American buffalo-horn-handled, front-ejecting stiletto knife and a very rare item.

'Yeah!' he yelled. 'What a knife, eh Orlando, what a knife!'

'Feen, mark-a my words: it's-a no good-a to have such a kneef. It's-a trobble,' warned Orlando.

Finn was grinning from ear to ear. 'Aye, you are right. It wasnae any help for Mad Mental Larry, now was it?' he laughed. 'Is my fish ready yet?'

'Two minutes, Feen. Two minutes.'

Revenge on the janitor

One night, when Finn was just leaving the Clachan Bar to make his way to the chippy, he saw a figure shuffling slowly towards him in a familiar fashion on the other side of the road near the Post Office. It was, Finn quickly realised, his old school janitor, Joe Durkin.

It was ten years since Finn had last seen Durkin. His face screwed up and his cheeks tightened as painful flashbacks of his time at school and the abuse he'd suffered at Durkin's hands leapt into his mind.

He did not have to think long and hard to remember. The bad memories ran through his head like a fast-rewinding film, only pausing when it reached the image of himself as a youngster standing humiliated outside Durkin's office at school, having just been told he was a daft bastard and would never get the football trial he craved. Finn saw himself back then, furiously warning Durkin that his day would eventually come. *I have waited a long time to get this man for what he put me through*, thought Finn.

By this time, Durkin was in his early fifties and had put on a pound or two around his middle; Finn, meanwhile, was a well-built, muscular young man in his twenties. Finn observed Durkin's familiar foot shuffle: one foot would swing left before hitting the ground and the other foot would slide on its shoe heel. Finn crossed the road and carried on walking toward Durkin, but the old janitor didn't recognise him as he walked past.

Turning on his heels, Finn gave Durkin a heavy slap on his shoulder and said, 'Hi, Joe, how are you doing?'

Durkin jumped. 'Fuck me, you gave me a fucking fright!' He looked Finn up and down. 'Who are you?'

'Can't you remember me? I'm that daft bastard who shovelled all of them tonnes of coke into that fucking cellar,' Finn answered. 'I bet you remember me now?'

Durkin stood shaking, unsure what to say or do. Like an electrical thunderbolt, a flash of fear ran down his whole body and tingled. 'What cellar? What coke? What are you talking about? Tell me, what do you mean?'

'Don't act the cunt with me. A cunt like you should know, you should always remember who you've abused – because later in life, they will always come back to bite your bum.'

'I don't know what you mean,' said Durkin.

'I am here to bite your bum – both for me and for them wee lassies that you bounced on your knee. They'll be young women now and able to tell their stories, I'm sure.'

'Now, wait a minute! I never—'

Finn interrupted Durkin, slowly placing his hand over the man's mouth and muffling his voice until he stopped speaking.

'Look at me. If you say you never touched the girls, I will give you a Glasgow smile – and I promise you that. You have fucked a lot of lives up, including mine, and I have waited ten years for this day. Do you remember me standing in the doorway of your hovel, declaring I would come back and get you when I was older? Well, here I am. You are not dealing with a wean now. Try dealing with the man!' snarled Finn.

Bellowing into Finn's face, Durkin cried, 'Who the fuck are you anyway?'

Speaking low and deliberately, Finn answered, 'I told you. I am the daft bastard that shovelled the coke for you so that I could get a football trial. My name is Finn McGill.'

Durkin's body jolted for a second time. His face turned ashen grey. 'Oh aye, Finn McGill. I do remember you.'

'I bet you fucking do! Because for you, Joe, the game is up.'

Durkin drew a deep breath and thought long and hard before he spoke. 'You were too shy and a wee bit backward for the team at the time. If I'd picked you to play, it would have broken your confidence even more. So I done you a favour by not picking you.'

'My fucking arse! Why did you have to say I was a daft bastard? And why would you regularly give me a slap or a kick when I passed you in the corridor? You had better answer me as you are making me angrier by the minute!'

'I never said you were a daft bastard, and I can't remember slapping you.'

Finn could not believe his ears. As a child, a week never went by without Durkin saying or doing something to hurt him mentally or physically. And now, face to face, Durkin was denying it all. Fury began to overwhelm him, the same fury that had ripped through him like a raging wildfire all those years ago and continued to burn inside him. Tonight, finally, he had a chance to douse the flames. He needed to get his own back. As his rage took grip, all Finn could see was a red mist that had descended like a sun blind pulled over his eyes. It was a red mist of revenge.

'You bastard that you are!' Finn screamed at Durkin, and he launched himself on top of him, grabbing him by the neck and then throwing his own head back and headbutting Durkin square on his nose.

Durkin stood motionless for a second, then his head flopped on to his chest and his legs gave way. He made a frantic attempt to grab hold of Finn before he fell to the ground. Once down, Finn laid into him, his fists pummelling like a pair of pistons on the wheels of a speeding steam train. Then he suddenly stopped for an instant.

'You bastard. How could you treat a child like you did?' he said fiercely. 'What about those lassies? They'll all have been scarred for life. You need locking up!'

Finn resumed his pounding of Durkin's face. Blood spattered from the man's nose and lips. Finn's mind kept flashing back to all the times Durkin had humiliated him. The trauma had affected him deeply, never really leaving him. He knew it had played a big part in knocking any last shred of confidence out of him. And the thought of him touching those young schoolgirls sickened him to the stomach. Finn could hold back no more. All the rage that had been bottled up inside him for so many years was unleashed. Screaming obscenities, he head-butted Durkin so hard this time that the man's nose cracked as loudly as a gunshot.

Finn finally stopped the barrage of blows when he felt no more resistance. Durkin was knocked out cold, lying flat on the ground with his arms outstretched. Finn looked around and saw there was no one else in the vicinity; they were all alone. The time, according to the Post Office clock, was nearing ten o'clock, and the evening light had darkened to an eerie grey dusk. Durkin began stirring and trying to sit upright, vigorously shaking his head from side to side in an effort to clear his head. Finn pulled at him by his lapel and placed him in an upright position against the Post Office wall.

226

'Stay there and don't move!' Finn ordered, before vaulting a wall into someone's garden where he untied a clothesline from its poles. He wrapped the rope around his elbow and hand and made his way back to Durkin, who was now swearing at the top of his voice.

'You cunt! When I get home, I will get the police on you. You fucking bastard!'

'No, you won't. You're not going home tonight.' Finn tied Durkin's wrists, dragged him over to the red telephone box nearby and tossed Durkin into it. Then he wrapped the rope around the outside of the phone box several times and tied it in a reef knot. 'There, get out of that, you cunt!'

Finn had often wondered what he'd do if he ever came across Durkin again. Now he knew.

The bus trip

Finn and Fiona hit it off in the few months before the bus trip and so she agreed to go. That morning, the Clachan was heaving with early arrivals enjoying a pre-outing drink. Davie was with his new girlfriend Betty, a pretty, petite woman with brown hair and glasses, and Tam was with Bridget, who was blonde and blue-eyed. They were all looking forward to spending time together.

'Drink up, everyone!' said Davie. 'We best get on the bus if we want the back seat.'

The six of them made their way out of the Clachan to board the bus. The sun shone brightly, warming the cool morning air, and there was barely a cloud in the sky. It set the mood for a good day ahead. The old Glasgow Corporation single-decker bus waited in the gravel car park with its doors open.

They all laughed as Tam pointed out the bus driver who was running around waving his hands in an effort to herd excited children on to the bus. His large stomach spilled out of his pale blue shirt and hung over his trousers. A tweed cap adorned his bulbous head, and heavy, black-rimmed glasses were wedged snugly on to his strawberry nose. 'All aboard for Saltport!' he called.

Finn looked at Fiona in dismay. The bus already seemed full of boisterous children, and yet more were outside, eagerly waiting for their parents to come out of the pub.

On the bus, Keeno stood by the steering wheel, looking nervous. He was fidgeting with his pen, turning it on its axis, and repeatedly wiping the sweat off his forehead with his hanky.

'What's with all the weans, Keeno?' Finn asked as he climbed aboard. 'Looks like there's hundreds.'

'Christ's sake, Finn. I've made an arse of it. I said three to a seat.' Keeno's voice softened as he mumbled through his embarrassment. 'The bus owner said I could do three kids to a seat.'

'Aye and what about it? Surely that's okay?' said Finn.

Keeno grabbed his hair with his two hands. 'No, it's not. It was three to a double seat and I have put three to a single seat!'

'You mean you have six kids to a double seat?'

'Aye, Finn, I have.'

'Fuck me, Keeno! How many people will be on the bus when it leaves?'

Keeno worked it out. 'Well, it's a fifty-six-seater. And fifteen seats have three kids, so that's forty-five, and the rest is normal seating … That's about ninety-six passengers altogether.'

Finn laughed, choking on his cigarette. 'Ach, don't worry yourself, Keeno. It will be an enjoyable day out. Just offer the driver some extra cash to take us, and stay cool, man.'

Walking up the aisle to the back of the bus, Finn was still laughing at Keeno's mistake. 'Christ, what a bus run this is going to be: forty-five weans all screaming blue murder!'

'Right, we bags the back seat,' said Davie, as they made their way through the multitude of children. They sat down and Davie opened a paper bag. 'There you go, lads,' he said, handing Tam and Finn a can of Tenant's lager and the girls a fancy Bacardi glass each. 'I took a loan of these out the pub,' he added, grinning.

'Pinched them, you mean!' laughed Tam.

'That's not all, ladies,' Tam declared as he put his hand into the bag and pulled out a bottle of Bacardi. 'Hold out your glasses. The party has just begun!' The girls clapped and cheered when they saw the bottle.

'That's awful nice of you, Davie,' said Betty. 'Pity there's no ice.'

'Hold on, Betty,' he replied, digging his hand into his jacket and smiling.

Betty's eyes widened and her mouth dropped open in disbelief as Davie pulled out a half-pint glass full of ice. Like a stage magician he gestured with a sweeping hand and sang, 'Ta- dah!' before placing a piece of ice into each girl's glass.

'No way!' exclaimed Betty. 'See, Davie Fleming, you think of everything!'

'Aye, and what else were you going to say?' he asked.

Betty stumbled over her words. 'Ach, well, you're just lovely.' She stood up and gave him a peck on the cheek. Davie grinned from ear to ear.

'There you go, lads and lassies, the princess has spoken. It's official: I'm just a lovely, nice guy who thinks of everything.'

'Wait a minute,' said Bridget, 'you're not that clever! You forgot the—' Before she could say anything else, Davie pulled out a bottle of coke. 'You don't mean this, by any chance?'

The girls looked at each other before lifting their knees and erupting in laughter. They all gave Davie a hearty round of applause.

The bus set off and the air was filled with a sound like fireworks as cans and bottles were cracked open. Tam held his can high and thrust it forward. 'Here's to a great day!' They all clinked, echoing his toast.

Their mood was happy as they sat back and settled in their seats, looking forward to their trip to the seaside. Finn and Fiona sat nearest the driver-side window, and Fiona turned her back to the glass and slung her legs over Finn's lap. Bridget and Tam sat together in the middle seats, while Davie and Betty sat by the window on the other side. Forty-five young children burst into song before the bus had barely turned the first corner from the Clachan.

'Oh, you cannae shove your granny off the bus!
Oh, you cannae shove your granny off the bus!
Oh, you cannae shove your granny
'Cause she's your mammy's mammy
You cannae shove your granny off the bus!
Singing aye aye yippy yippy aye …'

Everyone on the bus was in the same party spirit. Whisky glasses could be heard clinking, while empty beer bottles and cans were flung into an empty crate at a frequent rate. They had barely travelled ten miles, with at least another eighty miles still to go, before all the cans and pre-trip drinks at the bar began to take their toll on the group.

'Hey, driver, can you stop the bus?' someone soon piped up. 'One or two of us men need the toilet.'

'Aye, I will,' replied the driver. 'Give me ten minutes to find a safe spot to stop with some trees for cover.'

'I'm bursting,' said Tam.

'Aye, me too,' said Finn.

Both looked at Davie, who nodded. All three then looked at the girls, but they shook their heads from side to side.

'You three not needing a pish – I cannae believe that!' said Tam.

'Well, we've not been drinking pints like you; we've been on the shorts,' said Betty. 'Anyhow, yous can never hold your water.' The girls laughed, and the lads looked at each other and burst out laughing too.

232

Fifteen minutes went by and the bus continued to roll through the countryside without stopping. 'Hey, driver, I am really bursting!' one annoyed passenger shouted out.

'Aye, me too! You said you would stop and we are all bursting,' said another.

'I know! But we left the Clachan not much more than half an hour ago. And I am still looking for a safe place,' replied the driver.

'Just stop anywhere!' was the general consensus, and just at that moment the driver noticed a suitable area and pulled over. 'Right, lads, there you go: a lovely big hedge. Enjoy yourselves.'

There was a mad rush to get to the door. Tam, bursting at the seams by now, saw the bottle neck in the aisle and knew there was no immediate prospect of getting out to relieve himself. 'Fuck this! I'm going to pish myself if I don't get off this bus,' he said, and he grabbed the handle of the rear emergency exit window, unlocked it, threw the window wide open and launched himself out of it.

'Are you two coming?' he shouted as he disappeared.

Finn gave Davie a side glance and flung himself up to the window and side-vaulted out. Wee Davie climbed out and was lowering himself down on to the road when he looked up and had to quickly cover his face with his arm as a barrage of men leaped out over him. A peppering of exclamations could be heard as the men lined the field behind the hedge and relieved themselves.

'Thank God. Another five minutes and I would have burst.'

'Aye, I was about to pish myself!'

Everyone was pleased that they were able to empty their bladders without incident. One by one, they returned to the bus. The driver put his hand out in front of Finn as he stepped aboard. 'My buzzer is going off its head, so shut that emergency window and don't do that again.'

Finn grabbed the driver's cap off his head, saw he was bald, and replied in a loud voice, 'Aye, okay, keep your hair on. Oh, sorry, I see you haven't got any hair.'

The driver grabbed his hat back. 'Cheeky bugger.' He turned to the rest of the passengers.

'Right, everybody, now! Since the bus stopped for this comfort break, some of you have had to go out to relieve yourselves more than once,' he said, glancing at his watch, 'and now twenty-two minutes have passed. That means it's already near to one hour since we left the Clachan. So try and hold your water now or we will not get there at all.'

He sat down again and fired up the bus. It had scarcely turned a wheel before the children burst into song again.

'Ten green bottles hanging on the wall
Ten green bottles hanging on the wall
And if one green bottle should accidently fall,
There'd be nine green bottles hanging on the wall …'

Finn and the others joined in with the kids, with Davie singing 'Ten green blokes banging on the wall'.

Bridget dug Fiona gently in the ribs and nodded at the three boys. 'Keeno must have miscounted,' she said, 'because there's not forty-five weans on this bus – there's forty-eight. And these three are the biggest weans of them all!' The girls all laughed. 'Aye, mine will need his nappy changed soon,' added Bridget to more laughter.

'Bloody cheeky grown-ups,' said Finn, pointing his two index fingers upwards and wiggling them, gesturing to the boys that they tickle the girls. Wriggling and thrashing about, the girls' laughter and shrieks cut through the air, adding a happy ambiance to the already joyful bus. All six sat with tears running down their cheeks.

'That was so fun,' said Fiona, wiping away her tears with a lace hanky.

'You want some more?' asked Finn, holding his wiggling fingers in the air.

'No! No more! I couldn't take it.' Looking out of the window, she exclaimed excitedly, 'Look, everyone, a pure white horse!' They all started clamouring at the window to get a look.

'Where?' asked Betty.

'I just caught a glimpse of it!' cried Tam.

'Did you see it, Finn?' asked Fiona.

'No, I had my eyes closed.'

'What a shame. Goodness me, that was something to behold. I have never seen a pure white horse like that before. It was so beautiful, galloping alone in the meadow. I'm so glad I saw it.'

They all relaxed back into their seats. Laughing to herself, Fiona turned to Finn. 'You know, Finn, for a moment then when I saw the horse, I pictured you as a Cheyenne Indian and you were riding the horse bareback. It was so funny – I saw you naked except for your underpants! You were charging up the meadow towards me, and I was standing on a rock waving my lace hanky.' She waved her hanky to demonstrate. 'You seized me by the waist and sat me on your speeding white stallion and off we rode. You saved me from the baddies who wanted to have their wicked way with me!'

Finn was enthralled by her story. 'Oh Fiona, that is so sweet. Did you really imagine that?'

'Well, not the underpants part. But I did visualise you rescuing me and us riding off into the sunset. I thought how romantic that would be. I would have loved it to really happen. Oh well, we can only dream!'

'Ah, you've forgotten already that I truly *have* saved you. Aye, from all of them soft boiled turnips you've been seeing in the past. What's more dangerous than them soft numpties?' he said.

Fiona started to laugh. 'Soft boiled? Yes, they were. So true.' She moved closer to Finn and whispered, 'You know, Finn, I think you did save me,' and she laid her head on his chest.

Not long after, a cry could be heard down the bus. 'Hey driver, my wee Andrew needs the toilet. Can you stop, please?'

The driver sighed, annoyed. 'For God's sake, this is beyond a joke,' he muttered to himself, lifting his cap and wiping his brow. Then he responded in a calm manner, 'Aye, nae bother.' He saw a small thicket and pulled over. 'Right, the women and children first.'

The bus almost emptied, and the driver sat in his seat, glancing at his watch and shaking his head. They'd been stopped for nearly another ten minutes already. He was never going to get back to Glasgow on time. He had been behind the wheel for nearly one and a half hours and had only managed to travel about forty miles – and there were another sixty-five miles or so to go. He was livid. But he knew he would get no joy from the drunken mob behind him and kept his mouth shut.

The sound of bottles and cans opening continued constantly, and it wasn't long before another voice piped up, requesting yet another toilet stop. The driver's blood boiled. This journey should have taken two hours at most, but they'd set off two hours ago now and were not even halfway there.

Again, he stopped without protest. Yet again, all the men rushed for the door. *I can't go on like this*, the driver thought. *I will never get to the next pick-up on time*. His face was red with worry. But as soon as the men returned to the bus, the women and children all ran into the woods.

'Jesus Christ!' the driver cried out in exasperation. And he stood up and raised his voice so that everyone on the bus would hear. 'Look, everyone, I am paid by the Corporation to get you safely to Saltport on time and in one piece, so that you might enjoy your wee day out and your Tunnock's purvey.' He took off his cap and held it with two hands in front of him, shifting his weight. 'You may think there's no hurry. And, well, normally I wouldnae bother – but I have a schedule to keep today. I have another job back in Glasgow, taking people to a wedding reception, and then I have to run back here for seven o'clock tonight to take you lot home, before returning to the wedding reception at eleven thirty.

'I do all this so that you lot can enjoy your day. All this stopping and starting won't get us anywhere. My head is thumping with screaming kids but, hey, that's all part of the job. But we should by now be near enough to Saltport that you and the weans would be getting off soon – but we are still nearly fifty miles away and we are already a good hour behind schedule. So I have an idea.'

The driver walked up to the back of the bus and waved his arms toward Finn and the others. 'You lot on the back seats will have to move over or sit beside someone else. I will need to set up a toilet up here. I need you all on my side. Shall we do this?'

There was a lot of loud mumbling. 'Aye, that sounds a good idea,' said Keeno. 'We are all for it.'

'Has anyone got a spare shawl or a beach towel they could lend me?' asked the driver. Plenty of passengers were willing and before long he had several long beach towels.

'What's going on?' asked Finn as the driver returned to the back of the bus.

'I am making a bit of a toilet here on this side of the bench seat. Here, shift up now!' he demanded.

He began to construct a bivouac with the towels, giving Finn, Tam and Davie some string to help tie them on to the parcel shelf so that they draped down to the floor.

There was a lot of mulling by the passengers, wondering what he was going to use for the toilet. They could hear the luggage compartment opening, a lot of banging about and the sound of something being poured. The driver had emptied his reserve five-gallon drum of fuel into the tank.

'What is he up to, Finn?' asked Davie.

Peering out of the window, they saw the driver carrying a large oil drum.

'I am not sure, but whatever it is, we are not going to like it,' said Finn.

The driver placed the red metal five-gallon drum behind the towels and in between the rear seat and the last double seat. He unscrewed the four-inch lid, and placed a large fuel funnel into the hole. He then secured the funnel by wrapping string around it.

'Right, everyone! If you need the toilet, use the oil drum,' he shouted. 'But no solids!'

A chorus of 'Aww, for God's sake!' could be heard down the length of the bus.

'Any wee weans must go with their mother or father,' added the driver. 'All this will save precious time. All I ask is that you to go behind the towel tent and relieve yourself without the bus stopping. Otherwise, I won't be able to get you there in time to collect your refreshments. And I'll be late for my next job. I know it's not the ideal situation but it's all I can think of.'

There were shouts of approval from the passengers, and most felt reassured that it was the way forward.

Here comes the tsunami

Finn and his friends, though, were now all huddled together on the back seat with scarcely any real space to move – and they weren't happy about they were about to endure.

'Fuck's sake!' Tam shouted. 'Everyone will be taking a pish right next to us!'

'Well, we'll have to put up with it if we want to get there,' said Finn. 'Anyway, let's see how it goes.'

'I can't believe this is happening,' giggled Fiona. 'You couldn't write it, could you?'

There was a steady stream of people in the aisle waiting to use the drum, and Betty needed to use it too. When it was her turn, she popped her head round and was horrified to see the drum had little more than a four-inch hole in it with just a large funnel to do her business in.

'No!' she said firmly. 'I cannae do it in that thing. It's not right. And there is nowhere to sit. I am bursting though! I won't be able to hold it in!' she wailed. Agitated and feeling bloated, she shuffled her feet in an effort to stop any leakage and was about to call the driver to stop.

'Ach, everyone else has had to manage using the drum, so you need to manage too,' said Bridget.

'Aye, okay, you're right. I will give it a try, but I don't want any of you listening to me.'

I can't do this, she thought to herself. *They will hear me just like I've heard everyone else using it*. A sudden thought hit her. Betty pulled the shawl to the side and she started singing at the top of her voice, 'Ma maw's a millionaire, blue eyes and—'

The children on the bus immediately erupted into song:

'... and curly hair,
Sitting amongst the Eskimos,
Playing a game of dominoes.
Ma maw's a millionaire ...'

Betty smiled to herself as she made use of the drum.

'I'm next,' said Tam.

'Oh, we're nearly there,' said Finn. 'And, besides, that thing in there will be near full with all the weans drinking their ginger and us lot having a swally.'

'Aye, maybe so, but I'm bursting.'

Betty emerged, her face scarlet. 'You know that bloody thing was gurgling at me when the bus bumped on the road. I'm dreading the road back,' she shuddered.

Tam went next into the bivouac. Meanwhile, everyone sensed the bus was nearing the seaside as it cut through the streets. Though tall buildings obscured the shoreline, the smell of sea air permeated the bus and stirred the children. They could see other children walking in their plimsolls and swimwear, each holding a pail or a spade. Most of the children on the bus stood up excitedly as the sea became visible on the horizon.

Their shouts of, 'I can see the sea!' and 'I saw it first!' and 'No, I saw it first!' broke the driver's concentration. His view via the rear-view mirror was obscured by the children standing on seats, and he looked back and yelled, 'Will all you weans sit down, now!'

At that moment, a little Ford Anglia came out from nowhere and cut across the front of the bus, causing the driver to pull violently right on the steering wheel to avoid a serious collision. The passengers at the front of the bus all shrieked in terror. This momentum, in turn, caused the rear of the bus to skid in the opposite direction. The passengers shrieked as the driver frantically fought to get the bus under control.

Meanwhile, Tam, who was still relieving himself in the bivouac, was jettisoned out of the tent with such force that he was flung out towards the others, still urinating and holding his penis. He landed on top of

Bridget who screamed in horror. Then she saw what was following him and screamed again. 'Oh my God!'

A split second later, the drum was bouncing through the air towards the six of them. It hit the last two seats in front of them with such force, it imploded on contact, spewing a yellow fountain of urine into the air that splattered the ceiling before cascading back down in a huge deluge that covered the horrified six.

'Oh my God!' Fiona screamed, her hands held out in front of her and her face dripping with amber fluid.

The brakes squealed and smoked as the driver pressed down hard on the pedal, bringing the bus to an abrupt halt and sending the still very full five-gallon drum bouncing down the aisle towards the front of the bus. The violent tumbling of the canister caused urine to discharge from the filler cap like a huge geyser erupting. Pints of urine sprayed over the passengers and seats. It passed each individual, spewing forth like a Chinese fire dragon, soaking everyone in its path. No one was spared.

Finally, the drum slammed against the engine cover, bounded off and came to rest upside down on the stairwell where it lay motionless with the last few pints of urine gurgling out. The spray of urine had not missed anyone apart from the driver who had barely been touched.

'For fuck's sake, I'm covered in pish!' Keeno screamed as the shock and trauma kicked home. 'The whole bus is swimming in pish!'

Fiona was screaming in between spitting, puffing and blowing the urine from her mouth. 'Are you okay?' asked Finn as she began to weep.

'Are you kidding me? No, I am not okay!' she shouted at him. 'Look at me and my new dress!' She was still coughing dregs out of her mouth. 'I can't believe this is happening to me! It's in my mouth, hair and everywhere!'

Finn tried to console her. 'Don't worry, it's only pish. It will wash.'

A bead of urine sat at the end of Fiona's nose like a newly formed morning dewdrop clinging to a flower petal. She pushed out her bottom lip and blew it off her nose. Then she screamed at Finn in full-blown anger. 'Only pish! Only *pish*! You are kidding me! Look at me! I am covered in the stuff. Ninety-six people's "pish" as you call it! All over me. And you say it will wash! Oh, God help me! I just want to go home.' She leaned into Finn's shoulder and continued to cry.

Davie stood for a moment, his mouth agape. His arms were outstretched in front of him as though he was about to do an impression of Max Bygraves singing 'You Need Hands'.

'Fuck's sake, I am drenched!' he shrieked. 'Even my socks are soaked!' He was completely stunned, having been asleep with his head on Betty's knee when events took place. He tried to shake the liquid from his hair. 'What the fuck happened?'

Betty wailed and kept spitting, trying to remove all trace of urine from her mouth. Tam, who had taken the full force of the yellow fountain in his face, sat shocked. Not one part of his body had escaped. He looked like he had just emerged from a swimming pool.

Finn pulled down the towels from the makeshift curtain and handed one each to Betty and Bridget and another to Tam and Davie to share. He wrapped the last towel over Fiona's shoulders and tried to dry her off as she sobbed into her palms.

The bus was in pandemonium. Children were crying. Women were screaming obscenities at the driver, blaming him for the disaster that surrounded them. The floor was swimming in urine. And everyone in their own way tried to rid themselves of the amber slurry.

The driver tried to take charge. 'Is everyone all right?' he asked. 'And is anyone hurt? All I can say is I am so sorry about that. But to tell you the truth, that idiot in the Ford Anglia caused it. Did anyone here witness his reckless driving? And did anyone happen to get the number plate?'

'You must be fucking joking!' said an infuriated woman.

'No, we didnae!' butted in another. 'You're a fucking arsehole. You covered me and my weans in pish, and now you expect us to have taken down a number. Well I am so sorry, I never took his number – I was preoccupied wiping a gallon of pish out of my eyes!' she screamed.

'Again, all I can say is it wasn't my fault!' said the driver.

'Not your fault!' bellowed Keeno. 'We have paid you good money to get us here safe and sound, and we are neither safe nor sound. The day is ruined and it is all down to you!'

'Aye and I have got you here safe and sound,' insisted the driver.

'Oh yes, sir, we are here all right, but if you haven't noticed, we are all drenched in fucking *pish*!' Keeno shouted back. 'And I will tell you another thing: there will be no payment from me because I am giving everyone a refund!'

'Now, listen, I need not have taken the bus this morning with ninety-six passengers, but I did it and did all of you a favour. I never gave a second thought to the consequences for me if I were caught. Because it wouldnae have been any of you lot that would see the wrath of the police! So now give me a chance to make it right, for sanity's sake,' pleaded the driver.

'I suggest you all visit the Oxfam shop in Saltport and grab some clean clothing,' he added. 'It's on the high street – you can't miss it. It's next door to Boots the chemist. Then take a short walk down to the open-air swimming baths and get changed there. In less than an hour you will all be sorted again. I say it again: I am so sorry to you all. Sit down and I will run you all into town and drop you off at the charity shop.'

'Well, you better hurry up and get us there then,' demanded Keeno.

As the bus accelerated away, a tsunami of urine charged straight for the back of the bus, dragging along with it cigarette butts, spent matches, Spangles sweet papers and practically everything else that was on the floor. A couple of wine corks kissed each other as they bobbed their way down the aisle.

The wave had caught itself in the void between the rear of the stairwell and the lip at the front of the aisle. With nowhere for the flood to escape, the river of urine ran backwards and forwards under the seats like a small river every time the driver braked or accelerated. The passengers all lifted their feet.

'Fuck's sake, driver, we can't sit in this sea of pish!' a passenger yelled.

'No, we cannae!' exclaimed another. 'We need it mopping up!'

'We don't want this bus on the way back!' someone shouted.

'Aye, you are right. We want a clean bus to go home in.'

The driver approached a roundabout. He'd had another bright idea to jettison the now frothy and thickening sludge out of the bus.

'Right, everyone, hold on to your seats! There's a roundabout ahead.' He opened the bus's automatic doors as he proceeded to circle the roundabout, then he hit the brakes heavily, forcing much of the sludge out of the double doors. As he accelerated again ever so slightly, the remaining urine rushed back to the rear of the bus and built up a momentum so that on its return to the front it could break over the aisle lip and pour out of the open doors as well. He continued to control the flow of urine out of the bus like this until it had diminished to no more than a small drip.

Content that he has jettisoned as much of the urine out as he possibly could, the driver stopped at the nearest convenient spot and addressed the passengers.

'Right, everyone, do we carry on to the charity shop or should we make our way home? The answer to that is in your hands. Raise your hand if you want the bus to return home.'

He counted the votes and was surprised to find the majority of passengers were in favour of staying in Saltport. He took them to the Oxfam shop.

In an effort to dry out the bus, he had turned the bus's heater on to full flow, and now everyone was complaining of the smell coming from the seats and floor as they began to dry out.

Oh fuck, please God get me out of this mess, thought the driver, flustered. He turned off the heating and opened the doors again. Passengers were standing up and opening all the windows and the three sunroofs. Even the back emergency window was being held open by Finn and Tam. The buzzer signal was buzzing in the driver's ear but he said nothing. He knew he was lucky to be alive: some of the passengers were baying for blood.

'Right, everyone, we are nearly there,' shouted the driver. 'I am going straight home to change the bus. If any of you want to go home, stay on board.'

A minute or two later, he stopped directly outside the Oxfam shop. Virtually everyone piled into the shop looking for a bargain. Finn went straight for the jeans and found a pair of Wrangler's. He held them to his waist and they were about his size. He also picked up a T-shirt that was embossed with the 'ban the bomb' sign. Fiona flicked through the hangers and came across a beautiful maxi skirt and a yellow top to match. Davie and the others found outfits that suited them too.

Making their way to the swimming baths, Finn declared, 'I don't know about you lot, but this will stick in my mind forever! A pishy day out at Saltport! People will think we mean it rained. No! When we say pishy, we *mean* pishy!' For the first time in a while, they all laughed.

'Wait a minute,' said Fiona. 'I have not got a swimming suit.'

'Don't worry. They have remedial baths where we can have a private bath or shower,' said Betty.

'Thank goodness!'

They all had showers and got clean, emerging afterwards in their new clothes, relieved that the stink of urine was gone.

Sitting on some grass, they ate their sandwiches quietly, privately reflecting on the morning's traumatic events. It was Davie who finally broke the silence.

'Fuck. When I woke up and found myself on the floor covered in that yucky mess, I thought it was the end of the world.'

Finn thought for a minute and said, 'Aye, it might have been. If it wasn't for the skill of the driver, it might have been the end of the world for a lot of us. I just think everyone – including myself – has been a wee bit too hard on him. And I think we should get him a half bottle of whisky for when he finishes his shift tonight. It will calm him down a wee bit.'

Fiona was taken aback by Finn's statement, and she felt her heart melt inside her. She put her hand flat on Finn's chest and kissed his cheek. 'Oh Finn, that is so sweet of you. Everyone was so against the driver. I am ashamed that I was running with the other passengers, too. No one gave a thought as to how he was feeling, poor man. I think it should be an apology and a full bottle from all of us.'

They all agreed. 'After this morning, things can only get better,' said Finn. 'Let's make it a day to remember and enjoy it.'

'No, let's make it a day we want to forget!' said Davie.

They walked towards the beach laughing. It was most definitely a day that none of them would forget.

The goldfields

Finn was walking downhill to Fiona's house in Blackwood Gardens. It was a mild dusky evening, and the streets were empty except for a small black and white spaniel. When he saw it, Finn laughed out loud: it seemed to walk almost sideways like a crab. He was enjoying his evening walk, but when he was nearly halfway it started to rain and quickly turned into a deluge. Within a minute or two, the drains couldn't cope and the overflowing water raced down the hill.

 Walking at a faster pace, Finn slipped his hands into his pockets and put his head down, his posture resembling a half-closed penknife. With no jacket on, the cold rain penetrated his white shirt, stinging him and gnawing at his skin like a swarm of biting midges. Wrapping his arms around himself as protection from the downpour, his thoughts turned to

Fiona. He didn't know what was wrong with her lately but she had been acting funny.

He turned into the long drive, his shoes crunching over the white marble-stone chippings as he fought his way through the wind and rain to the front door. He rang the bell and waited shivering for what seemed an eternity under the dry porch. The lobby light lit up, and he noticed a stained-glass window above the door, depicting the Hood battleship.

Fiona's mother opened the door with a happy smile plastered on her face. Finn noticed her cheeks were cherry red and smiled to himself, knowing instantly that she'd been on the sherry.

'My goodness, come away in, Finn! Goodness me, look at you. You're soaked to the skin. I will away and get you a towel.'

Finn entered the grand hallway. It was as big as the Clachan Bar, with polished smoked-oak panelling halfway up the walls and up the staircase. A massive gilt mirror was on the wall straight ahead of him and he glanced at his reflection: sodden and shivering, he was a pathetic sight. Finn's eyes followed the staircase up to the middle where it split in two, branching off to either side. He chose the left-hand branch and stood on his tiptoes to get a better view of the high landing. He knew Fiona's room was on the left, but there was no sign of her.

Although Finn had met Fiona's parents a few times for a meal or a coffee, this was the first time he'd been invited to the house. He was in awe of its size. Mouth agape, he looked at the portraits that adorned the walls. It was obvious they were of family members from times gone by, and he speculated what sort of people could have afforded such a house back in those days. Maybe someone in Fiona's family had been high up in the shipyards and had perhaps helped in the designing and building of HMS Hood. Or maybe they were shareholders or lawyers like Fiona's father. He was certainly impressed by it all, and he wondered what the hell Fiona was doing with the likes of him. Eventually she would inherit all this, while he had nothing but the clothes he stood up in and his motorbike.

His thoughts were interrupted by Fiona's mother returning with the towel. 'Here you are, Finn. Give yourself a good rub down. Fiona won't be long. She told me to tell you to give her five minutes. Go stand by the fire and dry yourself. You will catch your death of cold if you stand here any longer!'

Upstairs, Fiona was sitting fidgeting. She didn't like confrontation and was afraid of upsetting Finn, but she knew she had to say her piece, and say it soon.

She was beginning to really resent Gallows Hill. She knew in her heart that Finn was wasting his life, and hers, by hanging around the Hill with his so-called friends. He was better than that; when she was alone with him you could not meet a sweeter or kinder man. But with his gang, he was a different person, and she did not always like his ways when he was with them.

She loved Finn, but his life in Gallows Hill wasn't the life she'd envisaged for herself, and she felt disappointed. There was no real prospect of making a better life for themselves there. It was the same places, the same faces, the same ways, the same days. Nothing had changed in all the time she had been with him. It was like being in some kind of time warp. Their lives revolved around the Executioners and the Clachan Bar. But she wanted more. Either he needed to give up the gang and walk away, or she felt her relationship with him was over.

Almost a month earlier, when she was having her hair done, she'd read a magazine article about the goldfields in Australia and was amazed and excited by the opportunities they had to offer a young couple. She wanted to talk to Finn about moving out there and starting a family. A new beginning for them both, she thought. A chance in a lifetime. She wondered – and worried – how Finn would respond.

But it would have to wait. Tonight they were having a meal at home with her parents. She would discuss it with him tomorrow. Her heart filled with dread.

The next day, Fiona waited for Finn at the Gallows Fill Café, eating the one indulgence she could never resist, a rich homemade chocolate cake. With her eyes fixed on her *Vogue* magazine, she took a sip from her coffee cup. The caffeine kick was just what she needed. Her hand shook as she checked her watch. Finn should have been there fifteen minutes ago. *I really do need to talk to him and get this off my chest*, she thought. But then she heard the distinctive roar of Finn's motorcycle nearly quarter of a mile away.

Finn pulled up outside the café and took off his open-face helmet and dark riding glasses. When Fiona heard the motorcycle's side stand go down, she shivered with trepidation. She had rehearsed what she was going to say a little earlier at home, standing in front of the biggest mirror in the house, but now anxiety wiped her memory. She rubbed at the nape of her neck with a trembling hand as she waited, her brows furrowed. If Finn genuinely loved her, surely he would understand. She ordered him a coffee and his favourite, a Paradise biscuit.

He walked through the door, a beaming smile lighting his face when he spotted her.

'My, Mr McGill, you do look handsome in your biker leathers.' She smiled nervously at him.

'Ach, so I have been told,' he said. 'You okay?'

Having had little sleep with all her worrying, Fiona felt dizzy and faint. She just wanted this conversation to be over with, but she startled even herself with her reaction to this question. 'Why should I not be okay? You tell me!' she snapped aggressively.

Finn had never heard Fiona raise her voice before for anything and he was shocked that she was now doing so with him. He held his palms up in a surrender pose. 'Easy now, girl, I was just asking,' he snapped back. 'But okay, while we are at it, you have been acting just a wee bit funny for a week or two, and to tell you the truth, I cannae abide all this huffiness. I have nae time for it.'

Fiona took slow, deliberate sips of her coffee, not looking at him. She looked straight ahead, poker-faced, as she deliberated what to say. 'Listen, Finn,' she blurted suddenly. 'I enjoy going to the Clachan Bar, but it's hardly paradise now, is it?'

Finn was astonished. 'Are you serious? What do you mean it's not really paradise? It's all right, isn't it? You enjoy it, don't you?'

'I just said I enjoyed it. But we never really go anywhere nice together because you are too well known in and around the city, with all that carry-on you get up to …'

'Aye, go on! You were saying? I get into …?'

'Well, the gang stuff … it's just not really you, is it?'

'Just not me? What's brought this on? I take you to the coast on my bike, don't I?'

Fiona flicked her head, throwing her hair down her back. 'Oh yes, we have been once, but even then we had to meet up with Tam and his woman,' she retorted. 'But anyway, never mind that. Look, Finn, I know you better than anyone: you are a sweet and lovely man with not one bad bone in your body. I also know – because you have told me – that you only *act* the hard man. It's not really you. You said yourself that you don't start fights, you only finish them.' Fiona looked Finn directly in the eye. 'I was proud of you for saying that. Because I believe in you, Finn. But there is more to life than hanging about Gallows Hill—'

257

Finn could not believe what he was hearing. He was the boss. He was the one to wear the trousers! His brow creased into a scowl. 'Wait a minute, Fee!'

But Fiona was fired up now. She had waited far too long to get her words out, and there was no way Finn was going to stop her saying what she had to say. She slapped her hand down on the table.

'No, Finn, you wait a minute! Let me finish,' she demanded. 'Then you can have your say. There is more to life than Gallows Hill … What about us moving over to Australia? There is a growing community in Kalgoorlie in western Australia where they have immense areas of goldfields. There are plenty of prospectors out there selling their nuggets and panned gold.'

Her voice softened and she gave him a hesitant smile. 'With my qualification pending, assuming I pass of course, along with your paperwork for your welding and burning and your crane driver's licence, I believe we would be accepted for immigration into Australia … There, I've said it now! Now it's your turn. What do you say?'

Finn sat back in his chair and threw his arm over its back. 'Whoa, wait a minute now, Fiona. What I say is, apart from the cost of moving over there, it is heavy stuff asking me to just up sticks and go! Aye, maybe you've thought hard about it, but it's the first I have heard about it! You can't expect me to make up my mind just like that to leave all my friends and family. You have another thing coming if you think that,' he said.

Fiona leaned over the table, took Finn's hand and clasped it tight. 'Look, Finn, I have a few pounds put away. Also, my mam and dad, bless them, told me that though they would not like it if I emigrated, they wouldn't stand in the way of any prospect of us having a better life together. They said they'd give us £5,000 to help us on our way. Having that sort of money would be fantastic. Together, we could set up a gold office, buying and selling raw gold. This is an opportunity I wouldn't want us to miss. And it's only ten British pounds with assisted passage to get there.'

Taken aback by Fiona's plan and her newfound confidence, Finn felt vulnerable. There was no way she was going to get the better of him, he thought. Enraged at what she was asking him to do, he pulled his hand from under hers and shouted, 'I don't know about all that! You really are moving fast.' He stood up from his chair, swung it behind him and pointed at his chest. 'What about me? What about what I want? Have you thought about that?'

Fiona was surprised, too, at how confident she was feeling. Her nerves had ceased to rattle, and calm now enveloped her. She believed this was the way forward and she was fighting for her man. 'Okay, go on then,' she said. 'You tell me what you want.'

'I want to travel and do things, too,' Finn started. 'I have dreams and ambitions. But it seems like you've already decided and now you just expect me to drop everything and everyone in my life and bugger off to

Australia with you and live happily ever after!' he yelled.

Fiona's confidence started to wane. 'No, I never meant it like that,' she said softly. 'I knew you would take it this way.'

'How could I take it any other way? It's clear to me you have made your mind up.'

Fiona could feel the eyes of the other people in the café bearing down on her. 'Calm down, Finn, and listen for a minute. Of course I want you to think it over. It would be silly not to,' she said. 'But with my degree, I believe we could make money from gold. And good money, too.'

'You're bloody right I will think about it. But I can tell you now, my thinking is not going to be about emigrating, that's for sure. Anyway, what's wrong with here? We do all right, don't we?'

'All right! Well, if all right really is good enough for you, Finn, then you stay here. Besides, you know what's wrong with here! We can't go anywhere. We can't do anything. We are stuck in a rut with no way out! I love you, Finn, but this is not the life for me. And maybe Australia is not the life for you either. But I want more.'

Fiona put her hand over her mouth to stop herself from giggling when Finn slammed his coffee cup down on the table and the coffee, like an Arabian camel, spat it back in his face in defiance. She knew better than to laugh. This was serious and would maybe make them or break them.

Finn wiped his eyes with the back of his hand. 'Right, I have heard enough of this tosh. I'm off. Enjoy yourself in Australia, and may you have plenty of gold-bearing clients! See you about.'

'Yes, typical. Finn McGill, the big man, walks out when the going gets rough and he doesn't get his own way. Hard man my foot!'

This touched a nerve in Finn. He'd not been prepared for Fiona to rebel so powerfully. His chair squealed as he yanked it back to the table. He sat down, nodding his head. 'Now I see. This isn't about me at all. This is actually all about you and what you want.'

'What do you mean, all about me?'

'Well, what have you to lose anyway? What the hell are you going to give up compared with my own sacrifice? Nothing!'

'I've thought hard all week, wondering just what you would say and how you would react. Well, Finn McGill, now I know. Finn, this really is all about us. And how dare you say I am giving up nothing!'

Battling back her tears, Fiona found it hard to admit to herself what she was prepared to give up for Finn. Sobbing, she dabbed her eyes. 'I have to leave behind Linda and all my other friends, my family who I'm very close to, my job, my life as it is now. But, most of all, my mother and my loving father. For me to leave Scotland and emigrate to Australia ... well, I know it will break their hearts. They might never see me again nor meet their future grandchildren. Yes, it will break their hearts. But I can tell you this, it will break my heart even more to leave them.

'All this I'm prepared to give up to be with you, to live a happy and content life together. So don't you just sit there and accuse me of not losing anything! You go back to your precious empire and sit on your throne in the Clachan with your partners in crime – because that's all you care about, isn't it?'

'Aye, that's right. At least I have people who are loyal to me, and they always have been. I'm sorry, I shouldn't have said what I said, and I appreciate you offering to give up everything for me. But I can't, and I won't, give everything up for you. I have always wanted to fit in and maybe be someone. And now I am someone who people look up to. There is no way I am giving that up. I wish you all the best and I am truly sorry we had to finish this way.'

Fiona lowered her head and gave a heavy sigh. 'Do you really want that life, Finn, pretending to be somebody you're not? If you carry on going down that road, it will only lead to misery. I appreciate we are finished. But, if not for me, then do yourself a favour and get out of the gang while you can.'

Finn cupped Fiona's chin in his hands and attempted to give her a farewell kiss on the cheek. Fiona turned and looked away. He held out his arms, palms up, and shook his head.

'Well, there is nothing more to be said,' he said, and he strode out of the café and didn't look back.

Fiona dropped her head and sobbed into her hanky, listening as the roar of his motorcycle faded into the distance. The coffee shop owner rushed over. 'Are you okay, lassie? Oh, here now, no man is worth all those tears! Can I get you another coffee? On the house,' he said.

It took Fiona half a minute to compose herself enough just to say, 'No, thank you. I have to be going.' She stood up to leave but her legs buckled beneath her and she fell backwards on to the chair. She threw her palms to her face and wailed.

As he rode home on his bike, Finn was arguing with himself. He felt he should have been a bit more diplomatic and sensitive with Fiona – but even if he had been, there was no way he was giving up his status in the gang. And there was definitely no way he was emigrating. His face scrunched up as he headbutted the oncoming wind.

'Why would she even ask me to do that?' he yelled. Then, mumbling under his breath, he said, 'I have earned my status through protection and defence, and I am proud that I have never been the instigator in any gang fight. So what is she on about, saying the gang's not really me? Well, it's her loss! Fuck her!'

Finn dropped a gear in anger and twisted the throttle grip as far as it would go. The bike's engine roared and popped as he sped down the road.

Looking for revenge

There was to be a dance over in Castletown and Jed was keen for the gang to go. One of the Executioners had recently been beaten to a pulp in the city centre in broad daylight by some of the Castletown Too gang. This was happening too often lately and he wanted to do something about it.

He looked over at Finn sitting in the corner of the Clachan talking to Tam, and caught his eye before lowering his gaze to the ground. He cracked his knuckles as he tried to find the right words. Jed knew this was really a big ask.

'Ach! It doesnae matter,' he muttered.

Finn looked over his pint glass at Jed as he sipped his beer. 'What doesnae matter? What are you talking about? Spit it out, man!'

Jed began swirling the dregs of beer around his own glass, making a whirlpool. His words came out reluctantly. 'Well, ah, I was just wondering … well, eh …'

Sitting himself upright in his chair, Finn slapped the table. 'For fuck's sake, Jed, spit it out! What's the matter with you?'

Everyone in the bar turned and looked over towards Jed, and he knew he had to say it. 'Aye, right, okay. There is a dance over in Castletown Town Hall this Saturday night. Norman and the Nutters are playing. You like them, Finn, don't you?'

'Aye, I like them but you know that's bandit country!' scoffed Finn. 'We'd be asking for trouble going over there. Dutchy Holland and the Toonies rule that place.'

'Aye, I suppose you're right.' Despondent, Jed let out a heavy sigh and laid his head down on the table. 'Aye, you are right as usual.'

Swallowing the last dregs of his pint, Finn gave Jed a glassy glare. 'Why the fuck would we want to go over there anyway?'

Jed looked serious. 'I am just fed up that the Toonies have taken out another one of the gang and we still do nothing about it. That's why.'

Crossing his arms, Finn replied, 'I am not even contemplating getting the gang to go over there. Have you forgotten what happened when me and Tam went over to Bridgetown on our own? I let my guard down for a woman and dragged Tam into a hornets' nest. We were both lucky to get away from the BMB gang in one piece. If it weren't for that soup ladle handle, well, who knows what would have happened to us. And you are too much of a firebrand, Jed. You would start trouble in an empty house.'

'What do you mean, firebrand? I won't sit back and let them Toonies run rings around us, if that's what you mean. Knife the bastards, that's what I say!'

'That's exactly what I mean, Jed. You are too much of a troublemaker and that's a threat to the whole gang. You go delving in with your head down with no thought for the safety of anyone else. And it's too risky. Sorry, Jed. I can't ask the lads to go over there, so the answer is no. Anyhow, if we bide our time, we'll get our revenge one day. But not this way, sorry.'

Sweat dripped from Jed's brow and his face reddened. He began to pace the floor, then turned to Finn. 'You have always said I'm second in command and that I can always have my say. So let's put this to a vote this Friday night. I will send out the word to the boys to meet here in the Clachan, and we will see what happens then.'

He was all fired up and Finn knew no amount of persuasion would convince him to drop the idea. He nodded towards Jed and lifted his glass. 'Aye, okay, big man. It's your call.'

Friday night soon arrived, and Finn, Davie, Tam and Jed all sat in the far corner of the lounge in the Clachan where they could see all the comings and goings. All but two of the gang turned up.

'Right, where's Charlie?' asked Tam. 'Anyone know where he is?'

'He cannae make it and sends his apologies,' said Winker. His real name was Norman Ward but he had a bad tic to his eye and blinked several times a minute. 'He is at the hospital with wee Hilda. She's in labour!'

'For fuck's sake, she's only a wean herself,' said Finn.

'If they are old enough to bleed, then they are old enough to breed,' piped up Big Jed. Laughter erupted and echoed throughout the bar as the banter flowed.

'Aye, she has always liked her hole, that one,' said Brodie knowingly.

'How the fuck would you know?' asked Peem. 'You have never had your hole except for Pam and her five sisters!' More laughter filled the room.

Everything was running smoothly and everyone was happy, and then the mood suddenly changed. An eerie silence descended and, like a dark cloud, it hung above the bar. Finn knew he had to take control. He composed himself by breathing slowly and got himself into character. He continued to play the hard man for the sake of his own self-esteem, honour and pride.

'Right, lads, it's time to get on to our business! Jed has something to say.'

Standing in front of the gang, Jed held a strong posture with his head held high and his shoulders back. 'You all know where we are going tomorrow night,' he said. 'Castletown! So if any yous have any objections, keep your mouth shut because we are going anyway!'

'Well, I have!' said Micky Dobbs. He was dubbed Micky, or the Mouse, by the gang because of his small stature, sticky-out ears and sharp, pointy nose. Micky always seemed to have something to prove. He needed to make sure the gang took him seriously and was a force to be reckoned with. In any street battle, he got stuck in and gave as good as the rest.

Micky stood up with his hands at his sides. 'We all must be off our heads going anywhere near that place. There is no doubt that Dutchy Holland and the Castletown Toonies will be there in force.'

The gang mumbled amongst themselves, some agreeing they should give the Toonies a visit, and some firmly against the idea. Finn knew it was a near split decision and he jumped out of his chair. He had not seen Fiona since that day in the café and felt he had nothing left in his life but the gang. To be part of it all, he had to keep up his image as the hard man.

'Aye, you lot, listen to the Mouse! Going near that place is just asking for trouble.' He threw his hands up in the air in frustration. 'It's not as if we have a fucking Trojan horse that we can use for a surprise ambush! They will see us as soon as we step through the door. You all know what will happen: they'll send out for reinforcements and before we know it, we will be fighting the whole town. Can't you see? When that happens, we are all fucked! Common sense tells you that!'

Shrugging his shoulders, Jed bellowed out, 'No!' He puffed his chest out and appeared calm and unworried. He had their attention now and felt like their leader. He opened his arms wide and then pulled them together, urging the gang to come closer.

Standing in the middle of them all, Jed said, 'Listen, look around us. There's twenty-two of us here. Twenty-two! And if every one of us stands our ground, we can make sure we do ask for trouble, 'cause it's about time we settled the score!' Letting out an exaggerated sigh, Jed shook his head. He knew what he was doing. 'Remember when Wee Eric went over there to Castletown to see his dying granny?' he said, deliberately riling the others. 'The bastards got a hold of him. They never gave him a chance. They just done him over. And for what? Just for living here in Gallows Hill.'

Looking around the room, Jed softened his voice. 'I am sorry, boys, but you all know that dirty bastard Dutchy drew a knife over him.' Jed jabbed his finger angrily and now raised his voice. 'That fucker knew Eric's granny was dying, and the cunt never had any sympathy for him. The woman died while Wee Eric was laid up in hospital.'

The gang stood listening to Jed, simmering in anger. His speech had touched a nerve and their hearts.

Shaking his head in disapproval, Jed added, 'Poor Eric. He never got to see his granny before she passed, the bastards that they are. We never avenged him or his granny. So, fuck this! We go over there and we shove it right up their fucking arses. Because we are the Gallows Hill Executioners!'

The gang whooped and shouted obscenities at the Toonies.

Finn dismissed Jed's speech with a wave of his hands. 'This is ridiculous and pure suicide. For those of you who have never seen Dutchy, he is one mean bastard. There's no doubt about it, he will fucking rip you open like he'd gut a fish. That cunt is unhinged. That's what we are up against.'

But it was no good; Jed had the Clachan buzzing like a bike of angry wasps. Realising he had most of the gang on his side, Jed excitedly shook his fists and continued to rant. 'And what about Geordie Geddes? The bastards saw him in the town when he was just looking for a watch strap and they dragged him into a close and kicked the fuck out of him. They left him unconscious.' Jed looked over at Geordie. 'What d'you think, Geordie? Should we go to the dance or not?'

Geordie looked startled, but Jed's' speech had lit a fire inside him too and he said with determination, 'Oh, aye, you're right. We should go! Let's get the bastards!'

Jed surged on. 'I tell you this, the fucking bastards need seeing to! You all know what's been going on. I say fuck them all!' and the room erupted with whooping and cheering.

'We all sit up in Gallows Hill like prisoners in our own district, not able to go anywhere for fear of other fucking gangs. And we sit back and let them fuck our own kind – Wee Eric and Geordie for two. So fuck them Toonies! Let's make a stance and show them we are no pushovers. We're the Executioners, and we stop for no man! As Robert Burns said, let us do or die!'

Some of the gang jumped about in a high-energy frenzy at this, screaming obscenities. But Finn frowned, knowing serious trouble was fermenting.

Jed smirked to himself. He'd cracked open the Gallows Hill jail block, and the prisoners in the room were angry and ready for a breakout. He had them in the palm of his hand. Gathering his thoughts, he concluded, 'So, tomorrow night, boys, let's show them bastards who the daddy is!'

The pub erupted once again. A heavy static electricity had taken the place of the once-dark cloud, and lightning would strike.

Keeno, the barman, muttered to those at the bar, 'Those boys are mental and on the warpath. Thank fuck we are on their side!' Numerous heads nodded agreement.

Finn groaned. He could not get Fiona's last words to him out of his mind. Was this really the life he wanted? And was he really the hard man the gang perceived him to be?

Toonies yah bass!

Saturday night came around so quick, no one in the gang had time to properly contemplate what was going to happen that night. In fact, no one cared, such was the frenzy Jed had induced. His speech had made them all feel invincible, just as he'd intended.

The Executioners all gathered in the Clachan Bar and Finn spoke first. 'Listen, you lot. You know I don't think this is a good idea, but the vote was to go, so I am with you. But this is Jed's command so let the big man speak.'

Jed refused to be put off by Finn and raised his voice to give his commands. 'Right, when we get in there, Geordie, the Mouse, Gregory and Peem, you give us back-up – so you lot hang about at the back of us. Sammy, Rab and Preston, you make sure you keep any cunt from getting near me and Finn.

'The rest of you stay in the wings,' he continued. 'We are gonnae do these cunts in! I want to hear it!' Jed waved his arms like an orchestra conductor, scooping his hands up for the crescendo as he shouted, 'What are we gonnae do?'

They all shouted in unity, 'Fuck them!'

'Again!' said Jed, and again the room erupted. 'Fuck them!'

Jed was enjoying the response from the gang and knew the majority were right behind him in this, but he didn't like the way Finn was sitting on the fence. Nor did Geordie Geddes.

'That was a brilliant speech, big man,' Geordie said. 'It's a shame but it looks as though Finn has shit his drawers. He is definitely not with us on this.'

The pair had grown close in the past few months. Since his kicking by Dutchy and his mob, Geordie had made a point of hanging around with Jed, and the gang understood he was seeking refuge. But they also knew that in a fight, Geordie would stop for no man until he could fight no more. He was of the same breed as Jed – very irrational, a bit of a troublemaker and not someone you could not trust. Finn always said he wasn't right in the head and urged people to watch their backs when he was around.

But it was clear no one was listening to Finn. He was losing confidence and was less sure of his status in the gang. He would go along with Jed and the gang on this ludicrous plan, though he knew it would all end in a bloodbath. As ever, he just wanted to fit in.

The gang assembled outside the bar and the mood was one of emotional hysteria.

'There's only three motor cars. Pile in the best you can and follow us,' said Finn.

They made their way down to Portside Road, a few streets away from the town hall. 'Stop here, Geordie! It's looking like it's all clear here. We might need a clean getaway. Besides, if they bastards see us getting out of these cars, they will wreck them. The cars will be safer here.'

As they walked towards the hall, Jed asked, 'Are we all carrying?' A solid 'Aye' came in response. 'Good stuff, lads. Good stuff.'

Finn, though, was concerned that they would be frisked at the door. 'We will need to stash it all outside 'cause the council has got the door policed with a few heavies. There's no chance we will get it in.'

The gang amassed outside the hall and encircled a small dry-stone wall. Peem removed a stone from it. 'Stash your chibs in here. We can collect them when we come out.'

'Fuck's sake, there is no way I am not carrying in there,' said Jed.

'No, you cannae,' said Finn firmly. 'If you get caught with that, they bastard police will hang a charge on the lot of us.'

'Aye, you're right,' said Jed. He handed his knife to Peem.

'It looks like it's headers, toe steelies and knuckles tonight. This will be easy!' said Gregory.

They were frisked in the entrance lobby as anticipated, but Finn was surprised to see only a few of the Toonies gang present.

'Watch that Finn boy! Make sure you frisk him good!'

It was Boaby, a square-faced and block-shouldered Toonie who was well known for being unafraid to use his chib. Finn had always said that Boaby was another one who was not right in the head. Even most of the Toonies were scared to get too close to him; he'd been known to knife his own kind.

Holding his head high and standing with his legs wide, Finn glared at Boaby. 'I know you. You're one of the cunts that done wee Eric McNally in that night, along with Dutchy Holland. Where is he then? 'Cause I want a word with him.'

Boaby stared Finn down in an attempt to scare him. 'He's got better things to do and won't be here tonight. Do want me to take a message then?'

Jed jumped in front of Finn and jabbed his finger at Boaby. 'Later! I will see to you later. Now fuck off out of my sight!'

What am I doing here? thought Finn. Fiona was right: I am not cut out for this. I'll go with it and support the lads tonight, but after this is all over, I want out.

The dance was in full swing. Scanning the hall, Finn saw that Norman and the Nutters had most of the women up dancing. Jed pointed out the Toonies in the far corner, eyeing up the Executioners. 'Right, boys, there is less of them than there is of us. Enjoy yourselves but keep close,' he said.

Finn and Jed each ordered a pint of heavy and a double whisky.

'Do you clock your woman then, Jed?' asked Finn.

'Aye, she is over in the corner near the stage.'

'Well, away over and see her then. And hurry up!'

Walking over with bottle of beer in hand, Jed's face lit up when wee Bella spotted him and smiled. 'How's it going, hen?' he said to her. 'I haven't seen you for ages. Where you been?'

Finn watched Boaby approach him with a weird stare in his eyes. 'The atmosphere in this hall is thicker than Sammy's ma's cock-a-leekie soup,' muttered Finn. He knew it was on. He was expecting it.

'Hey, Boaby, I'll ask you again. Where is that cunt Dutchy?'

Boaby looked at Finn with a contemptuous side-lipped grin and shook his head from side to side. He held his palms up, shrugged his shoulders and cleared his throat. 'You no understand Glaswegian? I told you: he's not here.'

This bastard is taking the piss, thought Finn. He knew the Executioners were looking to him to do something about this disrespectful bully. Finn felt his heartbeat quicken, a great pounding in his chest like a sledgehammer trying to burst through an armoured door. Adrenalin coursed through his body like a river in spate, gushing at his mind. It sharpened his thoughts but it also made his insides shake.

Though he had always said he would never start a fight, this was different. A fight was inevitable. As he had predicted, the hall had filled up with Toonies and men who were likely their fathers. Indeed, it looked like the Executioners were about to take on the whole town. Finn had to stand up to the bully boys who kept beating his boys up, and he had to make the first move before any more reinforcements arrived.

'Well, you give him this message from me,' Finn gestured to Boaby to come closer so that he could whisper in his ear, and Boaby leaned in to hear. Finn whipped his head back and headbutted him square on the bridge of his nose. There was a sickening crack. 'That's for Geordie, Eric and the rest.'

Boaby reeled back, grabbing his bloodied nose. 'You bastard!' he screamed through the blood, launching himself straight at Finn. Finn overpowered him easily, punching him to the ground and, like a pack of wolves, the rest of the gang set about him. Finn thought it might have been Wee Eric who, in the midst of the melée, had kicked Boaby's head like a football, leaving him laid out cold.

Everyone began fighting then. Chairs were flung, women were screaming and running towards the stage area for safety, and all hell let loose.

Regaining his faculties, Boaby shouted, 'Gerry, get the tools!'

The Toonies had hidden weapons in the cisterns of the toilets earlier in the week when the hall was being used for the Wednesday night bingo. Within minutes, a wall of armed men ran towards the Executioners shouting their war cry, '*Toonies yah bass!*'

Not realising they had weapons, Jed ran towards the Toonies and launched himself into the brawl. 'Fuck! The bastards are tooled up!' he shouted. 'I fucking told you, Finn, that they would be!'

Davie and Finn were both holding chairs as shields, and beer bottles were bouncing off them. Finn shouted, 'We've been tricked! Get out of here quick! We cannae defend ourselves with only our fists!'

The gang's only way out was through the small door into the entrance lobby. In their panic, they tried to squeeze through the door two or three at a time, jamming up their escape route. When they were finally all through, Finn ran to the main door and yanked at it but it was locked. 'The fucking Toonies have locked us in! And they are tooled up!'

Jed threw his fists down to his sides in anger. 'We fucking fell for it. We walked straight into a fucking trap!'

'We need to think!' said Finn. 'Break the door down, lads!' He turned and looked at the small doorway they'd all run through. A few of the Executioners were fending the Toonies off with chair legs. Finn opened a cupboard door and found brooms and mops. He threw them to Davie, Tam and the others.

'Take the heads off these and use the shafts as long clubs!' Finn broke the brush head off a broom and ran towards the Toonie gang, smashing the shaft into them. The rest of the gang quickly followed suit and they held the Toonies at bay with ease.

A Glasgow smile

The rest of the gang kicked and charged at the large entrance doors until they eventually gave way, and the Executioners poured out into the street like canal water through opened lock gates. Finn and a few others continued to fend off the enraged Toonies with their broom shafts, while the rest used the lobby desk and chairs to barricade the hall door. The Toonie gang wanted blood, and behind the barricade they snarled and bared their teeth like rabid dogs. 'You are dead, and we will fucking kill you!' they screamed.

Brodie and Peem ran to collect the chibs and weapons from the wall. When they returned to the lobby, only Davie, Tam and Finn were there; the rest of the gang had scattered out on to the road. 'Peem, you and Brodie get out of here,' said Finn. 'We will hold them back.'

The full moon lit up the night sky and the Executioners were clearly visible to the Toonie gang spilling out from the rear door. There was a scramble as some of the Toonies tried to get away from the knife-wielding Jed, who was by now in a frenzy. He ran at the Toonies in short bursts like some crazed gorilla, waving his arms erratically and beating his chest. 'Come on then!' he shouted, daring the Toonies to come for him and face his knife.

Peem shouted over to him, signalling that he should follow the others back to the cars. But Jed, irrational as ever, was having none of it. His hatred of the Toonies just fuelled his erratic behaviour. Standing with his legs apart and his eyes wide and bloodshot, he looked like a maniac. There was no way Peem could prise him from this stance, and though he was worried about Jed, he was also worried for himself. He couldn't understand Jed's reasoning for staying there, and if he hung about and stood with him, then he would be in grave danger, too. If the whole gang hung back, they would all be in grave danger. They had to get out of there, with Jed or without him.

More of the Toonies turned the corner, running straight for Peem and what was left of the gang. The Executioners made a valiant attempt to protect Jed, but there were too many Toonies to deal with. In all the confusion, they scattered in all directions, some heading for the cars as weapon-brandishing Toonies thundered after them. Peem realised he could not be responsible for Jed's actions now. His stomach churned in despair, but he could see they would have to sacrifice Jed in order to save the rest of the gang.

The remaining Toonies ran forward to attack Jed, chasing after him as he turned and ran up a close and into a brewery's yard. The yard was contained by a high barbed-wire fence. Frantically, Jed scrambled along the fence, looking for a way out. His heart pounded as panic set in his stomach.

Dutchy and the Toonies surrounded him, standing three deep in a large semi-circle. There was nowhere for him to go. Jed knew there were too many of them, even for him. But in his demented mind, he believed he could get at least two or three of them before they beat him down. With a look of hatred in his eyes, Jed snarled as his brain exploded in ferocious fury. He raised his arms, brandishing his knife, and made a futile heroic attempt, lunging into the middle of the raging mob, screaming, 'Executioners yah bass!'

A few swift blows and a crack from someone's bike chain and it was all over. Jed lay sprawled on the ground, ashen-faced, blood gushing from his nose. Dutchy stood over him and put a foot on his chest. He pointed at Jed, then swung his index finger and pointed it towards the road.

'Right, Heidle, you and Hammy drag this bastard out of this yard and under the streetlight,' he commanded.

The two of them grabbed an arm each and hauled Jed backwards. Jed screamed in pain as they slid him across the ground, grazing his back and buttocks. He managed to bend his legs and get both his feet on the ground, his body bent double.

'I've done nothing! Let me go,' he pleaded with Dutchy.

'Shut it! Done nothing, eh? Well, I'm not gonnae do nothing; I'm gonnae do you over. Did you really think that you fucking lot could come over here to our town and challenge us? My name's Dutchy Holland and I don't give a fuck who you are.'

Boaby held a knife to Jed's face, wanting to slit him, but Dutchy pushed his hand away and brought out his own cut-throat razor. Without any compassion, he slashed Jed right across his cheek. Just a red line showed at first. Jed hadn't even felt it, and didn't realise Dutchy had done anything until his cheek opened up and he saw the blood. He grabbed his cheek and screamed.

Some of the gang recoiled. They knew from Dutchy's cruel and disturbed inclinations in the past that this was not over. One of them tried to get Dutchy away from Jed. 'Come on to fuck. The police will be here in a minute or two.'

Lying on the floor curled up in the foetal position, Jed was trying to stem the blood flow from his cheek with the palm of his hand. Dutchy's voice now softened in apparent concern. 'Hold on, lads, hold on. Are you all right, Jed?'

Jed whimpered, his body shaking in spasmodic jerks. He was oblivious to Dutchy's question, so Dutchy raised his voice. 'Do you hear me? This is the last time I am going to ask you. Are you all right?'

It was obvious to everyone that Jed was not all right. Dutchy grabbed Jed's hair and lifted his head. A smirk crossed his face before he moved in closer to Jed's, and he screamed, 'Fuck me, I will not fucking ask you again! Are you all right?'

Pushing Dutchy's face away, Jed spoke in a trembling voice. 'Leave me here. I'm all right.'

Heidle and Hammy were frantically pulling at Dutchy's coat, trying to get him into the waiting car. He was halfway in when he broke free from their grip and returned to Jed, who had now managed to get up on to his feet. Dutchy put his hand on Jed's shoulder and said in a calm voice, 'Are you positive you are all right?'

'Aye, I am all right.'

There was a venom in Dutchy's voice when he screamed back, 'Well, you fucking shouldn't be!' and he drew his razor down Jed's other cheek. Like a rag doll, Jed dropped to the ground. A gang member grabbed Dutchy by his coat collar, trying again to get him in the car.

'You let everyone know Dutchy Holland from the Castletown Toonies gave you your good looks and your happy smile!' He was still frenziedly threatening the terrified Jed with his razor. 'You bastard, you!'

'Do him in for good, Dutchy!' goaded Boaby as he swung his boot into Jed's abdomen. Jed screamed and doubled up in pain.

'C'mon, man,' said someone, still trying to pull Dutchy away. 'It's done.' Dutchy was wide eyed and staring into space, psyched up by the carnage he'd created and enjoying the power. He was like an animal after the kill who won't let go of its prey.

The police sirens were getting louder. 'Fuck's sake, Dutchy! You're gonnae get us all huckled!' cried Hammy.

Dutchy finally climbed into the car. He pointed a finger at Jed. 'Remember, my name's Dutchy and I don't give a fuck. Nobody can touch me, because I'm the man.'

The car sped off, but a mile or two down the road, Dutchy spotted his ex-girlfriend and shouted to the driver to stop.

'Fuck's sake, never mind Maggie! Come on, Dutchy, the Executioners are scattered all around and we can get a few more of them before they disappear,' urged Boaby.

'Aye, well, on you lot go then. I have better things to do than chase wee daft laddies. I will still be here when you get back.'

As though nothing had happened, Dutchy got out of the car and went over to Maggie. 'Hiya, how's it going?'

'We cannae leave you on your own,' said Boaby. 'I will leave a couple of the boys to hang about and watch your back.'

Double Dutch

Finn, Tam and Davie ran towards the cars with the Toonie gang hot on their heels, and managed to make a hasty getaway. Finn blamed himself for letting this whole thing happen and punched the car door in annoyance. He told Peem to watch out for any of their gang, and almost immediately they caught sight of Jed staggering down the street, holding his face and chest.

Peem pulled up alongside him, the headlights of the car illuminating his suit and shirt, scarlet from the stream of blood running down both his cheeks. He was mumbling to himself with a dazed, empty look in his eyes, oblivious to his friends and surroundings.

'Fuck's sake!' cried Peem. 'Look at his face!'

'God, he's in a right state,' said Davie, and as if time had stopped, they all stood still, shocked and unsure what to do.

'Give me your vest, Davie,' said Finn. Davie took off his vest and Finn wrapped Jed's head with it. Finn and Tam put a shoulder each under Jed's arms and led him staggering to the car.

'Who done it? Who got you?' Finn asked. Jed mumbled incoherently.

'I will tell you who done it,' said Brogan, appearing from the darkness. 'It was that cunt Dutchy! We saw it all from up on the hill. Don't worry, we'll get the bastard for you!'

Just then, Rab pulled up with about ten of the gang rammed inside his car. 'Are yous all right?' he asked.

'No. Big Jed has taken the knife across his face,' said Finn grimly.

'Fuck! Finn, the Mouse has been chibbed too! And a few of the other lads have been beat up bad with batons and chains. They're on their way to hospital.'

Finn felt a coldness enter his body that chilled him through to his bone marrow. Everything seemed to be moving in slow motion. He couldn't believe this was happening, but he knew he had to take control of the situation.

'Right, Rab, you take Jed to the hospital. We'll scout around and get Dutchy and as many of the bastards as we can,' he said.

'I have got about a dozen in my motor; it will be a tight squeeze,' said Rab doubtfully.

'Right then, who is gonnae come with us? We've got the tools from the dyke.' Three men moved over from Rab's car to Peem's.

'Which way, Finn?' asked Peem.

'Double back down Scots Street and you'll come out just about a hundred yards away from the hall.'

Peem set off at speed but had barely gone into top gear when Finn shouted out, 'Wow, it's that bastard Dutchy there on the corner! I'm sure it's him.' All six whooped.

Finn's fury was real; this was no act. Anger shuddered through his body and adrenalin pumped straight to his head. He took out his buffalo jackknife. 'Leave this cunt to me,' he said. He would get his revenge for Jed and for the others now scarred for life.

Peem stopped the car on the corner, out of sight, and they made their way, creeping low, towards Dutchy. Within minutes they had surrounded him and his henchmen, taking them by surprise. The Executioners brandished their knives and trussed the three Toonies up against the wall.

Maggie swung her handbag at Finn and tried to kick him, but he was too quick for her and grabbed her leg. He held it high, leaving her hopping on one stiletto. 'Leave him alone, you bastards!' she screamed. 'Leave him alone! He's done nothing to you lot!'

Finn was unsure what to do with this hot-headed woman at the end of his arm. He knew if he let her go, she'd attack him again. Instead he gave her foot to Davie who, keeping her leg high as she swore and spat at him, hopped her over to a garden hedge and tipped her over it. Maggie landed on her back and screamed.

Jackknife in hand, Finn stood before Dutchy and imagined slitting the bastard open. In his mind's eye, he saw the aftermath – saw himself regain supremacy in the gang. With nostrils flaring and a curled lip that showed gritted teeth, he thrust his clenched jaw in Dutchy's face. Dutchy twisted and turned, trying to free himself.

'You are one sadistic bastard, Dutchy. I know and you know what you did to my mate Jed. Well, I am not going to give you a smile; that would be far too easy. I am going to cut your cheeks out of your head, and then I am going to gut you like a fish. You are only a big man with a razor; you are fuck all without it. Prepare to bleed!'

Finn's wide eyes gleamed like small torches. He pressed the button on the knife in front of Dutchy's face. The blade shot out. Dutchy startled and then recoiled as Finn held it to his cheek. The two other Toonies were screaming at Finn, but soon quietened when he wielded his knife towards them. 'You two want the same?' he barked at them. 'Because you will get it if you don't fucking shut up!' Both dropped their heads and gazed down at the ground.

Geordie gave Dutchy an unkind smile before gripping his head with two hands, yanking it backwards and holding him still. Finn laid the knife to his cheek once more. The rage in Finn's body heightened. Every nerve end in his body was tingling. He would avenge his friends and show he was still worthy of being their leader.

Crazed with his own desire for revenge, Geordie screamed at Finn to do it. He pulled harder on Dutchy's hair, bending his neck back and exposing a throbbing purple jugular vein, proud against his pallid complexion. 'Cut the bastard, Finn!' he shouted, repeatedly nodding towards Dutchy's throat. 'Fucking cut the bastard! That cunt left me lying unconscious in that close. I could have fucking died. Rip the fucker open!'

Petrified, Dutchy was momentarily rooted to the spot, but he screamed and struggled when he realised Finn was about to cut him. It took four of the gang to hold him still. Weeping and shaking uncontrollably, he pleaded, 'Please don't cut me, Finn! I'm sorry. Sometimes my head starts nipping and I don't know what I am doing—'

'Don't fucking listen to him, Finn! Do him and do him now!' urged Geordie. 'Or I will do it myself!'

Finn saw the terror in Dutchy's eyes, and watched his head swing from side to side in a desperate attempt to evade the blade. Then a shock ripped through Finn's body as if he'd been hit by the tip of a cracking whip. In his mind's eye, he could see a misty silhouette of Fiona holding her hand out for the knife. Her words rang in his ears: *No, Finn, this is not you. I believe in you. Do you really want this life? If you carry on down this road, it will only lead to misery. I love you, Finn.* He felt as though he were outside his own body.

Finn held the knife in front of his eyes, then looked around at the gang. They were baying for Dutchy's blood. Turning it slowly, he inspected the knife and then let it slip from his hand. In a haze, he watched it fall in slow motion and bounce off the pavement.

The reality of what he'd just been about to do slammed into his brain, and he was horrified and shocked. His stomach felt as though it were filled with lead. Sickened, his whole body recoiled from Dutchy. *What am I becoming?* he thought. Without warning, another realisation slam-dunked into his brain. It was not what he was becoming; it was what he had already become. This was exactly what Fiona had predicted. He was on his road to misery.

The gang, standing dazed, regarded him in disbelief. Geordie stooped down and picked the knife up, immediately slamming it back into Finn's palm. His face was screwed up in anger. 'What the fuck are you doing, Finn? Do the fucker! He deserves it!'

Dutchy was slumped in his captors' arms, shaking his head violently and whimpering nonsensically. Regaining his composure, Finn pressed the button to retract the blade into the handle before slipping it into his pocket. Looking Geordie in the eye, Finn held his palms up and out, then he pointed at the quivering wreck that stood before them.

'Look at that pathetic sight! That is a beaten man.' Finn swung his finger towards the two other Toonies that were trussed up. 'Those two can now see him for what he is. He is nothing but a sad and weak coward. When the boot is on the other foot, and no knife is in his hand, he is not worthy of any status. We can walk away from this and be better men.'

Geordie, Tam and the others raged at this, and through the dissonance of conflicting words, Geordie stooped forward and screamed at Finn, 'For fuck's sake! What about what the bible says? He who lives by the sword will die by the sword!'

But Wee Davie was thinking hard. He trusted Finn's intuition; he had always stood by him. 'I am surprised at you, Tam,' he said after a moment, 'after what us three have been through together. Can't you see that Finn is right, and that two wrongs don't make a right? Take a look at us – we are all like fucking animals!'

Tam hesitated, then let out a loud groan. His posture slumped, his head bowed on to his chest. Despite himself, he knew they were right. Avoiding eye contact with the others, he walked over to Finn and Davie. 'Okay. I'm with you two on this.'

Finn turned his attention to the remaining five. 'You are better than them Toonies. Prove you are men and let the three of them go. Walk away with us.'

'Your fucking bottle has gone!' Geordie retorted, his faced creased in fury. 'You can fuck off, Finn, because there is no fucking way we are letting them go. You must be joking after what they done to Jed and our mates. Let them go my arse! You three are finished with the Executioners. I will see to that!'

Finn, Tam and Davie never knew what became of Dutchy. They walked away and didn't look back. As the three made their way home with hands in pockets and heads bowed, Tam kicked a stone on the road. They all knew that they were finished with the gang. It had been their life for almost a decade, and they didn't know whether to laugh or cry.

'To tell you the truth, guys, after that carry-on, I am glad to be done with the gang,' said Tam. 'It used to be a peaceful team we had, but now with Jed and Geordie at the helm, heating the gang up to boiling point, it's been like bubbling porridge in the Clachan. It doesn't look good for the future. I am better out of it.'

Nearing home, talking fast to one another, their mood had lifted to a euphoric high. Finn turned to Tam and Davie. 'I am proud of you two. You will never regret what we just done. Anyway, we didn't have it in us to do something like that. Now we will need to drink in the Moy Bar in Blackwood Gardens with all the toffs!'

Tam put his fingers under his nose as though he were an aristocrat twisting his handlebar moustache. 'Oh yes indeed, landlord, let it be the finest whisky and dry ginger for all the hooray Henrys in the room, and three pints of heavy and whisky on the rocks for us reprobates.' The three friends laughed and walked the rest of the way with their arms over each other's shoulders.

Finn's lament

On arriving home, Finn poured himself an extra-large whisky. Tipping it back, he poured it down his throat in one go, then sat on the edge of the bed and poured himself another. Staring at the floor, Finn dug his elbows into his knees and cradled his head in his hands as he reflected on the day's events, and his life as a whole. What would he do now?

He began to piece together his life like a jigsaw. When sudden clarity hit him, he cupped his hand over his mouth. He finally got it. Like a ray of sunshine entering his head and illuminating his mind, Finn finally understood. How could he have ever truly loved Fiona if he could not love himself?

He had carried resentment and bitterness inside himself all his life. He knew where it all stemmed from: his mother and his uncle Finlay. They had never allowed him to like himself. Their words and actions had taken away every last piece of confidence he had, and still ate away at his mind even now. Flashbacks haunted him. Finn had always hated himself; he couldn't forgive himself for letting his uncle Finlay do what he did.

Through the years, Finn thought he would never rid himself of the shame and the painful memories, but now his head was clear and he could see reason … He had been let down so many times. At last, he understood that the abuse he'd suffered was not his doing. It was not his fault. He had never allowed his uncle to do what he did. Uncle Finlay had used fear, force and manipulation to get what he wanted.

When it came to friends, Finn could see now that people did like him. But he was unable to trust anyone – not even Davie and Tam, his best mates. He had never let them get too close, had always kept them at arm's length. His heart sank at the barrier between them. But now he understood the barrier was always of his own making.

He was proud that tonight he, Tam and Davie had walked away from bloodshed. He looked up at his reflection in the mirror and allowed himself to like the person staring back, if only for being a decent human being.

Slipping off the bed, Finn dropped to his knees. He crawled along the floor on all fours, his mind disorientated, and let himself weep. He'd always been forbidden to cry by his controlling and abusive mother; he'd suppressed his emotions ever since. Now the dam had finally burst. He was lost in a wave of intense sobs. Like a sponge, his brain had absorbed every unshed tear over the years, and now they gushed from his eyes, finally clearing out all the pent-up emotion.

Finn awoke the next morning sprawled over the bedroom rug. It was Saturday. He turned his head to look at the clock and jumped to his feet and into the shower. It was a quarter to eleven, and Fiona always caught the number 44 bus into the city at five minutes to twelve on Saturdays to meet Linda.

He looked out of the bathroom window. It was a beautiful sunny morning with not a cloud in the sky. He gasped at the view below the hill. It had always been there, this view, but he had never really noticed it before. He realised, as with most things in his life and especially Fiona, he had taken it all for granted. The Clyde was in the distance, busy with little boats heading in all directions. The rusting skeletons of ships being built all along the river's banks looked like a large orange city. Finn's mouth fell open at the beauty of the rolling hills in the far distance. He had woken with a whole new mindset. Being popular and liked was nice, but it was no longer his priority. Now he recognised that life and love were privileges he'd never previously allowed himself to enjoy.

Turning his motorcycle into Blackwood Gardens, Finn saw Fiona's distinct outline waiting at the bus stop down the hill. She was sitting with her legs dangling over a small green telephone-exchange box, talking to her mother's favourite prospect for her, Victor MacBride, the accountant's son – one of her soft-boiled turnips.

The distinctive roar of Finn's motorcycle could be heard approaching from a good distance away. Pricking her ears at the sound, Fiona's heart started pounding so hard, it was as though it wanted to burst out and escape her rib cage. Maybe Finn had changed his mind and wanted them to get back together? Though she stuck by her words and still wanted more from the relationship, she had missed him so much. Three weeks without him had felt a very long time and she yearned to be with him. One Saturday, she'd even gone to the Clachlan. She'd stood outside shaking, about to push the door open, but the sound of his voice inside had left her rooted to the spot, barely able to breathe. What if he didn't want to see her? He had not tried to contact her. Nerves and fear of rejection had got the better of her. Returning home, she'd thrown herself on her bed, heartbroken, and had bawled herself to sleep.

Victor saw Fiona watching the brow of the hill and noticed her smile had become brighter than the morning sun. 'I was saying, do you fancy a …' he tried, but Fiona wasn't listening. She was craning her neck to see the top of the hill, kicking her heels against the box in excitement. Her excitement soon faded, though, as the roar of Finn's exhaust died away again. She gave a loud sigh and her body deflated, slumping down on to her legs. Maybe Finn had seen her talking to Victor and thought that she had moved on already? Maybe that was why he had turned and left?

In truth, Finn *had* stopped his motorcycle when he saw Fiona in the distance. Her slight frame was unmissable, and his heart had missed a beat. He'd been thinking of all the happy times they'd spent together. In particular, he'd thought of their bus trip to Saltport when Fiona had seen a white horse and had imagined Finn riding it bareback in his underpants, galloping towards her to rescue her from the wicked men. She had said how romantic something like that would be …

Turning his bike around, Finn thought, *I will show her romantic!* Grinning to himself, he sped off looking for somewhere to undress. Not too far away he spotted a red telephone box, and his tyres skidded and burned as he pulled hard on the brakes. Glancing at the clock tower, he saw it was eleven forty-five; the bus would soon be there. He swung the door open and chuckled. He was just like Clark Kent going into the telephone box to change into Superman.

Stripped to his psychedelic underpants and boots, he rolled his jeans in his T-shirt and tied them to his bike. An elderly couple walking their dog saw Finn emerge from the box. 'It's warm this morning, is it not?' he said to them. They gave him a side glance and scurried away, muttering, 'Aye, oh aye, very warm …'

Opening his throttle, Finn sped down the hill. As he approached second gear, he beeped his horn and wound the throttle back. The front wheel lifted off the ground like a rearing stallion. He continued to wheelie the motorcycle down the road towards Fiona. Holding the handlebars tight, he stood upright on the foot pegs and revealed his psychedelic underpants for all the world to see. He twisted his arm in the air as though about to throw a lasso and shouted, 'Yee-haw!'

Victor stood stunned and shook his head in disapproval when he saw Fiona bent double, screaming with laughter and tears running down her face.

Finn pulled up on to the kerb alongside her, and with one fell-swoop he scooped his arm around her waist and guided her on to the back of his motorcycle.

'Hey, you! Where do you think you're going with Fiona?' demanded Victor.

Finn nodded towards Victor and laughed. 'Well, Fiona, it looks like I have rescued you from another soft-boiled turnip. I might not be riding a beautiful white horse, but I am riding my own iron horse!'

Unable to stop laughing, Fiona threw her head back and covered her mouth with her hand. 'Oh, Mr McGill, you are a daftie at times! But so romantic!'

Victor snapped in annoyance. 'Hoy! I asked you where you think you are going with Fiona!'

Finn glanced at Victor, then turned to Fiona and looked deep into her eyes. Fiona saw his own were sparkling and shimmering like the morning sun's rays bouncing off a tropical sea. Holding her gaze, Finn spoke softly. 'Australia.'

Fiona's eyes danced with Finn's. There was no tango this time; this was a waltz. She threw both her arms in the air and screamed with joy. Finn laughed at her excitement. He knew what he wanted now. He'd always known deep down. He fell in love with her the day he met her. Throwing her arms around his neck, she kissed him long and slow. Then she gripped him tightly around his waist, laid her head on his shoulder and whispered in his ear, 'I love you. I love you, Finn.'

His heart stopped beating for a second. A tear of joy pumped all the way from his heart and sat on his eyelid. He smiled with delight as he watched it fall on to his petrol tank. Twisting the throttle back, the bike roared like a lion, and they sped off into the distance.

THE END

Glossary

babby	baby
baws	testicles
bawbags	scrotum
boaby	penis
chib	sharp weapon, e.g. knife or razor
gallus	bold, cheeky, brash
ginger	soft drink
greeting	crying
huckled	arrested by the police
jakey	homeless drunk
peelie-wally	sickly, pale
pish	piss
purvey	refreshments
snash	insolence, abuse
stoater	beautiful woman
swally	alcoholic drink
up to high doh	stressed
yah bass!	you bastards!

Acknowledgements

My thanks to Dave Savage for his excellent artwork on the book cover that helps capture the mood.

My sincere gratitude to my editor Alice Nixon (www.alicenixoneditorial.co.uk) for her commitment, vision and guidance in helping make this a book to be proud of.

Special thanks to my sister-in-law Sheila for her unwavering support even in the face of my brother David's adversity. It truly inspired me to finish this book.

And my thanks and appreciation to my partner Susan Deakin – the kindest and most beautiful woman in the world – for all her encouragement, and for enduring my nightly midnight typing.

My thoughts

Do you know that I am here
Looking at you, you so dear?
Don't ignore me, talk to me –
For I am lonely, can't you see?
Plenty of people going about;
Talk to me! I do shout;
Nobody stops to say how do.
I have nobody to talk to, only you.
Say that things will be alright,
Hold my hand, hold it tight.
Let me sleep in my own bed,
Let me rest my tired head.
You are the only thing I have in sight,
So help me, thoughts, through the night.

By Pete Laird

Printed in Great Britain
by Amazon

21943000R00175